The Shivering Turn

Sally Spencer is a pen name for Alan and Lanna Rustage, a husband-and-wife writing team. Sally Spencer is the author of the Sam Blackstone mysteries and the DCI Monika Paniatowski mysteries.

@SallySpencerebk sallyspencer.com

ALSO BY SALLY SPENCER

The Monika Paniatowski Mysteries
Echoes of the Dead
Backlash
Lambs to the Slaughter
A Walk with the Dead
Death's Dark Shadow
Supping with the Devil
Best Served Cold
Thicker Than Water
Death in Disguise

The Inspector Woodend Mysteries
Dangerous Games
Death Watch
A Dying Fall
Fatal Quest

The Shivering Turn

Sally Spencer

BLACKTHORN

First published in Great Britain, the USA and Canada in 2019
by Black Thorn, an imprint of Canongate Books Ltd,
14 High Street, Edinburgh EH1 1TE

Distributed in the USA by Publishers Group West and in Canada by Publishers
Group Canada

First published in 2016 by Severn House Publishers Ltd, Eardley House,
4 Uxbridge Street, London W8 7SY

blackthornbooks.com

1

British Library Cataloguing-in-Publication Data
A catalogue record for this book is available on request from the British
Library

ISBN 978 1 78689 495 3

Typeset by Palimpsest Book Production Ltd, Falkirk, Stirlingshire, Scotland

Printed and bound in Great Britain by Clays Ltd, Elcograf S.p.A.

In memory of Reg Cooper
1934–2015
A loyal reader – sadly missed

PROLOGUE

It was a quiet suburban avenue. A few children might play in the street in the daytime, but as soon as night fell, curtains were drawn, doors bolted and living rooms filled with the sound of the television. Thus it was that there was no one to notice the girl when she appeared at the far end of the street.

She was running as fast as she could – but there was no real purpose behind the effort, no destination she was rushing to reach. She was, in so many ways, like a wounded animal which does not understand why it is in pain, but desperately clings to the belief that one more burst of speed might just enable it to leave that agony behind.

She was barefoot, but she didn't take the time to wonder where she had lost her shoes, not even when she stepped on a sharp stone which dug cruelly into her flesh.

She did not *wonder* about anything. She was feeling, not thinking – experiencing her nightmare again and again, on a constantly replaying loop of misery and despair.

Her lungs were on fire, and though her instinct screamed at her not to stop, her body was giving her no choice. She came to a sudden halt, and clutched the nearest lamppost for support.

Her breaths started to grow more regular, and her brain slowly began to engage again.

She did not know the name of the street she had stopped on, but she was confident she'd have no difficulty in finding her way from there to one of those places which – until that night – had been the anchoring points of her life.

For a moment, she considered heading for her school, where she had been happy and felt confident of herself and her small world. But that was absurd, because her school would be bolted and barred – and anyway, it could never be the same again.

Home, then?

The very thought of going home filled her with dread.

Perhaps she would go down to the river. The gentle lapping of the waves against the bank might relax her.

And if it did not, then she could slip softly into the water, let it gently cover her, and wash away all her cares for ever.

She heard the sound of footsteps in the near distance. It had never occurred to her that she would be followed – but it would make perfect sense if she had been.

She gasped once – at the horror of it all – and then began running again.

ONE

It's a grey, depressing morning in Oxford – the sort of morning when even the enchanted River Isis has lost its magic for me. I'm sitting in my one-room office at the unfashionable end of Iffley Road. The calendar on the wall (provided free by the Gordon's Gin Co. Ltd, in recognition of my substantial contribution to the company's ever-growing profit margin) says it is 8 May 1974, and I have no reason to dispute that.

I'm hung-over – thank you, once again, Gordon's! – and as I look blearily down at my imitation leather appointment book, the blank pages stare reproachfully back at me.

It's been a lean business quarter so far. True, I was highly praised for my undercover work in Taverner's Department Store (Q: How does a shop assistant manage to keep stealing expensive dresses when she is checked by security every time she leaves the building? A: Simple – she doesn't! All she has to do instead is make it easy for her mates to shoplift them during normal business hours), but that was in the middle of April, and since then there's been zilch. Still, like Charles Dickens's admirable Mr Micawber, I live in hopes of something turning up.

My office door is closed, but that doesn't prevent me from hearing the doorbell ring down at street level, because we at the unfashionable end of the Iffley Road don't set much store by sound insulation.

Next, I hear a click-click-click of almost-impossibly high stiletto heels, which tells me that the tarty secretary from the exotic (or should it be erotic?) goods import-export company on the ground floor has crossed the hallway and is about to open the front door.

Once inside, the bell-ringer says something in a mumbled voice, and the secretary – who could, if she so chose, seek part-time employment as a maritime foghorn – replies with just three words.

'She's up there!'

I can picture her in my mind, gesturing up the stairs with a thumb which is capped with a violently purple artificial thumb-nail. It wouldn't have cost her anything to have been a little less abrupt, I think – to have said, for example, that the visitor would find Miss Redhead's office at the head of the stairs – but I don't pay her wages, so I suppose I'm in no position to complain.

The visitor begins to climb the stairs. I can tell from the sound of the footsteps that it's a woman wearing low heels, and that, given the rate of her ascent, she's probably somewhere between thirty and fifty.

And as always when I'm about to meet a potential client, I am now assailed by a wave of misgivings.

What will this potential client of mine – this woman who will be older than I am, but maybe not by that much – be expecting to see when she opens the door?

She'll already know I'm also a woman – it says that quite clearly in the Yellow Pages telephone directory, and in the small ads in the local newspaper – but, given the 'profession' I'm engaged in, hasn't she the right to imagine a stocky woman with a butch haircut, who dresses in sensible tweed?

I hope not, because what she will be faced with instead is a slim woman with flaming red hair, who is fighting a desperate rearguard action to stave off the approach of her thirtieth birthday, wearing a black cotton trouser suit (my concession to seriousness) and a lilac blouse.

The footsteps draw ever closer.

When I was first starting out in this business, I would blurt out my qualifications right at the start of an interview.

I have a degree from the University of Oxford itself, I would say, omitting the fact that it is in English literature, rather than criminology, and – alas – not a brilliant first but merely a competent upper second.

I worked for six years in the Thames Valley Police, first as a uniformed officer and then as a detective constable, I would add – and then move on quickly, before the potential client had the opportunity to ask why I wasn't *still* working for Thames Valley Police.

I don't do those things now. Now, I am myself, and if the clients don't like it, that's too bad for them (and, of course, for my overdraft).

The visitor knocks.

'Come in,' I say.

She opens the door and steps inside.

I was right about her age – not for nothing do I have the words 'Private Investigator' expensively engraved on the smoked-glass panel that forms most of the upper part of the office door.

She is, in fact, a thirty-eight- or thirty-nine-year-old brunette. She is wearing a tan jacket (over the collar of which the loose curls of her perm hang effectively), and blue skirt. Both the skirt and the jacket come, I suspect, from Marks & Spencer's by-no-means-the-least-expensive-available-but-still-not-costing-you-an-arm-and-a-leg range. She has an attractive face, though, for the moment at least, it is overlaid with a mask of worry which does her no favours.

'Miss Redhead?' she asks uncertainly.

Of course I'm Miss Redhead! Who else could I possibly be, given that I'm in an office bearing her name, in which, further-more, there is only one desk?

That's what my brain thinks, but my mouth, framed by an encouraging smile, says, 'Yes, I'm Jennifer Redhead. How can I help you, Mrs . . .?'

'Corbet,' she says. 'Mary Corbet.' She hesitates. 'It's about my daughter – she's gone missing.'

I feel my heart sink as I see any chance of making my bank manager a little happier slipping through my fingers, but I invite her to sit down anyway, and indicate the visitor's chair.

'If you'd just like to give me the details,' I say, taking a notepad and pen out of my desk drawer and sounding all crisp and busi-nesslike.

She doesn't need any more encouragement than that.

'Linda's seventeen and a half,' she tells me, and names the school where her daughter is studying. 'It was last Friday night that she went missing. We were all out that night . . .'

'All?'

'The whole family – me, my husband . . . and Linda. I went

6

to my regular meeting of the Oxford Garrick Players. That's an amateur dramatics society, you know. We're planning to put on Noel Coward's *Private Lives* sometime in the autumn, and there's a very good chance that I'll be cast as Amanda.' She comes to a sudden uncomfortable halt. 'Oh God, what am I doing? Why am I telling you all this? It's not as if it *mattered*, is it?'

'If we're to get anywhere, Mrs Corbet, then you really do need to relax,' I say. 'Just tell the story in your own words, and leave it to me to make a note of the details which matter.'

She nods gratefully, and takes a deep breath.

'Tom, that's my husband, is a Freemason, and he had a meeting at his lodge, and Linda was supposed to be going over to her friend Janet's house straight from school . . .'

'How far away from you does Janet live?'

'Not very far at all. We're all in Summertown. She's not more than a few streets away.'

'I see. Carry on.'

'I got home about ten. It didn't really bother me that Linda was still out, because it wasn't a school day the next day, and you know what girls are like when they get together, don't you?'

'Yes,' I agree, 'I do.'

'By the time Tom got home, at about a quarter past eleven, I was starting to get worried, and even though it was quite late, I rang Janet's house. Janet said she hadn't invited Linda round at all, and, in fact, she hadn't seen her since four o'clock, when they parted at the school gates. So then I rang all her other friends, and they hadn't seen her, either.'

'What was your husband doing while you were making all these telephone calls?'

'He'd got back in his car and was driving around, looking for her.' Mrs Corbet reaches up, grabs one of her curls, and gives it a sharp tug. 'I kept telling myself I must have got it wrong – that she'd gone to see some other friend, one she'd never told me about, and that she'd probably told me she was sleeping over, but it simply hadn't registered with me.' She gives the curl another tug. 'I've been very distracted recently, you see, because that bitch Cynthia Roberts is determined, by fair means or foul, to pull the rug from under me, and get the part of Amanda for herself. But I'm sure now that I got it right about what Linda said. I'm sure she told me she was going to Janet's house.'

I close my notepad as a way of signalling to her that it's pointless to go any further with this.

'It's not me you should really be talking to,' I say. 'You should report it to the police.'

Mary Corbet shrugs, helplessly. 'I've been to see the police. They're simply not interested. They say that she's probably run away. They say it happens all the time.'

Yes, they probably will have said that, I think – but, chances are, they won't have said it without first making sure of their ground.

'Are any of Linda's clothes missing?' I ask.

'No.'

'Has she been having problems at school?'

'No, she loves school. She's very popular. The other girls voted her house captain.'

'How about at home?'

'What do you mean?'

She *knows* what I mean!

8

'Has she been having problems at home?' I amplify.

'She's our only child, Miss Redhead. Me and her dad both love her with all our hearts.'

'That's not what I asked,' I say, sternly.

She shrugs again. 'There's been the odd bit of unpleasantness with her dad in the last few months.'

'What kind of unpleasantness?'

'They've not been getting on.'

'I'm afraid you'll really have to be a little more specific than that.'

'Tom wants the best for her. He always has – right from the moment he first held her in the hospital.'

'Go on.'

'The thing is, you see, he's always been a very serious person, even when he was younger. He wants Linda to be a doctor when she grows up.'

'And what does Linda want?'

'Oh, she wants the same as her dad, but she takes more after me, and she likes having her bit of fun, as well.'

I put the notebook and pen back in the drawer.

'Listen, Mrs Corbet,' I say, 'the police have experience in these matters, and if they think—'

'It's just occurred to me how funny it is that you're a redhead and you're also called Redhead,' Mrs Corbet interrupts. 'I suppose there's a lot of people say that to you.'

I know what she's doing, of course. This is her attempt to establish a more personal relationship with me, in the hope that it will make me more empathetic, and hence more inclined to take her case. And if that doesn't work, well, at least she's managed to postpone the moment when she hears me turn her down.

And for the record, it *isn't* funny being called Redhead.

Just having red hair is a big enough cross for any little kid to bear. It apparently gives bus conductors free licence to call you 'Ginger Nut' and old ladies the right to accost you in the street and ask you if you eat a lot of carrots. But if, in addition, your name actually *is* Redhead – well, imagine what kind of target *that* makes you in the school playground. So it's no wonder, is it, that as soon as I was old enough to take karate lessons, I signed up straight away?

My dad knew what I was going through.

'I never set out to have a redheaded daughter,' he told me in one of our rare moments of intimacy, when I was six or seven. 'We didn't know about recessive genes when we got married, and your mum's hair was the most glorious shade of dark brown – almost like rich dark chocolate – back then.'

Yeah, right, Dad! I've seen the old photographs, and, at best, Mum's pale brown hair could have been compared to Cadbury's Milk Tray.

I smile at Mrs Corbet in a way which I hope conveys that, while I am sympathetic and understanding, I am also still determined not to waste either my time or hers.

'A lot of girls run away from home,' I say, 'and many of them have good reason to. But the ones who come from good, stable homes are usually back within the week.'

'My daughter hasn't run away,' Mrs Corbet says and, though there are tears in her eyes now, her voice is steady and determined.

'Then what has she done?'

'My daughter is dead.'

'Now what on earth would ever make you think that?' I ask and, though I've not made a conscious decision on this, I can tell from the tone of my voice that I'm trying to jolly her out of this mood of black despair.

'What makes me think it?' Mrs Corbet repeats. 'I'm her mother. She's part of my very being. And now I can feel this great gaping hole inside me, so I know she's dead.'

'I have some good friends who work for the Thames Valley Police,' I tell her. 'If you'd like me to, I could talk to them and ask them to take another look at Linda's disappearance.'

'It wouldn't do any good,' Mrs Corbet says firmly. 'No good at all. Your friends can't bring her back to life. All I want is to know where her body is, so that I can give her a decent Christian burial. Is that too much to ask?'

She reaches into her handbag, and when she withdraws her hand again, it's holding a large roll of five-pound notes wrapped up in a rubber band.

She places the money on my desk.

'This is for you,' she says.

'That's a lot of money, Mrs Corbet.'

'I know it is. There's over a thousand pounds there. Take it.'

'I couldn't possibly.'

'Do you know how I got all that money?'

'How could I?'

'I've been saving it out of my housekeeping for years and years. I've denied myself all the little luxuries I might have had, and I've done it gladly, because that money was for Linda, when she went to college. And now it's no use to her.' Mrs Corbet takes out a handkerchief and brushes away her tears. 'Please just give me one day of your time, Miss Redhead, and that money is yours.'

'All right, if you insist, then I'll give you one day,' I say, finally worn down and defeated by the heartbroken woman who is sitting opposite me.

'Thank you, Miss Redhead, thank you.'

'But I'm not going to take a thousand pounds for one day's work,' I tell her. 'I'll charge you my normal rates, which are . . .'

'I don't care what they are.'

I quote the figure anyway, then add – though it seems a pointless thing to say in this situation – 'And, of course, my expenses will be on top of that.'

Mary Corbet stands up. 'If you don't want the money yourself, then give it away to your favourite charity,' she says. 'Or burn it if you like – I don't care. I don't want it myself, because even touching it is a reminder that all hope is gone.'

TWO

In normal lunchtime traffic, it should take me six minutes to cycle from my office on the Iffley Road to St Aldate's, but, as I dismount in front of the Bulldog pub, I see from a quick glance at my wristwatch that it has taken me all of seven minutes and twenty-eight seconds.

Now that's a warning I'd better heed – because an action woman like me simply can't afford to go soft.

The Bulldog is one of my favourite Oxford pubs, due, in no small part, to the painted sign which projects (from above the main door) over the pavement. On one side of the sign is a typical jowly bulldog, glaring challengingly at the world. On the other is a man with a bowler hat and wearing a no less ferocious expression. Visitors wonder about the sign, but it does not take newly arrived undergraduates long to learn that there are two kinds of bulldogs in Oxford – and it is the bowler-hatted ones they should be more wary of.

DS George Hobson is waiting for me in the pub doorway. He is a big man, with broad shoulders and a square jaw, and some people might even, without too much exaggeration, call him handsome.

Once, back in the almost-forgotten mists of time, George and

I were lovers. Now when we meet, our interactions mainly take the form of jokey, affectionate aggression – he treats me as the smart-arsed university girl, I talk to him as if he was no more than a ponderous, slow-witted copper. We tell ourselves (though we certainly don't tell each other!) that this is the best way in which two people who have painfully broken up – but are still quite fond of each other – *can* relate. But the real truth, I suspect, is that by sticking to the superficial, we avoid the painful process of analysing what went wrong between us.

As I securely chain the front wheel and frame of my machine to a low iron hitching post which was originally intended to tether gentlemen-farmers' horses, George says, 'Still riding that old bike, I see! That's the trouble with you university types – you spend your whole lives pretending you're the people you were at eighteen.'

And we're off on our routine!

I look down, and feign surprise that I'm holding my machine.

'Gosh, that was well spotted,' I say. 'I *am* still riding that old bike. What an eye you have, George – and what a brain! With talents like yours, you should be a detective.'

He's right about us university types, though. Almost everyone connected with Oxford University – from professors of the most obscure branches of moral philosophy, down through graduates like me to the very newest undergraduates – travels around the city by bicycle. We tell ourselves that we do it because, as a mode of transport, the bike is both quick and convenient, but there's something in all of us that imagines it gives us a cavalier – or perhaps bohemian – air.

The downside – as the double locking of my machine has

already hinted at – is that riding a bike also furnishes us with the opportunity of gaining first-hand experience of petty crime.

'You find a seat, and I'll go to the bar and get the drinks,' I tell George, as we enter the pub.

I make this offer partly because I'm a conviction feminist (though that conviction does not extend to leaving the clumps of ginger hair that sprout relentlessly from my armpits unshaven), but mainly because we both know George is doing me a favour.

I buy the drinks (a gin and tonic for me, a pint of Courage Directors for him) and take them over to the table he has selected. As I pass the door, I glance quickly at the street to make sure my bike is still there.

George notices the gesture – and grins.

'We can be justly proud of the fact that, relative to its size, Oxford has just got to be the bicycle-theft centre of the world,' he says.

I return his grin. 'One theory is that there's a single bike-theft ring, with branches in both Oxford and Cambridge, and the bikes stolen in Oxford are sold second-hand in Cambridge, and vice versa,' I say.

'But you don't believe it?'

'I used to – until I joined the police, and saw for myself just how many bikes are regularly hauled out of the river.'

'So what's your theory now?'

'I'm not sure I have one.'

George grins again. 'You'll have a theory, Jennie,' he says confidently. 'You have a theory about *everything*.'

He's right again, of course – I do have a theory about everything. I don't particularly like the fact, but there's nothing

I can do about it – like my red hair, it's a curse I must carry through life.

I glance through the window at the impressive frontage of Christchurch College, the only university college in the world (as far as I know) to have a cathedral *within* its walls.

'My theory is that it's not so much an act of theft as a gesture of defiance,' I say.

'Go on,' George says, giving the smart-arsed university graduate the opportunity to say something stupid, and thus feed him with the material he needs for his next foray into taking the piss out of her.

'There are quite a lot of unemployed young men in this beautiful city of ours,' I say.

'Yes, there are,' George agrees.

'They sit in bars like this one – nursing their half-pints, because it's all they can afford – and they watch other young men in tails (and young women in shot-silk gowns) swan in for a quick drink on the way to their expensive May Balls. Then, a month or so later, they're walking along the High – probably having been to the dole office to draw the pittance which has to last them a week – and they pass the Examination Schools, where these same young men and women, in mortar boards and gowns, are opening bottles of genuine French champagne and toasting the brilliant future they are all absolutely certain lies ahead of them. And these young men with no prospects at all look at those young men who have more prospects than you could shake a stick at – and they resent them.'

'Yes, I think they do,' George agrees heavily, having found nothing in my words to mock. 'I'm in a good job, one that I enjoy, but there are times when even I catch myself resenting it.'

'So they steal the bikes belonging to these privileged "shit-heads", and dump them in the river. It's only a minor inconvenience for the bikes' owners – the thieves know that – but it is an inconvenience of some kind, and that has to be worth *something*.'

'And it's a whole lot better than them deciding to beat the crap out of the students,' George says.

This is suddenly getting far too serious and philosophical for my purposes. I decide I'd better lighten the mood before applying the mental thumbscrews of manipulation.

'The town did experiment with rioting and beating the crap out of the students once, but it didn't really work out,' I say. 'Oh, it's true that *some* of the students and their professors did panic, run away and establish a new university, but most of the university people just stayed put – because they knew that the establishment, which holds all the power, was very firmly on their side.'

'Hang about, Jennie,' George says. 'Did you just tell me that some of the students and professors ran away and established a new university?'

'Yes.'

'I don't remember that.'

'It was probably a little bit before your time on the force, though I can't be entirely sure about that.'

'I think it must have been,' George agrees. 'In fact, since I've never even heard any of the old-timers at the station go on about it, I'd guess it was pre-war. Am I right?'

'You are. Perhaps I should have mentioned that the university the runaways established was Cambridge . . .'

'Cambridge! Then it must have been—'

'And the year was 1209.'

George laughs. 'You really suckered me into that one,' he admits. He looks down at his glass. 'This appears – by some magical process that I don't quite understand – to be empty.'

'Would you like another one?' I ask.

'Not really,' George says. He pauses – though not for long enough to give me time to say anything. 'But, do you know, if I refuse your kind offer, I'm guessing you'll be offended.' He sighs. 'All right then, for the sake of our friendship, I'll just have to force another one down.'

I go up to the bar and buy him another pint. When I return with it, he takes a generous slug, then assumes his business face and says, 'So what can I do for you, Jennie?'

'I want to ask you about a girl called Linda Corbet. I know the name probably means nothing to you, so if you need to slip down to the station—'

'That won't be necessary,' George interrupts. 'What do you want to know about her?'

'She was reported missing, wasn't she?'

'That's right.'

'When I was on the job, if a girl of her age was reported missing, the force dropped everything else so it could concentrate all its resources on that one operation. Leave was cancelled, search parties were formed, and there were appeals on the television. So why didn't that happen this time?'

'That kind of full-scale operation only occurs when there's no plausible explanation for the girl going missing.'

'And there was a plausible explanation in Linda's case?'

'Yes. Her father was convinced that she'd done a runner. He said he'd been worrying it might happen for some time.'

'And you were prepared to take the father's word for it?' I ask – only a little short of horrified. 'Just like that?'

'Yes, he's a very level-headed sort of bloke and—'

'Even though the mother was convinced Linda would never do anything like that?'

'Have you met the mother?' George asks.

'As a matter of fact, I have.'

'Is she your client?'

I take a sip of my G&T. 'You know I'm not allowed to say who I'm representing.'

George nods his head in a knowing – and, I have to say, rather maddening – way.

'So she's your client,' he says confidently. 'She's a bit over-emotional, isn't she? A bit unstable?'

Up until this point, I'd have said exactly the same thing myself, but now – perversely – I find myself going in to bat for Mary Corbet.

'She's not so much over-emotional or unstable as distressed,' I hear myself say. 'Who wouldn't be if they found themselves in her situation? But you don't see it that way in St Aldate's – the last bastion of male chauvinism. The father shows much less feeling, which, of course, makes him easier to handle, so you prefer to take his word rather than hers on whether or not—'

'And then there's the canvas holdall,' George interrupts.

'What canvas holdall?'

'From the photographs I've been shown, I'd say it's about yea big.' He holds his hands three feet apart to indicate the size. 'It's the sort that has a zip along the top and two handles. There are three or four stalls in the market that sell something similar. You know the kind of thing I'm talking about, don't you?'

'Yes, I know,' I agree. 'So what about it?'

'It's missing – and so are some of Linda's clothes.' George smiles. 'Your client didn't tell you about that, did she?'

No, she bloody well didn't!

So if her bag's gone, the girl really has done a runner – that much is plain. And all I can do now – all I'm *able* to do now – is persuade Mary Corbet of the fact. And to do that successfully, I need more information.

So where do I start?

Part of Mary's argument is that Linda would never run away from home, because not only is she perfectly happy, but she's pretty near perfect herself. But how true is that?

'To your knowledge, has Linda Corbet ever been in any trouble with the police?' I ask.

'As a matter of fact, she has,' George replies. 'About three months ago, she was arrested in the company of several students from St Luke's.' He pauses, and shakes his head in mock disapproval. 'Still, I suppose we should expect that kind of behaviour from lads from St Luke's.' Another pause – just two beats. 'That's your old college, isn't it, Jennie?'

'What were they doing – these students from my old college?' I ask, ignoring the heavy implication.

'They were on Beaumont Street, near the Playhouse. They

were drunk and shouting abuse at passers-by. Then they got bored with that, and turned their attention to damaging several of the cars parked along the street.'

'What sort of damage are we talking about?'

'It was the usual mindless vandalism – breaking aerials, scraping coins or keys along the sides of the cars in order to damage the paintwork.'

'So were they charged?'

'No.'

'If they'd been a bunch of local working-class lads they would have been,' I say, switching – in the flickering of an eyelash – from Jennie Redhead, member of the intellectual elite, to Red Jennie, working-class lass and true champion of the proletariat.

'You're probably right,' George agrees.

'So *why* weren't they charged?' I ask, starting to get angry, as I always do when privilege raises its ugly head.

'The students denied they'd done the damage . . .'

'Well, they would, wouldn't they?'

'But that notwithstanding, they agreed to pay for the cost of repairing the cars anyway.'

'You're side-stepping the question, George,' I tell him. 'A criminal act had been committed, and they should have been charged, whether or not they paid for the damage. So why weren't they? Was it perhaps because one of them had a rich, important daddy?'

'It's certainly true that one of the "daddies" did intervene personally,' George says.

'Ah!'

'But if you're thinking it was some rich moneybags or politician from London, then you're wrong.'

'So who was it?'

'It was Linda Corbet's dad.'

'And how come Linda's dad's got so much influence with the cop shop?' I demand.

The question seems to take George by surprise.

'Well, because he's . . .' He stops mid-sentence, as if he's suddenly understood where the confusion has arisen. 'You don't know who Tom Corbet actually is, do you?'

'Is there any reason I should?'

'No, not when I stop for a minute and think about it, there isn't. How long ago did you hand in your papers?'

'It was nearly two years ago now – June 1972.'

'And Tom Corbet didn't arrive until – I think I'm right about this – August '72.'

'For God's sake, get to the point, George,' I say exasperatedly. 'Where was it that Corbet didn't arrive until August? Oxford?'

'Well, yes – but, more specifically, the St Aldate's nick.'

'You surely don't mean . . .' I begin.

'Yes I do – Tom Corbet's an inspector in the uniformed branch.'

Which was another interesting fact that Mary Corbet hadn't bothered to mention when she'd come to see me.

THREE

Oxford may be the city of dreaming spires, visited annually by hundreds of thousands of tourists, but its railway station – as bland and unimaginative as most of the other stations along the line – is something of a let-down. In fact, the only thing that distinguishes it from those other stations is the bicycles. There are hundreds of them – maybe even thousands – chained up in front of the station, left there by commuters who work in London but live in Oxford. It is, of course, a chancy business leaving your bike unattended at the station, as it is leaving it anywhere unattended in the city, but at least there, since a thief can only steal one bike at a time, the odds are several hundred to one against it being yours.

These are the thoughts that pass through my highly trained mind as I cycle past the station but, once I have crossed the river, I start to plan what I will say to the man I expect to find working on one of the Twenty Pound Meadow allotments.

These allotments lie just beyond the river. Once I turn off Botley Road, I am on a rough track which skirts the edge of the allotments, and can see for myself the patchwork of mini-fields cultivated by men who might live miles away from the meadow.

All the allotments are neat and tidy (if they weren't, the omnipotent allotment committee would repossess them) but, within the rules of acceptability, there are a variety of styles. Some of the plots look almost like private gardens, with lawns, neat wooden sheds which could almost be called chalets, and tables and chairs laid out for a comfortable picnic. Others are single-mindedly dedicated to the cultivation of marrows, turnips and butterbeans. These latter have sheds too, but, far from being chalets, they would blend in nicely in the slums of Caracas.

This being a Wednesday afternoon, most of the allotment holders are at their places of employment, but there are a few men – probably shift-workers – spreading manure on their flower beds or weeding between the cabbages.

The man I've come to see is a shift-worker of sorts. His allotment has a solid-looking shed – with no pretensions to being anything else – and a small greenhouse. Beyond these two structures are the beds of vegetables, laid out with almost military precision, and the man himself, wearing a blue boiler suit and heavy green wellington boots, stands in the middle of one of these patches, digging away as if his very life depended on it.

He is so intent on his task that he doesn't hear my bike rattling as it hits the ruts in the track, and doesn't even seem to notice me when I dismount next to his allotment.

I stand there for a moment, just watching him, and thinking that his combination of energy, strength and skill is really quite marvellous. I also decide – if I'm being honest – that he is quite handsome and rather fanciable.

Back to business, Jennifer!

Since I wish to attract his attention, I could just speak to him, I suppose, but I am English, and we don't do things that way, so instead I cough (quite loudly!).

He spins round. At first, he seems quite startled, then the smile of a gentleman welcoming you to his little kingdom fills his face, and he says, 'Can I help you in some way?'

'Am I right in assuming that you're Inspector Corbet?' I ask.

The smile stays fixed, but now it is edged with curiosity – and perhaps even a little caution.

'That's me,' he admits, 'and who might you be?'

'My name's Jennifer Redhead, and I'm—'

'And you're the private detective that my wife has hired to look into Lindie's disappearance,' he interrupts me.

'You knew about that?' I ask, slightly surprised.

'Why wouldn't I?' he counters.

'It's just that you weren't at the meeting we had this morning, so I assumed . . .'

'You assumed Mary hadn't told me about it? Is that what you were going to say?'

'Yes.'

'Do you have any grounds at all for making such an assumption, Miss Redhead?'

'Experience,' I say. 'A lot of women don't tell their husbands they're coming to see me.'

'And why is that, do you think?'

'Because the very fact that they feel the need to consult me is often a sign that the family decision-making process has broken down, and one of the members has decided to go rogue.'

'Clever answer,' Corbet says. 'Did you also assume that if I'd known she was coming to see you, I'd have tried to stop her?'

'Maybe,' I admit.

'I didn't come with her because I knew it would be a waste

of time – more than a waste, it would only have added to her emotional distress, since I would have felt obliged to contradict most of what she told you. I explained all that to Mary but, after I *had* explained it, I didn't try to pressure her any more, because she's an adult and it was her decision.'

'I see,' I say.

'You used to be a member of the force, didn't you, Miss Redhead?' Corbet asks.

'Yes, I did.'

'Why did you resign?'

I shrug. 'I wanted to try something else.'

He frowns. 'If this conversation of ours is going to go any further, Miss Redhead, you'll have to start being as honest with me as you expect me to be with you.'

He knows what happened, I tell myself.

Or, at least, he's heard the rumours that probably still linger in the corners of the police station like the faint buzz of a dying fly as winter approaches.

The faint buzz of a dying fly as winter approaches?

Yes, sometimes, that's just the way I think – it must be something to do with all that literature I've force-fed myself.

'Well?' Inspector Corbet asks.

'I began to suspect that one of my senior colleagues had been corrupted,' I say cautiously.

'That's an interesting choice of words,' he muses. 'Why did you say "been corrupted" instead of "was corrupt"?'

'Does that really matter?' I ask.

'Yes, it does matter, if you're trying to get the measure of someone like I'm trying to get the measure of you.'

'All right, I'll explain it to you,' I say. 'If you've got a natural inclination to be bent, then the chances are that the career path you choose will lead you to a life of crime, rather than one of crime prevention and detection. So I think that most coppers start out being honest – and maybe even idealistic. It's only later, when the prospect of incredibly easy money is being continually dangled in front of their eyes, that some cops go bad.'

'You're really quite the little philosopher,' Inspector Corbet says, favouring me with a smile which is more sardonic than amused. 'Now, about this copper who has, as you put it, "been corrupted" – we are talking about Chief Superintendent Dunn, aren't we?'

Oh yes, he knows, all right.

'We're talking about Chief Superintendent Dunn,' I confirm.

'And what did you think he was guilty of? Selling heroin? Running a prostitution ring?'

'You're playing games with me,' I tell him. 'You know it was nothing like that.'

'Then what *was* it like?'

'I suspected he'd been using his position – and the access to information that position allowed him – to give certain members of the business community an unfair advantage.'

'In other words, he'd been taking bribes.'

'Yes.'

'Tell me all about how it all started.'

IT ALL STARTED WITH Mr Khan, who ran a corner general shop which was on my route to work.

Mr Khan was a jolly man, a few stone overweight, and with

a white spiky beard you could have used as a yard brush. His shop was the kind that sells everything and, if whatever you wanted wasn't on the shelves, Mr Khan would disappear into the dark recess at the back of his store, and, after the sound of much clattering about, would emerge again with the rare shade of shoe polish you needed to make your interview shoes positively glow, or the plastic giraffe you wanted as the centrepiece of your daughter's birthday party.

I became a regular customer, partly because the shop was so convenient, partly because I liked talking to Mr Khan and – I flatter myself – he liked talking to me.

It was during one of these conversations that he revealed he had had an offer for his shop.

'Is it a good offer?' I asked.

'Oh yes, it is a very good offer – generous, even.'

'Will you accept it?'

'I think so.'

'So someone else will soon be running the shop,' I said, trying my best to hide my disappointment.

'No, no, my dear, it seems you've got quite the wrong idea,' Mr Khan said, waving his podgy index finger in the air as if he was conducting a massive orchestra. 'The offer has come from a property developer. He wants to buy the whole of Primrose Street.'

Primrose Street! For some people, the name might instantly conjure up images of a neat, bright road with a tub of flowers next to every freshly painted front door. Others, of a more cynical nature, would perhaps picture it as an ironically named northern industrial street, where even the sparrows have a smoker's cough. In fact, it was neither of those things, and, consisting as it did of just one row of six terraced houses, it was a bit of a stretch to call it a street at all. Still, I could see how it might easily appeal to someone wanting to build executive houses or luxury flats.

The next time I saw Mr Khan was about a week later, and he had changed his mind about accepting the offer.

'When I lived in Kenya, I had a small factory which employed thirty people,' he told me. 'Then the government changed the law, to encourage what it called Africanization, and I was not allowed to own my little factory any more. I sold the business for a miserable pittance . . .'

'Because people knew that as an Asian trader you *had to* sell, and they saw no need to offer you a good price?'

'Exactly. I came to England a broken man. As I walked down the gangplank of the ship which brought me here, I saw – even from the docks, which you would think were the same all over the world – that this was a country which was so clearly alien to me. I did not think I would ever have the will to start another business, yet – almost by a miracle – I did find that strength from somewhere, and this shop is the result. I like the shop. It is no Woolworth's or Marks & Spencer, but I am proud of it – and of myself. I do not want to move again.'

'And how do your neighbours feel about moving?' I asked.

'Two of the families would be quite willing to move, but the rest are happy where they are. They do not want money – they want the homes that, over the years, they have lovingly made for themselves.'

TOM CORBET, HIS BIG-booted foot resting on the top of his spade, has moved so little while I've been telling my story that I am almost convinced that he hasn't heard a word I've said.

Then he proves me wrong by asking, 'What was it that came first? Parking restrictions?'

'That's right,' I agree. 'Everybody woke up one morning to find that there were double yellow lines right down Primrose Street, and also a hundred yards in each direction along the Cowley Road. It wasn't necessary, and there was nothing like it either on – or just off – any similar stretch of road. Mr Khan's neighbours suddenly found that they could no longer park close to their own houses.'

'And Mr Khan's customers couldn't stop in front of his shop?'

'Just so! Whenever they did, a traffic policeman would magically appear out of nowhere.'

'You checked that was actually what happened?'

'I didn't need to – because it happened to me. I was only in the shop for a minute, and when I came out again, he was already filling in the summons. Then he remembered seeing me around the station, and he stopped writing. But I don't imagine for a second that anyone else was that lucky.'

'Is that it?' Corbet asks. 'Or were there other things which raised your suspicions?'

'One of the young couples who lived on Primrose Street was raided by the Drugs Squad – and not once, but twice. Nothing incriminating was found, either time, and when I spoke to them about it, they told me they were in the Salvation Army, and didn't even drink alcohol.'

'You verified they *were* actually in the Sally Army?'

'No, but there was a big bass drum with Salvation Army written on it in their hallway, and unless they kept it there on the off-chance they might need to fool an off-duty cop who dropped in unexpectedly, I think they were telling the truth.'

Corbet nods. 'Is there more?'

'The man at number seven was pulled over by the traffic police for a "random" car inspection a total of four times before they found anything wrong with his vehicle. The couple at number three soon learned that if they ever went to the pub, there'd be officers waiting in the car park when they came out, and that these officers would accuse them of being drunk and disorderly.'

'What you're suggesting is that there was a giant conspiracy,' Inspector Corbet says.

'No, I'm not suggesting that at all,' I counter. 'Traffic comes within Chief Superintendent Dunn's remit, and if he asks for more restrictions to be imposed, everybody assumes that – since he's the expert – he has a perfectly valid reason for making the request.'

'Getting the Drugs Squad involved would be trickier.'

'No it wouldn't – it'd be a doddle. All he had to do was to tell the Drugs Squad that he had information from a confidential source which would indicate that drugs were being sold on Primrose Street, and they'd automatically apply for a warrant and raid the place.' I pause for a second. 'Each individual action is only one tiny innocuous piece of the puzzle, you see, and it's only when you put them all together – as I did – that you can even start to get the complete picture.'

'And you're sure that Chief Superintend Dunn is your man?'

'I'm certain of it, because most of the harassment came directly out of his department. Besides, a couple of months after the residents of Primrose Street ran up the white flag, the developer who pulled the street down busied himself with building a rather splendid extension on Dunn's house.'

'Maybe Dunn paid for it.'

'I'm sure he did – he'd have been a fool not to. But I'm equally sure that it won't have been long before the money he paid over found its way back into one of his less conspicuous bank accounts.'

Corbet nods again. 'So you went after him?' he says.

'Yes.'

'What rank were you at the time this was happening? WPC?'

'No, I'd just been promoted to detective constable.'

'You were a mere DC, but you still went after a chief superintendent. Did you ask for help from anybody else?'

'No.'

'Why not?'

'Because I knew there was a more than fair chance of me going down, and I didn't want to drag anybody else with me.'

Corbet takes his hand off his spade, and gives his head a slow, thoughtful massage.

'So you knew you were likely to come out the loser, but you went for it anyway,' he says. 'Why?'

'Because I knew it was the right thing to do – and that really left me no choice in the matter.'

'What happened in the end?'

'What do you *think* happened?'

DUNN CALLED ME INTO his office. When I arrived, he pretended to be working, just – I think – to give me time to examine the numerous commendations which hung on the wall behind his desk. I declined the opportunity, and instead stared fixedly out of the window.

When he did finally look up, there was a look of almost sorrowful sympathy on his face.

'You've been investigating me,' he said softly.

'Have I, sir?' I replied.

'Yes, you bloody well have,' he said, the mask of reasonableness cracking just a little. 'I normally applaud enthusiasm in young officers. More than that, I actually encourage it.'

'But . . .?' I suggested.

'But for it to be effective, it has to be directed, intelligent enthusiasm – and yours isn't. You've shown a shocking lack of judgement, which may – in the future – endanger both you and your colleagues. And that is why I think it might be best if you resigned.'

'What if I refuse?' I asked.

'I prefer to look at things from a more positive angle,' he told me. 'If you show the good sense to resign, I will write you a sparkling recommendation for whatever more appropriate career you choose to pursue.'

'What if I refuse?' I repeated.

He sighed. 'You are temperamentally unsuited to police work, and if you insist on remaining in the force, then soon or later – and I strongly suspect it will be sooner – you will make a mistake which cannot be excused, and you will be dismissed – or perhaps even end up going to prison.'

'What you mean, sir, is that if I refuse to resign, you'll find a way to fit me up.'

'I'm not saying that at all,' he told me – and now there was a look on his face which could only be described as complacent sadism. 'But, for the sake of argument, let's assume that I was. Say I told you, right here and now – and in the most explicit terms possible – that I'd find some way to nobble you. Would the chief constable believe you if you told him what had passed between us?'

'I don't know.'

'Of course you do – and the answer is, you know he wouldn't. Or, say we lined up every officer in this station and asked them which of us they trusted more. What would their answer to that be?'

They'd say they trusted you, I thought – because they know which side their bread is buttered on.

'So all that leaves is the newspapers, doesn't it?' Dunn asked. 'You could easily go to them, and present them with your largely unsubstantiated story about a bent senior policeman, but would they print it? They'd certainly first consider the possibility that, if they ran with it, I might well sue them, and they'd be only too aware that they'd never be briefed from this police station ever again – so, on balance, I don't think they would.'

He slid a piece of paper across the desk to me.

'This is your letter of resignation, DC Redhead,' he said. 'Will you sign it now? You know it's for the best.'

'Yes,' I said heavily, 'I'll sign it.'

He reached for his pen, and was in the process of uncapping it when I said, 'Given how many crooked deals that pen has probably played a part in, I think it would be safer to use my own.'

I watched the look of pure rage spread across his face. It wasn't much of a victory – but it was all that I had.

*

'SO YOU RESIGNED,' CORBET SAYS.

I shrug. 'I like to think I can act heroically when the situation calls for it, but heroism wouldn't have done me any good at that point, and I'm not the stuff that martyrs are made of.'

'And do you still think Dunn's bent?'

'Yes.'

'I'm far from convinced you're right, but I suspect that if I thought he was bent, I wouldn't have the balls to go after him. And that's the only reason I'm willing to talk to you now, Miss Redhead – you've got more balls than I have, and that buys you a little respect.' He pauses and lights a cigarette. 'Ask me whatever it was that you came here to ask me.'

'Linda's mother thinks something terrible has happened to Linda in Oxford, but you think she's simply run away. Is that right?'

'Yes.'

'Yet the night she went missing, you spent hours driving round Oxford, looking for her.'

Corbet shakes his head, sadly.

'Is that what Mary's told you?'

'Isn't it true?'

'No, it isn't. What I did do was to go to the railway station and bus station, to find out if anyone had seen her there.'

'And it didn't occur to you – not even for a second – that she might have been attacked?'

'Not after I saw that Mr Dumpy was missing.'

'Mr Dumpy?'

'When Lindie was eleven, we went to Southend-on-Sea for our holidays, and one day, when we were walking along the promenade, she noticed this canvas bag in one of the gift shops.

It was only a cheap thing, but she was absolutely thrilled to bits when I bought it for her. She embroidered a cartoon of a man's face on the side of it, and she called it Mr Dumpy, because she could dump all her stuff in it, and when she'd done that, the cheeks on the face bulged like those on a dumpy person. That's the sort of silly thing that kids make up.'

'I know,' I agree.

'Anyway, she's stuck with that bag ever since. Every time we go away on holiday, she point-blank refuses to use the smart suitcase we bought her, and crams everything into Mr Dumpy. It means she has to do a lot more ironing, but she doesn't seem to mind that.'

'And you noticed Mr Dumpy was missing?' I ask.

He nods. 'While Mary was on the phone to Lindie's friends, I checked her room, and there was no sign of Mr Dumpy.'

'Why do you think she ran away?' I ask.

'If you asked her, she'd probably say it's because I've been putting too much pressure on her.'

'And what if I asked you?'

'I'd say I was doing my best to persuade her not to throw her life away.' Another pause, while he takes a drag on his cigarette. 'I suppose my wife has been telling you how well Lindie's doing at school.'

'And isn't she?'

'She was until just before Christmas – then her work suddenly started dropping off. And it went even worse in March, when she got mixed up with the wrong crowd.'

I have to tread very carefully here, because although I know he's referring to the St Luke's students she was arrested with, I can't let *him* know that *I* know without revealing that I have a source at the station.

So all I say is, 'The wrong crowd?'

'They're students from the university, but not the good students – the ones she should have been taking as an example if she ever wants to get into Oxford herself. No, she chose to pal up with the dregs – with a bunch of over-privileged, mindless vandals.'

'Did you have an argument with Linda over these new university friends of hers?' I ask.

'We discussed it,' he says cautiously.

'Discussions don't normally make people decide to run away from home,' I point out.

'Do you want me to say that I lost my temper with her – that I shouted at her and said things I regretted later?'

'Only if that's what happened.'

'All right, I may have lost my temper,' he concedes. 'I *did* lose my temper with her. I told her if she didn't show some marked improvement pretty damn quickly, I'd kick her out.'

I say nothing.

'Do you think I've been too hard on her, Miss Redhead?' he asks. 'From what I've said, have you already formed an impression of me as an unyielding Victorian father?'

'I haven't formed any sort of clear impression yet,' I tell him. Then I add, because this man seems to have a finely tuned radar for detecting insincerity, 'But the unyielding Victorian father is a possibility I've yet to rule out.'

For perhaps a minute, Corbet says nothing, and when he does speak, there is a bitter edge to his tone.

'My father was a useless drunk, and my mother was nothing

but a street-corner prostitute,' he says. 'Does it surprise you to hear me describe my parents like that?'

'Not if that's what they were.'

'I've had a little help along the way, when I was growing up. I won't deny that – but the man I am today is mainly of my own making,' Corbet says. 'I'm not claiming to be that exceptional – many other people have had to make the same journey – but by God, it was bloody hard, and all I ever wanted was to make sure that Lindie didn't have to endure the same herself.'

'Go on,' I encourage him.

'I was an inspector stationed in Abingdon, and I was in line for a promotion to chief inspector. Then, one day, Lindie's form teacher called me in. We met in Lindie's classroom. The teacher – Miss Eccles – said my daughter had great potential. Then she stood up, walked over to the door, and looked up and down the corridor, to see if any other member of staff was close enough to hear what she was about to say. And even then, when she spoke it was almost in a whisper.'

'What did she tell you?'

'She told me that to fully realize that potential, Lindie needed to be in a better school. She said she had contacts at St Margaret's in Oxford but, because it was a good school, it was also a very popular one, and in order for Lindie to get in . . .'

'You'd have to live in the catchment area, which would mean you moving to Oxford.'

'Which would mean us moving to Oxford,' Corbet agrees. 'When I put in for a transfer, my chief super called me into his office. He told me that if I stayed in Abingdon, I'd get my promotion within six months, but he'd done some checking on my behalf, and discovered that there wouldn't be any vacancy in Oxford in the foreseeable future. Looking at it from that perspective, I'd be a complete bloody fool to move, he pointed out.'

'But you did it anyway – which shows you've got a fair amount of balls yourself.'

Corbet shakes his head slowly from side to side. 'No, Miss Redhead, you don't understand. It wasn't balls at all – it was love. But I expected something in return – I expected Linda to make the best of her opportunities.'

'Where do you think she's gone?' I ask.

'She could have gone anywhere, but I expect she's headed for London – which is where most runaways end up.'

'And have you asked the London police to look for her?'

'Not officially, no. I've no grounds for making such a request, because she's seventeen and a half, and left of her own free will.'

'But unofficially . . .?'

'Unofficially, I know some coppers in the Met, because we've attended the same conferences and got on together, and I've asked them if they'll keep an eye out for her.'

'Do you think that she'll come home of her own free will?'

'That's what I'm praying for. But she's like me – stubborn – and she certainly won't come back until the money's run out.'

'She has money?'

'Oh yes. When she told me that she'd decided she wanted to become a doctor—'

'Was that her decision – or yours?' I interrupt.

'It was hers,' he says, with just a hint of anger. Then he softens, and adds, 'It would probably be more accurate to say it was ours.'

'Yours and Linda's?'

'Yes.'

'What did your wife think about it?'

Corbet sighs. 'Mary's not a very practical person,' he says. 'Her idea of self-fulfilment is to dress up and pretend to be somebody else.'

His cigarette has burned down almost to the filter tip. He snips off the still-burning ash with his finger and thumb, watches it fall to the ground and then stamps on it. As he puts the filter tip in one pocket of his overalls with one hand – a tidy allotment is a filter-free allotment – he is already reaching into another pocket with the other for his packet of cigarettes.

'It was because Lindie wants to be a doctor that I got her a part-time job – Saturdays and holidays – in one of the pharmacies,' he says.

I can see where he's going with this.

'And you let her keep some of the money she earned?' I ask.

'I let her keep *all* of it,' Corbet says, with a sudden hard edge to his voice. 'She's my daughter, not a lodger.' He looks around the allotment with a wistful expression on his face. 'Lindie loved this allotment when she was younger,' he continues, dreamily. 'We'd come here day after day, and never get tired of it. I'd never grown flowers – I'm a practical man, and I don't see the point in growing something you can't eat – but she asked me if she could try her hand at it, and I said yes. And you should have seen the results. She didn't just have green fingers – she had magic fingers!'

I do a quick survey of the allotment. There are lettuces growing in stiff, uncompromising rows, and the regimented tops of autumn potatoes thrusting out from their clayey grave. And in one sheltered corner there is a bed of flowers – blue and yellow delphiniums around the edge, red roses in the middle – over which butterflies dance in gay abandon.

'Did your daughter plant those?' I ask.

'Have you not been listening – or is it simply that you have no short-term memory?' Corbet asks, suddenly irritable. 'I've just told you that she doesn't come to the allotment any more. As she developed more interests of her own, the allotment lost its allure, which is, I suppose,' he pauses to sigh again, 'only natural.'

'So you planted them?' I ask.

'Yes,' he says.

'Recently?'

'Yes.'

He is speaking awkwardly – perhaps reluctantly – but I don't read the signals, because I am interested in his motives, and completely forget that he also has emotions.

'What *made* you plant them?' I ask, like a drunken elephant rampaging through an Indian village. 'Are you growing them for her?'

'Well, *of course* I'm growing them for her, you stupid bloody bitch!' he roars at me.

The sudden violence in his voice – the aggressive stiffness of his body – quite shocks me. But it passes in a moment. His stance loosens. His mouth – which was temporarily a vast cavern of rage – returns to its normal size.

'I'm sorry,' he says, in a voice which is now almost a whisper. 'That was unforgivable.'

'No, I'm the one who should be saying sorry,' I tell him.

And I truly mean it.

41

He was quite right to call me a stupid bitch. I have been very stupid – not to mention grossly insensitive. The allotment was where he and Linda were happiest together, and this flower bed is his equivalent of keeping a candle burning in the window for his missing daughter. It is a deeply personal thing – and *of course* he doesn't want to talk about it to an outsider.

'I'd like you to do something for me,' he says – and it is a plea rather than a request.

'What?'

'I'd like you to persuade my wife that nothing bad has happened to Lindie – that she's just run away. If you *can* get her to believe that, then you'll be giving her hope. And even if Lindie *never does* come home again, there's at least a slight possibility that Mary will be able to convince herself that, wherever she is, the girl is happy.'

'Is that what *you* think, Mr Corbet?' I ask. 'Do you think she might never come home again?'

'No, of course not,' he says, far too hurriedly. Then he shakes himself, as if he could shake off despair as a dog shakes off water. 'I don't know,' he admits. 'I tell myself that there's no reason she wouldn't come home eventually, but there's a part of me that says she never will.'

'I will talk to your wife,' I promise. 'But I'm not a family friend or a guidance counsellor, and all I can really do is to say that, in my professional opinion, she's gone away of her own free will.'

'Yes, of course, that's all I could expect you to do,' he says sadly.

As I start to walk away, I hear him say, 'Maybe I *was* too hard – maybe I was *too hard*,' but I don't turn around, because I know he isn't talking to me.

FOUR

The house is a large 1930s semi-detached dwelling on a leafy street in north Summertown – the sort of street which is the natural habitat of assistant bank managers, junior doctors, deputy head teachers and university lecturers. It has two bay windows projecting out from the main building, and the upper one is capped with a dinky triangular roof. The walls are painted white, as are the window frames and front door, and the curtains are a delicate shade of pale blue. If you'd asked me to describe the kind of house in which I thought the Corbets might live, I would have imagined something exactly like this.

As I walk up the driveway, I find myself thinking about the little flat I once owned over one of the many bookshops on Broad Street. It wasn't much (two-bed, one bath, kitchen/ lounge), but I'd grown quite fond of it, and when, as a result of having signed the letter Chief Superintendent Dunn had so thoughtfully drafted for me, I found I was no longer able to keep up my mortgage payments, I may have shed a tear or two.

Now, I occupy a bedsit near my office – and whereas, in my old flat, I had a cupboard in the bathroom, I now have a bathroom in a cupboard.

I hope to some day step on to the property ladder again, and there is no doubt the money Mary Corbet gave me would have been a huge help to that ambition. Unfortunately, the reason I'm here is to hand that money back.

C'est la vie!

I ring the doorbell, and instead of hearing the sound of footsteps coming down the corridor, I hear the bolt being drawn and the door opening.

It's almost as if Mrs Corbet has been hovering in the hallway on the off-chance that I might pay her a visit, I think – and maybe that's exactly what she has been doing.

I hadn't anticipated being angry but, looking at her now, that is exactly what I am.

'Have you found out anything yet, Miss Redhead?' she asks, almost breathlessly.

'Yes,' I reply coldly, 'I've found you've been playing me for the complete bloody fool.'

'I haven't . . . I never meant to . . .'

I hold out the roll of bank notes in my right hand.

'I'm returning your money,' I tell her. 'I haven't spent so much as a penny of it.'

'Oh please,' she says, cupping my right hand with both of hers – forcing it closed, so I am still holding the bank roll – 'I'm sorry I wasn't entirely honest with you the last time we talked.'

'Saying you weren't "entirely honest" is a bit of an understatement, don't you think?' I ask her.

'Just come inside, and I'll explain everything to you,' Mary Corbet implores me.

'I can't see there'd be much point in that,' I say. 'In my professional opinion, Linda has decided to leave home, and there's really not a great deal that anybody can do about it.'

'Please, I'm begging you,' she moans.

She has a grip on my right hand and is using that grip to haul me into the house.

Resisting would present me with no problems – I once dropped a fifteen-stone lorry driver armed with a crowbar – but, given the state she's in, it would seem almost cruel.

Besides, having one last shot at convincing her of the truth is the least I can do for her husband.

Once inside, Mary Corbet seems to decide that it is no longer necessary to apply 'force'. She relinquishes her grip, and shimmies around me so that she can close the front door.

'The lounge is that first door on the right,' she says, once we are both safely locked inside. 'Go straight in.'

I sigh, and do as I'm told.

Once we're in the lounge, she begins fussing over me like a mother hen.

'Do take a seat,' she says. 'I think you'll find that armchair over there very comfortable. Now, what would you like to drink? There's both tea and coffee, but I wouldn't the least mind – honestly I wouldn't – if you told me that you felt like having something a little stronger.'

'I don't want a drink, Mrs Corbet,' I say.

'Not even tea? Oh, and I've just remembered – there's fruit juice. Pineapple and peach flavours, I think.'

'I don't want anything to drink – but I would like to ask you a question,' I tell her.

'Oh, all right, then,' she says, sounding disappointed. 'What was it you wanted to know?'

'I want to know why you didn't tell me that, before Linda disappeared, she'd packed a canvas travelling bag – which apparently has also disappeared?'

Mrs Corbet laughs. I think she is trying to sound amused, but to me it comes across as close to hysterical.

'You've got it all wrong,' she says. 'If Linda had been packing a bag to take away with her, she'd never have put *those* clothes in it.'

'What do you mean?'

'The missing clothing is either old or else stuff that's gone completely out of fashion. Linda wouldn't be seen dead wearing . . .'

She stops, horrified at what she's just started to say.

'Oh, my God,' she moans, as she presses her knuckles hard against her teeth. 'Ohmygod, ohmygod, ohmygod . . .'

She's gone bright red, and I'm afraid that if she carries on like this, she'll have a seizure. I drop the money on the coffee table, and grab her firmly by the shoulders.

'Take deep, slow breaths, Mary,' I order her. 'Like this . . . in, out . . . in, out . . . in, out . . .'

She does as she's been told, and slowly the red colouring drains away, and she's pretty much back to normal.

I ease her into one of the armchairs.

'Stay there,' I tell her. 'I'm going to the kitchen to make you a cup of hot, sweet tea.'

'I'll make the tea,' she says, trying to get up out of the chair.

'No, you won't,' I insist, gently forcing her back again.

'But you don't even know where the kitchen is,' she protests.

'There can't be that many rooms on the ground floor,' I say. 'I expect I'll find it eventually.'

The kitchen is clean, tidy and organized. I wonder to what extent this is due to Mary's own inclinations, and to what extent she, like the root vegetables on the allotment, has had order imposed on her.

When I return to the lounge – one cup of hot sweet tea in hand – Mary is looking a little better.

'While I've been sitting here, I think I've managed to work it out,' she says in a calm, reasoned voice.

'Work what out?'

'Work out what happened to those missing clothes you talked about. Linda was such a responsible girl, and when she realized she was never going to wear any of the clothes again, she will have bundled them all up into a bag, and taken them down to one of the charity shops.'

She is consistent in only talking about Linda in the past tense, I note. Mary is convinced her daughter is dead, and nothing but cold hard evidence is going to make her think otherwise.

'Do you think she would have left Mr Dumpy at the charity shop, as well?' I ask.

Mary Corbet looks as if I've just slapped her.

'How . . . how do you know about Mr Dumpy?' she gasps. Then she nods. 'I know who told you.'

'Do you?'

'You've been talking to my husband,' she says – and makes it sound like an accusation.

'Of course I've been talking to him,' I agree. 'You must surely have known I was going to do that.'

'You shouldn't go listening to him, you know,' she tells me. 'He's got it all wrong.'

Or, to put it another way, I think, he refuses to buy into your version of events.

'So what *did* happen to Mr Dumpy?' I persist. 'She *won't* have left it in the charity shop, now will she?'

'She might have done,' Mary says, her voice that of a stubborn child who knows the game is up, but is still looking for a miracle to save her.

'Your husband told me that she took that bag everywhere with her – that she insisted on using it, even though you bought her a smart new suitcase.'

'It used to be like that, but she'd finally grown out of it,' Mary Corbet says. 'She told me so herself.'

'Can you remember her exact words?'

'Not exact, no, but it was something like, "I've grown tired of this old bag and I think I'll throw it out."'

She's lying – but I'm not sure that she actually *knows* she's lying. I think there's at least a part of her brain which is processing all the material to make it fit her theory. It's something we're all guilty of, though most of us don't do it on quite this grand scale.

I decide to approach the problem from a different angle.

'What did Linda do with the money she earned in her part-time job at the pharmacy?' I ask. 'Did she put it into her bank account, or did she give it to you for safe keeping?'

I realize I have just made a mistake. Questions should be open-ended, so that they harvest as much information as possible. What I've just done is not so much to ask her a question as to present her with two of my own assumptions and ask her to pick one.

It's all her bloody fault, I tell myself – she's making me lose all sense of judgement.

'Linda kept all the money that she earned from her job in her bedroom,' Mary Corbet says.

'She's been working at the pharmacy since she turned sixteen. That's right, isn't it?'

'Yes.'

'And she's worked there every Saturday and for a lot of every school holiday?'

'Yes.'

'So even though she won't have been paid as much as a grown-up would have been, it must still be a fair amount of cash.'

'It is.'

'And didn't it worry you that Linda kept so *much* money in the house, Mary?'

'It did, at first – but then she showed me her hiding place, and I had to admit that as long as she kept it there, it was perfectly safe.'

'A good burglar can find anything,' I say.

'A burglar, on average, is in a house from somewhere between ninety seconds and three minutes. He only has time to check out the most obvious hiding places – and Linda's was not obvious.'

Ah yes, I mustn't forget that her husband's a copper who probably lives and breathes criminology, even when he's at home.

'I'd like to see Linda's room,' I say.

'Why?' Mary asks, defensively aggressive.

'Because it's possible that it may contain some clue as to what's happened to her.'

'Well, if you think it will help,' Mary says.

She is suddenly much more relaxed. And no wonder – because she's getting exactly what she wanted.

You're an idiot, I tell myself – you came here with the sole purpose of making it clear to her that you want nothing more to do with the case, and yet you're allowing yourself to get sucked in even further.

But now, having made the request, I feel obliged, for politeness' sake, to at least go through the motions.

LINDA'S BEDROOM COULD HAVE been lifted straight out of the Ideal Homes Exhibition (Children's and Teenagers' Section) of 1973. The pale-wood wardrobe, chest of drawers, bookcase and dressing table are a matched set with clean functional lines – modern furniture for the modern young lady. The room also contains a desk with a flexible desk lamp and an office chair – a reminder, if we needed one, that this is not just a bedroom, it is also a study.

A small teddy bear – ears ragged, black cotton thread smile worn pencil thin – sits at one corner of the desk. He is quite cute – though nowhere near as cute as ReadyTeddy, who keeps my bed warm for me when I am not there.

One thing does surprise me about the room – the choice of posters that the girl has chosen to Blu-Tack to the wall. I might have expected pictures of Mud and Suzi Quatro, or – if she had already put her teenybopper tastes in music behind her – Cockney Rebel and Eric Clapton. Instead, there are engravings of men in seventeenth-century garb. I recognize two of them immediately – George Herbert and John Donne, both of them giants of the

Metaphysical movement (which wasn't really a movement at all, but we won't get into that now). The third just might be Sir John Sucking, a minor Metaphysical poet who stands in relation to Donne and Herbert in much the same way as Gerry Marsden (of Gerry and the Pacemakers) stands in relation to John Lennon and Paul McCartney.

'Had Linda been studying the Metaphysical poets at school?' I ask.

Mary Corbet shrugs. 'I wouldn't know anything about that. She'd long ago got beyond the stage where I could understand what she was studying. If you want to know the answer, you'll have to ask her dad. She always talked about her school work to him.'

Would that be the dad that – just five minutes ago – she told me I shouldn't listen to?

This is one mixed-up lady.

On the chair beside the dressing table there's a white girl's blouse and a sewing box. I pick up the blouse, and see that Linda has started to embroider something on the back of it: '*And dare you face your urges*'.

'She was always good at embroidery,' Mary Corbet says. 'She won prizes for it at junior school.'

'Does this phrase mean anything to you?' I ask, holding up the blouse for her to see.

'Is it Shakespeare?' Mary Corbet asks. 'I know she had a big thing for Shakespeare at one time.'

No, it isn't Shakespeare, or rather – taking into account the fact that the Bard of Avon wrote so much that only someone with a really big head would claim to know it all – I don't *think* it's Shakespeare.

I spot the clue (I am a detective, after all) on Linda's desk. It takes the form of a single sheet of A4.

'Is this Linda's handwriting?' I ask.

'Yes, it is,' Mary Corbet replies, with a catch in her throat.

What's written on the piece of paper is part of a poem.

> And dare you face your urges and desires
> Embracing both the good and bad you own
> Or will you, like a cold and errant coward
> Abandon all and make a shivering turn?
> Robert Cudlip 1612–1659

By the date, another of the Metaphysicals, though not one I have ever heard of.

It occurs to me that I've almost forgotten one of the main reasons I came up here.

'Where did Linda hide the money that she'd earned at the pharmacy?' I ask.

'You don't want to bother about that now,' Mary Corbet says, with a definite hint of uneasiness in her voice.

'But I do want to bother,' I insist. 'And if you want me to be your investigator, then you're going to have to allow me to investigate in any way I consider appropriate.'

She points to the bookshelf. 'It's in there. She hollowed out one of those books.'

I'm impressed by Linda's collection. There's Shakespeare, though almost every bookshelf in the world will have Shakespeare (even if most of them go unread), but there's also Ibsen, Chekhov and Aristophanes. She has a number of Dickens' novels, but these are supplemented by Dostoyevsky, Kafka and Proust. This collection is not exactly a mirror version of my own, but the two certainly strongly overlap.

I notice two other things: the first is that the only science books on the shelves seem to be school textbooks, and the second is that there's a copy of Enid Blyton's *Five Go To Smuggler's Top* incongruously sandwiched between George Eliot's *The Mill on the Floss* and Jane Austen's *Emma*.

'Which book is it that she hollowed out?' I ask.

'I don't remember,' Mrs Corbet says.

She's lying, of course. And the *reason* she's decided to lie is because she's starting to realize that she's made a serious tactical error in bringing me up here – an error that could seriously damage her campaign to get me to accept her version of what happened to Linda, rather than her husband's.

It doesn't matter that she's lying, because I don't need her help. I already know which one is the hollowed-out book – it's the one that simply doesn't belong on these particular shelves.

I reach out for *Five Go To Smuggler's Top*.

'What's the point in looking for the money Linda saved up?' Mary Corbet asks, verging on the desperate now. 'It won't give you any clues about what happened to her.'

No, it won't – not if it's still there, snugly concealed in its hiding place.

I flick the book open. It has indeed been carefully hollowed out – and it's empty.

'Maybe she moved it somewhere else,' Mary Corbet says.

'Now why would she have done that?'

'I don't know. Maybe she'd decided it just wasn't safe leaving it there any more.'

'And what might have led her to the conclusion that it wasn't safe where it was? Could she perhaps have seen a number of suspicious-looking characters lurking around her bookcase?'

'It's not funny!' Mary Corbet says.

'I wasn't trying to be funny,' I tell her. 'I was just trying to show you how absurd your explanation is. Let's face it, Mary – she took her clothes, and she took her money. She's run away.'

'Linda wouldn't do that,' Mary says. 'She'd have been going to university next year – and she was so excited about it. And even if she *had* run away – and she'd no reason to in this world – she'd have found some way to contact me, so I wouldn't worry.'

'I have to go,' I say, heading for the door.

She moves quickly, to block my way.

'If she'd run away, she'd have been sure to take Theodore Bear with her,' Mary says. 'And where's her school uniform? Why would she have taken that with her?'

'When was the last time she wore it?'

'The night she went round to Janet's house . . .' She pauses. 'The night she was *supposed to* go round to Janet's house,' she corrects herself. 'The night that she went missing.' She takes another pause – this time for breath. 'So how do you explain that, Miss Redhead? How do you explain the fact that Theodore Bear is still here – and her school uniform isn't?'

I can't explain, but though those two things provide some slight counterweight to the theory that Linda has run away, they are nowhere near heavy enough to tip the scale in the opposite direction.

'I'm sorry, Mary . . .' I say.

'I wasn't going to tell you this, because I was afraid you might think I'd gone a bit mad, but I went to see a medium last night.'

'Oh, for God's sake, Mary!' I groan.

'You shouldn't mock mediums, Miss Redhead. The police use them all the time.'

'No, they don't. They *very occasionally* listen to what mediums have to say, but usually, when the truth is uncovered, it's a million miles from what the medium told them.'

'I . . . I spoke to Linda. She said that she was dead, and that she was lying close to water. Why would she have said that if it wasn't true?'

'Two rivers and a canal run through this city, Mary,' I say. 'If Linda was dead – which she isn't – then of course she'd be lying near water. None of us in Oxford is ever very far from water.'

'And she said that we shouldn't bother to look for her, because what happened to her is all her own fault.' I'm tempted to say that we should respect Linda's wishes then, and stop looking for her – but that would only feed Mary's delusion that she'd actually talked to her daughter.

'The medium may have genuinely been trying to help you, or she may just have seen you as an easy mark but, whichever it is, you can't trust what she told you,' I say.

'She didn't tell me anything. It was Linda who told me.'

'No, it wasn't.'

'She doesn't want me to look for her, but I have to. Her soul will never rest until she's given a decent Christian burial.'

'I have to go, Mary,' I say.

'If you don't help me, I'll kill myself,' she screams, her fists clenched into tight little balls. 'I'll do it – I swear I will.'

I don't exactly believe her – she is, after all, an *aficionada* of amateur dramatics – but the problem is that I don't exactly *disbelieve* her, either.

I am not in the business of tracking down runaways and dragging them back home. Linda is of an age at which she is entitled to make her own decisions but, even if she wasn't, the law simply does not give me that power.

And anyway, if Linda *has* gone to London, I will never find her, because London is a very big city, and I simply don't have the resources at my command.

But, I argue to myself, if I can at least come up with some proof that the girl has left Oxford of her own free will, then I will have done all that is humanly possible – and if Mary Corbet still chooses to top herself after that, it will have nothing to do with me.

She's looking at me. She knows she's broken down my resolve, and she's doing her very best not to give me a last-minute escape route by seeming too triumphant.

'I'll give the investigation another two days of my time,' I say.

'But two days may not be—' she starts to protest.

'Two days,' I repeat firmly, holding up my hand to emphasize my determination. And then, to make sure I've left no loopholes open, I spell it out even more clearly. 'That's forty-eight hours, Mary.'

'I know.'

I make a show of examining my watch. 'Forty-eight hours starting from right now.'

'Oh thank you, Jennie,' she says with a humility that makes me want to curl up and die. 'Thank you *so* much.'

FIVE

The senior tutor at St Margaret's High School for Girls is called Mrs Conner. She wears purple-tinted half-moon glasses, which could, I suppose, be for a medical condition, but they blend in so well with her tightly curled blonde hair and her suede waistcoat that I'm guessing they're more of a fashion statement. She is in her late thirties, and exudes an air of brisk efficiency which, as I look at her across the desk, I perversely find both admirable and annoying.

'You say that you're acting on behalf of Linda's parents, Miss Redhead,' she says.

'That's right.'

'Do you have anything in writing to confirm that?'

No, I think, *but I've a pocket full of bank notes to prove how serious Mrs Corbet is. Will that do?* What I actually *say* is, 'I'm afraid not. They didn't seem to think that would be necessary.'

'Ah, then we find ourselves in a rather tricky situation. I wouldn't want you to think I'm questioning your integrity . . .'

When people feel obliged to say that, what they actually mean is that – damn right – they're questioning your integrity.

'No, of course not,' I say, to make things easier for her.

'. . . but, given the confidential nature of whatever I might impart to you in this room, I'd feel much happier if the parents could confirm that you're acting as their agent.'

'Fine with me,' I tell her. 'Why don't you give the mother a ring?'

'I'd . . . err . . . prefer to talk to the father,' Mrs Conner says.

Ho-hum, nobody trusts Mary – and nobody wants to deal with her, unless they absolutely have to.

'Inspector Corbet may be difficult to contact,' I say.

'And why is that? Is he involved in a major policing operation at the moment?'

'No, he's up to his knees in manure.'

'I beg your pardon!'

'He's out on his allotment – doing a bit of digging.'

'He has an allotment!' Mrs Conner asks, incredulously.

'Yes.'

'What an extraordinary thing for a fairly senior police officer to be interested in,' Mrs Conner says. She pauses for a moment, as she weighs up her options, then – no doubt recalling other conversations with the over-dramatic Mary Corbet – she continues, 'Well, perhaps we can just assume that you have the parents' authorization. What, exactly, would you like to know, Miss Redhead?'

'We could start with you sketching out Linda's academic background,' I suggest.

'Linda has a good brain – but not a first-class one,' Mrs Conner tells me. 'She'd never make a research scientist, but fortunately she appears to have no desire to become one, and there's no reason at all she couldn't become a perfectly acceptable medic.'

'Do you think that studying to become a doctor is what she really wants for herself?'

'What do you mean?'

'Well, she does seem to have a very real passion for world literature, doesn't she?'

'Does she?'

I think that I've got Mrs Conner's number now. What she likes about her job is the title (and possibly the money). It's the actual tutoring – getting to know the kids you're dealing with – which is a bit of a drag.

'She's got a whole bookcase full of serious books in her bedroom,' I explain. 'And they're not just any old serious books – you can tell they've been selected to encompass a wide literary panorama.'

Mrs Conner wrinkles her nose, as if I've just broken wind.

Then she laughs. 'Well, I'm afraid the world needs competent doctors much more than it needs wild poets,' she says in a patronizing manner which really gets right up my nose.

Biting back the obvious comment, I content myself with saying, 'I'm sorry, I seem to have got us off the point. You were telling me that she should make a perfectly acceptable medic.'

'And so she will – but not if she continues on as she is. Even without this disappearing stunt she's apparently decided to pull, the standard of her work this year has fallen far short of what I've come to expect of her.'

'Are we talking about the standard over the whole year?' I ask.

'No, it was shortly before the start of the Christmas holidays that the rot seemed to set in. It wasn't that the work she started turning in was bad – it was just well below the standard I knew she was capable of. Then, sometime in March, she showed signs of really going off the rails – and it's not just her work I'm talking about now.'

So Tom Corbet was right, and Mary Corbet was wrong, rather than the other way round, I think. I can't say I'm surprised.

'Would you like to explain to me what you mean by the term "going off the rails", Mrs Conner?' I ask.

'We have a strict school uniform policy here, and – unlike in many other schools – this is not relaxed when our girls enter the sixth form. This code is quite clearly spelled out to parents when they apply to have their children admitted, and it is rigorously enforced.'

Memories of my own school days drift back uninvited – me, a twelve-year-old, standing in front of Miss Chapman's desk, and thinking that the way she perches her glasses on the end of her pointed nose makes her look just like an owl; Miss Chapman, glaring up at me as the fingers of her right hand beat out a declaration of war on the desktop.

'How would you describe the knot in your tie, Jennifer Redhead?'

'I don't know, Miss.'

'Did someone teach you to do up your tie in that flamboyant manner?'

'Pardon, Miss?'

'You look like what we used to call a spiv. Do you know what a spiv was, Jennifer Redhead?'

'No, Miss.'

'They sprang up just after the war – although "crawled out of the woodwork" might be a better way to describe them. They sold goods

– *usually* stolen *goods* – *that it was impossible to get on the ration card. They had pencil-thin moustaches and wore loud suits and ties with ridiculous knots like the one you've tied. You wouldn't like to be mistaken for a spiv, would you?'*

It had seemed to me that since I was a girl – and had neither a flashy suit nor a pencil-thin moustache – it was unlikely that I ever *would* be mistaken for one, but I understood the rules which governed Miss Chapman's narrow little universe, and so I replied, dutifully –

'*No, Miss, I wouldn't like that at all.'*

'*So who did show you how to tie that knot?'*

'*Nobody showed me. I made it up myself.'*

'*Well, we do not "make up" things in this school, Jennifer Redhead. We use a half-Windsor knot when we fasten our ties. Is that clear?'*

'*Yes, Miss.'*

And here I am, nearly two decades later, talking to a woman who doesn't look – or dress – like Miss Chapman, but who, I suspect, has the same ice-cold contempt for children's creativity pumping through her veins.

'I take it from what you're saying that Linda *did* infringe the uniform regulations in some way,' I say – and it is only with great effort that I avoid adding 'Miss' to the end of the sentence.

'She did indeed infringe the regulations,' Mrs Conner says gravely. 'She started wearing badges.'

Oh dear, dear, dear! I'd feared it might be something truly horrendous, like coming to school topless, with her nipples dyed bright green, but it's even worse than that – she started wearing badges!

'A prefect's badge or a house captain's badge would have been permissible,' Mrs Conner continues. 'In fact, having taken on the responsibility of the office, she was almost obliged to wear them at all times on school premises, but these new badges she started wearing were clearly unauthorized.'

'What were they like?'

'Most of them were cheap quotations, taken, I would imagine, from the half-intelligible utterances of greasy-haired pop singers. I really can't recall what most of them said, but one did stick in my mind.'

'Oh?'

'It said, "Nothing that is worth knowing can be taught." Now what kind of degenerate would ever come up with a thought like that?'

'Oscar Wilde,' I say.

'I beg your pardon?'

'It's a quote from Oscar Wilde.'

'Well, there you are then. He was a degenerate, wasn't he?'

'Perhaps he was,' I agree, 'but he still managed to write some bloody witty plays.'

She gives me a vinegary stare. If I had been one of her pupils, she'd probably have had me running around the hockey pitch a dozen times for daring to use such language in her esteemed presence.

'However, I did manage to counter that quotation with a rather telling one of my own,' Mrs Conner says complacently.

She sits back and waits for me to ask what it was – typical teacher's trick – but, given the context, I don't think there's any need to.

'"Genius is one per cent inspiration, and ninety-nine per cent perspiration." Thomas Edison,' I say.

'Exactly,' she says – but she looks rather miffed that her opportunity to enlighten me has been snatched away from her. 'And Linda's problem of late,' she ploughs on, because having worked a pretty good line, it's a pity to waste it, 'has been that she's been starting to think it's one per cent perspiration and ninety-nine per cent inspiration.'

'Were you surprised when she ran away?' I ask.

'I think it's fair to say that I was more disappointed than surprised,' Mrs Conner tells me.

'Do you have any idea what brought about her change in attitude round about Christmas time?'

'I'm afraid I don't.'

I am not amazed by the total unhelpfulness of her answer – but I think I know someone who *will* be able to help me.

IT'S NEARLY FOUR O'CLOCK, and I'm standing outside St Margaret's.

The school is one of those Victorian buildings which, with fewer windows, might easily have been one of the dark satanic cotton mills of my Lancashire heritage – and with a few more could just about pass itself off as the 'little palace' that the cotton magnate who owned that mill would have built for himself.

St Margaret's is surrounded by high railings, each one topped with a wicked spike, which is pretty much guaranteed to keep the innocents inside protected from the lecherous and lascivious world which exists outside. Ah, but when the bell rings, the gates are thrown open, the teachers go home, and the innocents not met by their parents are left to fend for themselves!

As the girls stream out, I remember what Mrs Conner said about the dress code, and find myself conducting a critical examination of the school uniform. The blazers are purple – a revolting purple, I quickly decide – and just looking at the thick grey woollen stockings is enough to make my knees start to itch.

It is certainly not the sort of outfit I would take with me if I were running away to London – but then I've never been a great one for uniforms of any sort, and one of the happiest days of my life was when I ditched my WPC uniform for plain clothes.

The younger girls are allowed out first – probably to avoid them being trampled in the rush – but gradually the escapees get taller and taller, and when they reach the right height, I put my hand into my pocket and bring out a photograph that Linda's mother has given me.

I soon spot the girl I've been waiting for. As her picture fore-warned me, I couldn't call her exactly ugly, but it would be quite a stretch for me to describe her as attractive.

But what the photograph hasn't prepared me for is the way she walks. Her gait does not reflect her looks at all, being neither overly diffident nor blatantly aggressive. Rather, she moves with a confidence which is not designed to impress anybody watching, but is simply an expression of her. She is, as my American friends would say, comfortable in her own skin.

When she draws level with me, I step in front of her and tell her who I am, and what I am doing there.

'Would it be possible for us to have a little talk – maybe over a cup of tea?' I ask.

'Yes, I don't see why not,' she says easily, without any sign of suspicion or guile.

THE TEA ROOM IS CALLED the Mad Hatter's, a reminder (as if anyone living in Oxford really needed one) that this is the city in which Lewis Carroll – a man who, under his real name, Charles Lutwidge Dodgson, was supposedly no mean mathematician – wrote his famous fantasy adventures.

Once we step inside the tea room, it becomes apparent that, apart from the name over the door, there is little connection with *Alice's Adventures in Wonderland* – and I look in vain for dormice peacefully asleep, March Hares going completely crazy as only March Hares can, or Red Queens who employ decapitation as a way of expressing their displeasure.

There are only two tables occupied. At one sits a group of four blue-haired old ladies, talking about a fifth absent old lady called Marjorie, who, it appears from their conversation, is such a nasty piece of work that she would make Attila the Hun seem like Mother Teresa. At the other of the occupied tables are two star-crossed adolescents, whose love blinds them to the pimples of youth which sadly heavily afflict them both.

I lead Janet to the table which is as far as possible from both the bitching circle and the lovers, and order a pot of tea from a waitress who is dressed like a maid in a period drama.

'Have you got a cigarette?' Janet asks.

As a matter of fact, I have. I don't smoke myself (overly competitive hockey players shouldn't), but I carry a packet of Benson & Hedges Special Filter around for just such occasions as this one.

I take out the cigarettes, offer one to Janet, and light it for her. She sucks the smoke down into her lungs, showing no sign of discomfort that I am not joining her in her habit.

'You gave Linda Corbet an alibi for the night she went missing, didn't you?' I say.

Janet shakes her head.

I've been expecting this response, because now that it's obvious something has gone seriously wrong, it's only human nature (and especially teenage human nature) that she should do everything she can – tell whatever lies are necessary – in order to keep *herself* out of trouble.

'Are you quite *sure* that you didn't offer to alibi her?' I ask, in a tone in which I intend to suggest that whilst I will insist on the truth come what may, I will not be too condemnatory when she finally feels herself compelled to confess it.

The look on her face tells me she thinks I'm talking down to her – and I have to admit that she's right.

'I'd have been no good as an alibi, because I wasn't at home that night,' she says.

'I'm not quite following your logic,' I confess.

'You mean that you can't see why the ability to provide an alibi is dependent on me being at home?'

'Exactly.'

Janet grins. 'I thought private eyes were supposed to be really smart,' she says. 'They certainly are in all the movies I've seen.'

'What have I missed?' I ask, with a touch of humility which might just compensate for my earlier misjudgement.

'Say Linda's parents had decided to ring up, and I'd been out,' Janet says. 'They'd have asked my parents if Linda was there, and my parents would have said that no, she wasn't.'

'But if you'd been there . . .?'

'If I'd been there, I'd have made damn sure I got to the phone ahead of my parents.' She mimes picking up a telephone. 'I'd say something like, "Oh, hello Mrs Corbet, it's Janet speaking. Linda's on the loo at the moment. Shall I ask her to call you back?" Then I'd ring the number of the place where Linda really was, and tell her to call home.'

'Has that ever actually happened?'

'No, it hasn't.'

'Is that because you refused to do it?'

'No, it's because she never asked me to.'

'What if she *had* asked you for an alibi? Would you have provided her with one?'

'I might have done,' Janet says. 'But before I did, I'd have needed to know exactly where she was going.'

'*Why* would you need to know that?'

'Because I couldn't stop her doing something stupid or dangerous, but I certainly wouldn't be prepared to make it any easier for her.'

'So you really have no idea where she went last Friday night?'

'None at all.'

'Has she contacted you since she went missing?'

'No.'

'Do you think she ran away to London?'

'I couldn't say – one way or the other.'

I don't get the feeling that her lack of responsiveness is because she's either stone-walling me or sulking. In fact, I'm almost certain that the reason she is not saying much is because she doesn't have much to say – and I find that really rather strange.

'I always thought that best friends knew everything there was to know about each other,' I prod.

'Who says we're best friends?' Janet counters.

'Aren't you?'

'Not any more.'

'So what happened?'

'She drifted away from me.'

'You mean that you drifted apart?'

'No, I mean she did the drifting, while I stayed anchored and hoped she'd decide to drift back.'

'When did this happen?'

'Just before Christmas.'

Just before Christmas!

About the time that Mrs Conner – she of the tinted glasses and trendy suede waistcoat – says that Linda's school work started to take a dip!

'And what caused her to drift away?' I ask.

'I was probably too honest with her.'

'Would you like to explain that?'

'She asked me, shortly before the end of term, if I thought she had a good chance of getting into Oxford, and I said she had no chance at all. I really tried to say it as gently as I could, but . . .'

She stops talking, and waves her arms helplessly in the air, thereby creating a swirling pattern of cigarette smoke.

'Even if you were very, very gentle when you said it, it was still a bit mean of you, wasn't it?' I ask.

'No, as I said, it was honest.' Janet stubs her cigarette out in the ashtray, grinding it perhaps a little more than is strictly necessary. 'Look, Linda's a smart girl,' she continues, 'but Oxford is one of the world's three or four top educational establishments – and it simply doesn't operate like most universities do.'

She's not wrong. Oxford is a collegiate university. Its structure is more feudal than federal – which is to say that, while each college pays homage to the university (much as feudal barons paid homage to the king), it is virtually independent. You don't apply for admission to the university – you apply to the individual college, which is where, if you are accepted, you will receive most – if not all – of your instruction. Furthermore, the person who interviews you – and who alone has the power to accept or reject you – is probably the man or woman who will be your tutor for your entire college life.

But what really matters here is the size of the colleges. Walk along the High or Broad Street and look at the splendid buildings in which the colleges are housed, and it is easy to fall into the trap of thinking that each college must have thousands of students.

Wrong!

The bigger colleges, like Christchurch and Keble, have fewer than five hundred undergraduate students. The smaller ones, like Oriel, have just over three hundred. So in any one year, there just aren't many places to be had. And given that many of the places which *are* available have already been earmarked for applicants whose fathers and grandfathers attended the college, or are a shoo-in for pupils from the major public schools, whose whole educational career has been shaped towards getting them into Oxford (and these two groups have a substantial overlap), there aren't many perches left for the rest of us chickens to occupy.

I don't mean to suggest that the people who get in through the back door are so dumb that their knuckles scrape the ground – many of them are very bright indeed – but it's not a level playing field, and if life has placed you at the bottom end of the slope, you need to be pretty damn good if you're going to get in.

'So Linda wasn't good enough to get into Oxford,' I say to Janet.

'Sadly not.'

I find her certainty irritating.

'And the reason you're in a position to judge this is because you *are* good enough?' I ask tartly.

'Yes,' Janet says, without hint of bravado. 'I am.'

'So you'll be expecting to go to Oxford yourself?'

She shakes her head. 'No, that's far too close to home for my liking. I'll be going to Cambridge, instead.'

'And you're sure you'll get in?'

'I'm *already* in. I took the entrance examination a year early.'

This girl has the ability to make me look foolish without really trying – and I don't like it.

'What happened after you'd told Linda that she simply wasn't clever enough?' I ask.

'At the time, she just looked disappointed. I tried to give her a reassuring hug, but she pushed me away. The next day she was sort of back to normal, but there was something missing.'

'Missing?'

'It was as if there was suddenly a black hole in our relationship – as if she no longer considered herself my best friend, but had decided to keep on playing the *role* of my best friend. I think, if I'm honest, that she didn't really like me any more, but felt she needed to stay close to me.'

'Why?'

'Because even though she didn't like me, she still trusted me – and most people need a confidante. And, of course,' she laughs bitterly, 'she was waiting for the opportunity to try and prove me wrong.'

'And did she get that opportunity?'

'She thought she did.'

'Tell me about it.'

'It was in early March. We'd pretty much stopped leaving school together by that point, but on this particular day she stuck close to me. It didn't take me long to work out why – when we got to the gates, there was a good-looking young man standing there, waiting for her. She kissed him – not a deep kiss, just a peck on the lips – then she turned to me and said, "This is Jeff. He's my boyfriend." So I said hello to him, and he said hello back – but I got the impression that he'd rather not have been there at all.'

'What happened next?'

'She said, "Jeff thinks science is a waste of time. He thinks that only dull people – people with no spirit – study science." That was a dig at me, of course, because I'm a physicist. And, of course, she was also giving herself a face-saving device. So what if she wasn't good enough to study medicine at Oxford? Medicine was science – and science didn't matter.'

'How did Jeff look as she was saying all this?'

'He was looking more and more uncomfortable as time went by. But she hadn't finished yet. "Jeff says I've got just the right sort of brain to be a wizard at literature," she said, "and he should know, because he's *already* a student at St Luke's"!'

'I imagine that, by this point, Jeff was really squirming,' I say.

'He'd practically melted with embarrassment.'

'But he probably considered it was a price worth paying, if it got him into her knickers?'

Janet laughs – and it's the deep, hearty laugh of someone who's really amused.

'You surely don't think she's letting him screw her, do you?' she asks.

'Don't you?'

'Positively not! Linda has some very old-fashioned notions. She'd never uncross her legs without a ring on her finger – and I'm talking about a wedding ring, not just an engagement ring.'

'Unlike you?'

Janet shrugs, as if she thinks it's a stupid question to ask – and probably pointless.

'I lost my cherry on a summer holiday in Tuscany, when I was fourteen,' she says. 'He was a waiter at the hotel that my family was staying in. His name was Mario, but then that's hardly surprising, because most waiters seem to be called Mario, don't they?'

'Did you enjoy it?'

'Not a lot. I think it's just amazing how much the sociological and anthropological aspects of our culture have focused on a fleshy tube between a man's legs which happens to harden when it's engorged with blood.' She shrugs again. 'But I suppose it's still a man's world, so men get to set the agenda.'

'Tell me about Linda's family,' I suggest.

'Her mother's a nice enough woman in her way, but she does tend to see the whole of life as a drama – with her acting in the starring role.'

'What about her father?'

'His main problem with her is that he seems incapable of recognizing the fact that she's growing up.' Janet pauses. 'Mind you, in a way, he's right. She's terribly naïve.'

'Is that why you'd insist on knowing where she was going before you gave her an alibi – because she's terribly naïve?'

'Yes, I suppose it is.'

'Do you know about the incident in front of the Playhouse – the one where the police were called in?'

'Oh yes – she told me about that. Some of Jeff's friends from St Luke's College got filthy drunk and started behaving badly, and Linda – because she's so easily influenced – went along with them.'

'After that particular incident, her father threatened to throw her out, you know.'

Janet laughs again. 'He would never have thrown her out – not in a million years. He's devoted to her. He worships the ground she walks on.' She is suddenly more serious. 'And it works the other way as well,' she continues. 'One of the reasons she so desperately wanted to get into Oxford is because she thinks that's what he wants.'

'When I asked you if you thought that she'd gone to London, you said you didn't know.'

'And I don't.'

'Her mother says she would never have run away.'

'Her mother would, wouldn't she? And actually, I'm rather surprised myself, because she's a very conventional girl – but if she isn't here, she has to be somewhere else, and unless she's been abducted by Martians, she's in that "somewhere else" because that's where she chooses to be.'

On the surface, Janet seems to have been very open with me, but I'm still not sure to what extent I can trust what she's told me. I don't mean that I suspect she's been deliberately lying to me, but the truth as she sees it may not necessarily be all that close to reality.

The thing is, I've experienced myself what it feels like when your best friend gets a boyfriend before you do.

It warps your perspective.

It challenges your niceness.

You want to say he's a waste of time. You want to cast an unfavourable light on what he does and what he says, so that she'll decide he's not good enough for her, and things can go back to what they were.

It takes a great deal of willpower to overcome your resentment and to be really – *really* – happy for your mate now that she's hitched up. I like to think I succeeded, but I'm sure there are half a dozen girls back in Whitebridge (maybe even my then-best friend herself) who will say that I didn't.

And there are other matters over which Janet might be jealous. Linda is very pretty, and Janet is not. Is it possible that, in some hidden part of Janet's brain, there lurks the feeling that it is unfair Linda should have both the looks *and* the academic success, and that when she told Linda she wasn't good enough for Oxford, she unconsciously did it to hurt her?

'You remember you said that you told Linda she'd never get into Oxford?' I ask.

'Yes.'

'Most girls – most people – wouldn't have done that to a friend. Even if they weren't prepared to tell an outright lie, they'd have fudged things by saying that she might be lucky with the questions on the entrance exam, or the don interviewing her might see hidden potential.'

'I know,' Janet agrees.

'So why didn't you do that?'

'I wanted to,' Janet says. 'I knew it would drive a wedge between us if I told her the truth.' Tears have started to appear in the corners of her eyes. 'But when you love someone – *really* love someone – you have to sacrifice yourself to protect them. And that's what I was doing – trying to protect her by preparing her for the disappointment I knew was coming.'

SIX

It is a sunny Thursday morning, and I am cycling down Broad Street (known locally as the Broad), which is my favourite thoroughfare in the whole of Oxford. It is one of only two streets (the other being the High) which dissect the heart of the university, and on it – or just off it – you will find Blackwell's famous bookshop, the History of Science Museum, the Bridge of Sighs and the Sheldonian Theatre.

But I'm not making this journey for my own pleasure. It's strictly business – and that business is Linda Corbet.

My current thoughts on Linda run thus: (i) Linda is very keen on literature, but agrees to study medicine in order to please her father; (ii) her friend Janet tells her she will never get into Oxford, and she decides that no other university is worth the candle, but (iii) she doesn't immediately abandon her science studies, because she is too timid to make the grand gesture, and so she simply begins to take less care over her work, then (iv) she meets a student from St Luke's and this doesn't just revive her interest in literature – it makes her fall head over heels in love with it, and most especially with Robert Cudlip (1612–1659), and finally (v) last Friday she tells her parents she's going to visit a friend, packs her bag, takes her money out of its hiding place in the Enid Blyton book, and runs away.

What I don't yet know is what was so special about last Friday. And there just has to have been *something* special about it to push her into a course of action that neither her mother nor her best friend thought she was capable of.

For a moment, I toy with the idea that she's eloped with this boy Jeff, but from Janet's description of them together, it's clear that they were more like an unexcited Darby and Joan (and him a very reluctant Darby at best) than they were Romeo and Juliet, consumed with passion.

I'm beginning to wish that I had never taken her case on (*beginning to wish: that's a laugh!*) because sooner or later I'm going to have to pay Mary Corbet another visit, prove to her that Linda ran away, and leave her with the knowledge that her daughter cares about her so little that she cannot even be bothered to let her know that she is safe and well.

I search for a distraction (who wouldn't?) and fix on Charlie Swift, the man I'm on my way to see.

I ONLY HAVE A FEW true friends, which is due, no doubt, to my sceptical detached nature (or possibly my terror of being let down), but Lord Charles Edward George Withington Danby Swift is one of them. Charlie is the bursar at St Luke's, a post which, in most educational institutions, would mean he was little more than a bookkeeper. But not here! Within the context of an Oxford college, being bursar makes a man a power to be reckoned with, because he does more than keep accounts and post bills – he controls the wealth.

And make no mistake about it, most of these colleges are

wealthy. Much of the wealth is based on land, often gifted to them by the various warriors, cowards, wise men, drooling idiots and plain homicidal maniacs who, over the centuries, have worn the British crown. And land in England (a very small country with a very large and increasingly pressing population) is hugely expensive, especially when it lies as close to London as Oxford does. Nor, when I talk about land, do I mean a couple of large fields – it is said (though I've never checked this out myself) that you can walk from St John's College, Oxford to St John's College, Cambridge without once stepping on land which is not owned by one of those two colleges.

I met Charlie – the man with the power! – during my first week in Oxford, at a reception in the Master's Garden.

To say that I felt out of my depth at that reception would be as huge an understatement as calling what sunk the Titanic 'an ice cube'.

For openers, I was a woman in a college which had only started admitting women the previous year (and still had precious few).

But that was nothing compared to the other disparities.

I was a northern girl, and when I looked around me, I still half-expected to see smoking factory chimneys, not Matthew Arnold's dreaming spires of the Oxford colleges.

I was lower middle class – it was years since Dad had push-biked around collecting insurance payments at people's back doors but, even so, his trousers still bunched at the ankles, as if his body retained a physical memory of cycle clips.

I was state educated and talked with a heavily vowel-based regional accent, whereas most of the people around me spoke in that lazy drawl which is almost the secret language of the more expensive public schools.

And last but not least, there were my clothes. We were all wearing subfusc, which is a strict requirement whenever the Master is present at an event. That meant I was dressed in a dark jacket, white blouse, black bow tie, dark skirt, dark stockings and black shoes, as well as a commoner's gown which only reaches down as far as the top of the buttocks, and so is generally known as a bum freezer – all of which should have helped me to blend in.

Right?

Wrong, because all the other girls' outfits were top-of-the-line Jaeger, and mine had been purchased at Ramsbottom's ('Down-to-Earth Prices for Down-to-Earth Folk') Spring Sale.

As I stood there on that lawn, ignored by all these people who seemed to know each other – and had no interest in ever knowing me – I had never felt so alone in my life.

I was just about to attempt to slip away unnoticed when I felt someone tap me lightly on the right shoulder and heard a plummy voice say, 'Hello, you seem to be a little down in the mouth. What's the matter, my dear – won't the other children play with you?'

I swung around, furious at being so openly ridiculed, and saw Charlie for the first time.

He was in his early forties then – a tall, stately looking man with hair the colour of pale straw. I was on the point of telling him what I thought of him (I may well have been about to use the word 'arsehole' once or twice) when I saw that, despite his words, the expression on his face was completely free of malice.

'I'd ignore them, if I were you,' he continued. 'They're so terribly cliquish. But then, the *nouveau riche* always are.'

'The *nouveau riche*!' I repeated incredulously.

'That's right,' Charlie confirmed. 'Take that chap over there.' He pointed to a young man whose face could not have been more flushed with aristocratic arrogance if he had put a saddle on a convenient serf and was riding him around the estate. 'I happen to know that only a couple of centuries ago, his family hadn't even got a pot to piss in.'

'Only a couple of centuries ago!' I repeated, teetering uncertainly between gratitude at being rescued and a protective belligerence which had not quite gone away. 'Is that meant to be some kind of joke that only people already in the know would really understand?'

'Most certainly not,' Charlie said. 'In Oxford, as you'll find out for yourself when you've been here a while, we tend to take the long view on such matters.' He paused, and looked down at the glass of white wine he was holding in his hand. 'This Pinot Gris is perhaps just a little too fussy for my taste,' he continued. 'What do you think of it?'

I thought it was only the third glass of wine I'd ever drunk in my life, and I was in no position to judge.

'I've tasted better,' I said, casually.

Charlie just grinned.

'Have I said something funny?' I asked.

'No. I'm smiling because I'm embarrassed.'

'Embarrassed? What about?'

'About putting you in a rather difficult position.'

'I don't understand.'

'I said the wine was a Pinot Gris, but now I realize it's a Chablis, and you – having known from the first sip what it really was – have been wondering whether to correct me or just let it pass.'

My first impression had been the right one, I thought – the only reason he was talking to me was that it gave him the chance to humiliate me.

'What kind of sick bastard—?' I began.

'There's no shame in not knowing about wines, you know,' Charlie interrupted me.

'There might not be, but it certainly feels like there is here,' I replied.

Charlie looked around him.

'Perhaps you're right,' he agreed. 'What I'm really in the mood for now is a pint of best bitter in the Eagle and Child. Would you care to join me?'

'I would,' I told him. 'I'd like that very much.'

AS I GET CLOSER TO St Luke's, I find myself pondering on the architectural mélange that is the University of Oxford.

The Taj Mahal, or the Church of Notre Dame de Paris, to take just two examples, are the products of a single magnificent vision, but Oxford colleges are much more piecemeal add-on affairs – less overarching concept, in other words, and more Lego – and St Luke's is a perfect example of that.

When the college was founded in 1208 (the founder being Guy de Torre, 3rd Baron Forshaw, a noble lord who had made his fortune in the sacking of the ancient city of Constantinople and the slaughtering of its inhabitants), it consisted of no more than three private houses and a small chapel. And so it remained for over a hundred years, until, using an endowment from Thomas Cosgrove, a wool merchant, the college bought the houses behind it, and, by the simple expedient of building between the two rows, created the first of the college's quadrangles. The second quad, built in the fourteenth century, was Gothic, and has gargoyles of nightmare ferocity staring down disapprovingly over the lawns below. The third was built in the Renaissance style, the fourth was Baroque, the fifth Neoclassical, the sixth Gothic again (it had come back into style) and the seventh and final quad is a Victorian mishmash. Thus from tiny acorns do mighty hybrids grow.

I wonder if, when he was assuaging his guilt by spending his blood money, our founder, Guy, ever imagined that he would one day give the opportunity to a girl from the sooty north to have her already fine mind polished and refined, thus equipping her for the life of a private detective with a one-roomed office and an overdraft.

I suspect not.

A GROUP OF TOURISTS – FROM the way they're dressed, I'd guess they are Americans – is clustered around a guide near the gate; as I push my bike past them, I hear the guide say, 'And, of course, even today, and despite all the changes we've seen since the war, well over half of the students come from public schools.'

'Oh I think that's just wonderful,' says one of the tourists – a woman in her forties with a kindly face.

'Wonderful?' the guide repeats, confused.

'Why yes,' the woman says. 'We're standing in front of this marvellous college, which I'm sure offers a truly great education, and you tell us that well over half of the students in it come from the public schools. Don't *you* think that's wonderful?'

'Well, not exactly,' the guide says.

'I mean to say, we Americans pride ourselves on being democratic and coming from a land of equal opportunity, but I'd be real surprised if over half the students at Harvard or Yale attended public school rather than private school.'

The guide looks slightly embarrassed, though whether it's for her or himself, I'm not quite sure.

'The public schools are private,' he says.

'Excuse me?' the woman says.

'The public schools are private. They're mostly boarding schools, and they're usually very expensive.'

'So what do you call the schools that aren't private?' the woman asks, mystified.

'They're state schools,' the guide says.

'Private schools that are called public schools and public schools that are state schools,' she says, slowly and carefully, as if trying to get it straight in her mind. 'It seems a little bit crazy to me.'

You've got a point there, lady, I think, as I push my bike around the group and into the archway.

The porter comes out of the lodge, and smiles at me.

'Good morning, Miss Redhead,' he says. He pauses. 'Or should I be saying "Good morning, Mrs . . ."?'

'It's still Miss Redhead,' I tell him.

He shakes his head in mock despair. 'It's a crying shame, so it is. In my opinion, any young gentleman who doesn't try to snap you up wants his head looking into.'

'I dare say you're right,' I agree. 'And how are you feeling yourself, Mr Jenkins?'

'I can't complain. Not that it would do any good if I did. The last college servant to complain was my great-grandfather, and if they didn't listen to him then, I don't see why they should listen to me now.'

And he winks at me – something I've never seen him do to any other member of college.

I am one of the few students or ex-students I have ever heard put a 'Mr' in front of the porter's name, I remind myself as I park my bike against the porter's lodge, and I do it not because I am a natural rebel against the great traditions of the college, but because I just can't bring myself to call a man who is my father's age only by his surname.

I pass beyond the gate and cross the de Torre Quad, heading for the Fellows' Quad, where Charlie Swift has his rooms.

From the entrance to Charlie's staircase, I can see the Master's Garden through the archway, and I feel a shudder run through me – because the garden still reminds me of the desperate state Charlie was in when he walked into the Lamb and Flag, that day in the late spring of 1964.

IT HAD BEEN OVER seven months since the garden party, and Charlie and I now met regularly for drinks. We were a strange couple, divided as we were by age, background and place in the college hierarchy, but the simple fact was that we enjoyed each other's company and had become real mates.

I'd already grabbed a table when Charlie walked in through the door, and I was shocked in the change in him. He looked much smaller, greyer and older than the last time we'd met, only days before, and when the barman shouted out, 'A pint of the usual, Lord Swift?' he seemed barely to have the energy to nod.

He sank down into the chair opposite me.

'I'm in trouble,' he said, without any preamble.

'What kind of trouble?' I asked.

'I was in the Master's Garden late last night. I had a friend with me.' Charlie hesitated. 'We went into the bushes.'

'Went into the bushes?'

'For sex – all right! We went there for sex!' Charlie said, with uncharacteristic aggressiveness.

I felt an unworthy stab of jealousy. I didn't want to go to bed with Charlie, and would almost certainly have turned him down if he'd suggested it – but still, I was a little miffed that he hadn't at least asked me.

Charlie put his hands to his head. 'Oh, why didn't we just go to my rooms? It would only have taken a couple of minutes.'

'What went wrong?' I asked – because it was becoming plain that all his troubles emanated from what had happened in the garden.

'Apparently, there have been complaints from some of the dons that the undergraduates had been using the Master's Garden after dark, and because of the complaints, the bulldogs decided to conduct a random check last night. We – my friend and I – were right in the middle of things when the bulldogs' torches hit us. My friend ran away, but I couldn't, because my trousers were around my ankles.'

It was hard not to laugh. It must have been embarrassing for Charlie, certainly, but as a senior member of the college he'd been perfectly entitled to be in the garden with his guest, and the most he could expect from the Dean's Committee was a slap on the wrist.

'The bulldogs have reported to the dean that my companion was male,' Charlie said.

'Well, why don't you just tell the dean that they're talking bollocks?' I asked lightly.

'I can't – because he *was* male,' Charlie said.

Three years later, none of this would have mattered, because by then the Sexual Offences Act would have passed through Parliament, and Charlie would have been legally able to screw any man he fancied, as long as that man was over twenty-one and consenting.

But this was 1964 – the year that the four loveable mop-heads called The Beatles conquered the United States and Cassius Clay, the world heavyweight boxing champion, changed his name to Muhammad Ali.

'If the dean reports it to the police, Charlie, you might well go to prison,' I said.

'He *will* report it to the police – he has been made aware that a criminal act has been committed within the college grounds, so he has no choice in the matter – and I *will* go to prison,' Charlie said, gloomily.

'How many bulldogs were there, Charlie?' I asked.

'Two.

'And did they get a good look at your companion?'

'Not a very good one, no. It was dark in the garden, and all they had was their torches. Besides, Adam was wearing his duffel coat because, at that stage, there was no need for him to get undressed, and when he ran away, he'd already pulled his hood up.'

'Would they have seen the colour of his hair?

'Probably.'

'And what colour is it?'

'He's a blond – but darker than me.'

'I'm going to go to the dean and tell him I was the one who was with you,' I said.

'You can't do that!' Charlie protested. 'Think of your reputation.'

'And think of yours if I don't do it,' I told him.

AS I STOOD THERE IN the corridor, with only an ancient oak door between me and the Dean's Committee for College Discipline, I reflected on the fact that within a short space of time, I might no longer be a member of the college I'd worked so very, very, hard to get into.

Was I regretting voluntarily putting myself in this position?

No, emphatically not – because, whatever happened to me, I couldn't let sweet, gentle Charlie go to prison.

The heavy door swung open, and I found myself looking into the eyes of a grim-faced bulldog.

'You may enter,' he said – as if he was reluctantly doing me a favour.

I entered.

The dean and two senior fellows were already seated behind a large table. A bulldog – even grimmer than the one who had admitted me – stood behind them, rigidly at attention. The second bulldog joined him, and now there were five pairs of eyes burning into me.

'Sit down, Miss Redhead,' said the dean, indicating a chair facing the table, which, unlike their chairs, did not have hundreds of years of history carved into its back.

I sat on the modest, modern chair and, as I did so, I felt the devil enter me – he does that sometimes – and I determined that if I was going to be sent down anyway, I might as well have some fun.

The dean – a stout man who has always reminded me of Dickens's beadle – looked me up and down.

'Is it your contention, Miss Redhead, that last night you were in the Master's Garden with the bursar?' he asked.

'Yes, sir,' I replied.

'And . . . err . . . was some act of intimacy taking place?'

'If you mean by that, sir, was I down on my knees, about to give Charlie Swift a—'

'Just answer yes or no,' the dean interrupted, hastily.

'Yes.'

'The bulldogs think it was a man on his knees in front of the bursar,' the dean said. He turned to one of the bulldogs. 'Isn't that right?'

'Yes, sir,' the bulldog said.

'It was me,' I insisted. 'I was wearing my duffel coat – and duffel coats are such bulky things that it's almost impossible to determine the sex of whoever's inside them, especially in the dark.'

'Are you sure it was you?' the dean asked ponderously.

'I'd hardly expose myself to this humiliating interrogation if I wasn't sure, now would I?'

The three wise men put their heads together, and talked in whispers. The bulldogs, rigid as ever, stared at the far wall.

After a couple of minutes of whispering the three wise men looked up, and the dean delivered the verdict.

'We have dismissed the charge of trespass against you, since you were in the garden as a guest of a senior fellow,' he said.

He seemed to be expecting me to say something. My first thought was to tell him I would be eternally grateful that they had found me not guilty of something I was plainly – by their own argument – not guilty of, but prudence prevailed, so all I said was, 'Thank you, sir.'

'We have also dismissed the charge of moral turpitude, since, when the bulldogs interrupted you, you hadn't quite . . . you hadn't quite . . .'

'I hadn't quite . . . ?' I asked.

'But there was no doubt that you intended to commit moral turpitude, is there?'

'No, sir, I was certainly going to—'

'Thus, you are clearly guilty,' the dean said, interrupting me for a second time – and for the same reason as he interrupted me the first. 'However, given your youth, we are minded to ascribe most of the blame to the bursar, and on this occasion we are prepared to issue no more than a warning. But we will expect exemplary conduct from you in the future, Miss Redhead.'

'Thank you, sir,' I said, suitably meekly. 'Thank you very much.'

I left the room with only a slight stain on my character. I don't think it was so much that they believed me, as that they needed to *appear* to believe me, because, if they hadn't, Charlie would have ended up behind bars – and really good bursars like him are hard to find.

I MET CHARLIE LATER that afternoon, in the Eagle and Child.

'How did it go?' I asked, though I already knew it could not have gone *too* badly, because he was back to being almost his normal self.

'Oh, they lectured me about being *in loco parentis*, and I pointed out to them that you were of an age at which, legally, no such requirement did – or could – apply. Then they told me that the decent thing would have been to take you to my rooms, and I replied that my doctor had prescribed both fresh air and sex to me, and I was simply combining the two.'

'You really said that?' I asked.

'Oh yes. And finally, when all else had failed, they pointed out that we might have damaged some of the flora, and I agreed, but countered with the point that because of the bulldogs' intervention, we'd had no opportunity to roll about crushing the Master's precious marigolds.'

'So how did it end?'

'They invoked the college statute of 1345, under which I could be fined five groats – and not just any five groats, but ones produced by Edward III's royal mint. I think the reason the statute is so specific has something to do with Edward's groats having a higher silver content than those churned out by his father's mint.'

'And how do you intend to lay your hands on five medieval coins?' I chuckled.

'Clearly, I can't, but the statute seems to have thought of that, and allowed for an alternative.'

'Which is?'

'I'm to provide the dean with six leather feeding-bags, full to the brim with oats. They'll be no good to the dean – he's never owned a horse in his life – but he'll insist on it, because he's a real stickler for tradition.'

'I'll get you a pint,' I said.

'No, I'll get you one,' Charlie countered. 'And Jennie . . .'

'Yes?'

'I really appreciate what you've done, and I'll be forever in your debt.'

'You don't owe me anything,' I told him, offhand. 'I did it because you're a friend.'

'Then as a friend, I promise you this – if you ever need anything, you only have to ask.'

He meant it then, and he means it now, but there must have been times since I've become a private detective that he wishes he'd simply kept his mouth shut.

SEVEN

I turn my back on the Master's Garden – and on memories of the Dean's Committee for College Discipline! – and climb the staircase.

Charlie, like the gentleman he is, does not wait until I knock on his door but is there on the landing to greet me. He is wearing a Savile Row suit, a white shirt, and a tie which I believe identifies him as an officer in the Grenadier Guards. His black shoes are polished to a mirror shine, and when he reaches out to touch my shoulder, he exposes one of his solid gold cufflinks. He looks like a million dollars, and I would be flattered that he'd made the effort, if I didn't already know that he would be dressed like this even if he wasn't expecting any visitors.

'CT,' he says, and kisses me chastely on both cheeks, 'what an absolute delight to see you.'

CT is short for Carrot Top. If anyone else called me that these days, I would probably kick them right in the nuts, but Charlie is Charlie, and so he gets away with it.

He gestures to the open door of his rooms. 'Please enter my humble quarters,' he invites me.

Humble quarters!

Right!

Charlie's 'humble quarters' consist of two rooms and a bathroom. One of them is an immense living room/study with a desk and filing cabinets at one end – he does have a regular office in the administrative wing, but rarely uses it – and at the other, his antique furniture, lovingly collected over a forty-year period. The second room, the bedroom, must have been equally immense until part of it was shaved off, sometime back in the Fifties, when the college authorities decided that while St Luke's had many historic traditions which must be preserved at any cost, having plumbing was probably a good idea, and thus installed the bathroom.

No kitchen? you ask. *No utility room?*

Why would Charlie need either of those?

He lives a privileged life, but since he comes from an equally privileged background, he is scarcely aware of the fact. His rooms are cleaned, and his clothes cared for, by his faithful scout, who has worked for the college for over thirty years, and whose father and grandfather probably worked there before him. He eats in the Great Hall, except for breakfast, which his scout picks up from the kitchen and brings to his room. I doubt he has ever crossed the threshold of a supermarket, and though it's conceivable that he may know how to change a light bulb, I wouldn't put any money on it.

WHILE CHARLIE IS MAKING the tea (that much, he has learned to do!), I take the opportunity to slip into the bathroom, which is an Italian marble extravaganza that he paid for out his own pocket. And it is once I am on the loo that I notice the framed poster on the wall.

Actually, it is not a poster at all, but a blow-up of two of the inside pages of the *Daily Examiner*.

I gaze at the headline.

What a to-do, Milord!

It refers, of course, to the unfortunate incident in the Master's Garden. By rights, the whole affair should have been quietly put to bed with the ruling of the Dean's Committee. And no doubt it would have been, if the story hadn't been leaked by one of the college servants who was part of an experiment to discover whether it was possible to hire staff with no family tradition of serving the college (it turns out it wasn't). Even then, the actions of this latter-day Judas Iscariot (as he was affectionately labelled by other servants) might have led nowhere, had it not been for the fact that the local journalist who paid Judas a retainer for juicy information had the ear of a Fleet Street tabloid editor.

But given that the servant *was* on a retainer, and the journalist *did* have the editor's ear, the story landed on the editor's desk and, once it was there, there was no way he wasn't going to run it.

This Oxford tale had it all – a private police force, a noble lord, and sexual 'goings-on' in a garden normally reserved for pondering on the philosophical mysteries of the universe. It may even have been that my red hair was the cherry on the top of the cake, though that could just be me pushing my own significance a little too far.

At any rate, the story did come out as a double-page spread.

Below the screaming headline, there are two photographs. One is of two men – models, probably – dressed as bulldogs and looking very stern in their bowler hats. The second is of a garden, which would seem a plausible Master's Garden to anyone who didn't know what it actually looked like.

The story (?) follows:

Lord Charles Swift, the bursar of St Luke's College, Oxford, thought he was safe enough conducting his nocturnal hanky-panky in the Master's Garden of the exclusive college, but the financial wizard hadn't counted on his activities being disturbed by the bulldogs, the university's bowler-hatted private police force, which has the power to arrest anyone within four miles of a college building. So it must have come as a shock to him to find himself and his companion – sultry redhead Jennie X, a student at St Luke's – caught *in flagrante* in the bulldogs' torch beams.

There was more – at least another three columns – but I hadn't read them at the time, and I don't read them now.

BACK IN THE LIVING room, I mention the poster to Charlie.

'Ah,' he says, the hand which holds the exquisite china teapot freezing for a moment, 'I normally remember to take that down when I know you'll be visiting me.'

'But why do you have it hanging there at all?' I ask.

He shrugs, and a tiny splash of Earl Grey launches itself from the spout of the teapot.

'I'm not sure I really know why,' he confesses. 'Maybe it's just an old queen's way of sticking two fingers up at what used to be a highly disapproving world.' He frowns. 'But if it bothers you to know it's hanging there, CT, I'll take it down permanently.'

'It doesn't bother me – not now,' I tell him.

But it had bothered me – or at least created some very awkward moments for me – at the time.

IT WAS MY FIRST trip home to Whitebridge since the story had appeared in the tabloids. When I arrived on the Saturday, my parents were somewhat distant (no change there, then, distance being pretty much a way of life in my family), but made no mention of the incident. It was only on Sunday, over afternoon tea in the front parlour – an obligatory family ritual which the outbreak of World War III, and Russian tanks rolling down our street, would probably not have interrupted – that Mum decided to broach the dreaded subject. And, even then, she did it in that roundabout way for which she was justly famous.

Picture the scene.

There were fresh antimacassars on the chairs, and the place reeked of newly applied beeswax. We were all sitting with plates of cakes (the best china, because, after all, it was Sunday) balanced on our knees.

Suddenly Mum sighed.

'Was it you yourself who told that newspaper reporter that you were a sultry redhead,' she asked, 'because you're not, you know.'

'No, it wasn't me, Mum,' I replied.

'Then what *did* you tell him?'

'Nothing – I never even spoke to him.'

'Well, I'm not going to call you a liar, Jennie, but if you read what he wrote about you, it certainly *sounds* as if you talked to him.'

We both relapsed into silence, and the only sound to be heard was the ticking of the old grandfather clock which has counted off the lives of several generations of Redheads.

Tick-tock, tick-tock . . .

'You've put me in a very difficult position, and make no mistake about it,' Mum said finally, as she reached across to the cake stand for another scone. 'I just don't know *what* I'm going to say to the neighbours.'

'For heaven's sake, Mum,' I said, exasperatedly, 'why would the neighbours expect you to say anything to them? When was the last time you talked to Mrs Robertson?'

'I don't know.'

'Or Mr and Mrs Talbot?'

'It's been a while.'

'It's been ten years – at least.'

It's true – my mother doesn't talk to the neighbours. It would be wrong to say she thinks of herself as above them – that would be being snobbish, and she's no snob, as she will tell you herself at great length. It's just that, well, most of them are not worthy of her time.

It was Dad's turn to talk. He didn't want to – that much was obvious – but there is only so long that anyone can withstand my mother's glare.

'We expected better of you, Jennie,' he said.

At this point I could, I suppose, have told them the truth.

It's all right Mummy and Daddy, I didn't do all those naughty things with the nasty bursar, because he prefers young men.

But that would have really been to put the homosexual cat amongst the homophobic pigeons because, from their point of view, it was preferable to have a daughter who was a scarlet woman than to have one who was friends with a *queer*.

'Look, I'm very sorry the newspaper got hold of it,' I said, 'but this is the swinging 1960s, you know – you surely didn't expect me to still be a virgin, did you?'

'Parents always live in hope,' Dad replied, heavily.

More silence – more clock ticking.

'Still, I suppose that if you *had* to bring disgrace on the family, at least you did it with a better class of person,' Mum said finally.

And from that day to this, none of us has ever referred to the unpleasant incident again.

'SO HOW CAN I help you?' Charlie asks, as he awkwardly mops up the tea with an immaculately ironed linen napkin.

'I need some information on several St Luke's students,' I say, and hand him a list of the boys who were arrested on Beaumont Street with Linda Corbet. 'I thought you could tell me who to ask.'

'Is this for a case you're working on, CT PI?'

'Yes.'

'And what sort of information are you looking for?'

Aye, there's the rub. I don't *know* what sort of information. Trying to find out what exactly happened on the night Linda Corbet disappeared is like feeling my way around a blackened room, and not only do I not know where the light switch is, I'm not even sure what it looks like.

'I want some general information,' I say, so I don't appear a complete bloody idiot.

'I might have some "general" information myself,' Charlie says, abandoning his mopping with evident relief, and walking over to the filing cabinet which stands next to his desk.

He takes out a list, scans it quickly, and then reaches into the cabinet again and produces a thin blue file.

'All college societies are eligible for a grant to subsidize their activities,' he says, flicking the file open, 'but in order to qualify for it, they must register with the bursary. The six students on your list each belong to several college societies, just as you might expect. Is that the sort of thing you're looking for?'

'I suppose so,' I say, trying not to sound dubious.

'Two of them are in the Debating Society, and three of them are members of the Athletics Association. They all row, and – now this really is very interesting – they all belong to the Shivering Turn Society.'

The Shivering Turn Society! The name rings a recent bell with me, but I can't quite put my finger on where I've heard it before.

'In case you're wondering what the society does, it's dedicated to studying the works of a Metaphysical poet called Robert Cudlip,' Charlie says.

Of course – Linda's blouse embroidery project!

Or will you, like a cold and errant coward / Abandon all and make a shivering turn!

'Your degree was in English Lit, wasn't it?' Charlie asks.

'Yes.'

'So was mine. Did you get a first?'

'Regrettably not.'

'I did, which must mean I'm immensely clever.'

'Oh, it does, Charlie,' I agree. 'Your intelligence is matched only by your modesty.'

'The point is, I studied the Metaphysical poets, and yet I've never heard of this Robert Cudlip. Have you?'

'No,' I admit, 'I haven't.'

'Isn't that typical of the kind of undergraduates we're getting these days!' Charlie says in disgust.

'What do you mean?'

'They're all so bloody pretentious. They could have got together to study Shakespeare's sonnets – God knows, there's enough depth and meaning in the sonnets to keep them busy for a couple of lifetimes – but instead choose someone totally obscure, probably because they think that makes them look more profound. What pathetic little wankers they really are!'

'When did the society last meet?' I ask.

'That's almost impossible to say. When the bigger societies decide to hold a meeting, they have to book a room, and we'll have a record of it. But there are only ten listed members of the Shivering Turn Society, and so they could quite easily meet in one of the member's rooms.'

'Is that uncommon?'

'Is what uncommon?'

'That a society only has ten members?'

'No, it's not at all uncommon. As far as some of these insignificant little shits are concerned, the exclusivity of the society is its main attraction. In fact, there are half a dozen societies which could simply be called "The Only Reason I'm Forming This

Society Is So That When You Apply To Join, I Can Turn You Down and Feel Superior Society".'

So what have we got? I ask myself.

Linda has a boyfriend called Jeff; Jeff is a member of the Shivering Turn Society which concerns itself with studying the works of the poet Robert Cudlip; Linda was in the process of embroidering one of Cudlip's poems on to her white blouse, and everyone arrested with Linda outside the Playhouse was a member of the society.

I'm beginning to think that since the Shivering Turn Society has begun to play such an important part in Linda's life, the society – or at least some of its members – might have played a significant part in her decision to run away. Perhaps they did no more than encourage her. On the other hand, they might have actively helped her – finding her a job in a company that one of their fathers owned, for example. It may even have been more negative than that – perhaps they ridiculed her because she didn't have the courage to do what she really wanted to do, and that tipped her over the edge.

'I think I'd rather like to talk to these boys,' I tell Charlie.

'Then why don't you just go ahead and do it,' he suggests.

'The thing is, though I want to talk to them, I'm not convinced they'll be awfully willing to talk to me.'

'Why wouldn't they be?'

Simply put, they won't want to own up to an action which they must know will have seriously pissed off an inspector in Thames Valley Police, because – however rich or important their fathers are – a local copper, if he really sets his mind to it, can still make their lives very uncomfortable.

But I don't want to explain any of that to Charlie, partly because he'll probably pick so many holes in my theory that I'll start to doubt my own instincts.

So I just say, 'I'd like to tell you, but I can't really do that without breaching client confidentiality.'

'And we wouldn't want that,' Charlie says. 'So let me see if I've got this straight – you want to talk to them, but you think a certain degree of compulsion will be necessary?'

'Yes.'

'If you need someone to crack the whip over them, then we'll have to go to the dean, 'cos he's the chief whip-cracker in this here college,' Charlie says, in what I assume he fondly supposes to be an American cowboy's accent.

'The dean and I don't exactly get on,' I say. 'I know he *wanted* me to lie about what went on in the Master's Garden, but I think there's a part of him that feels I should have been too *terrified* to lie to the almighty dean, and he still resents the fact that I did.'

'The dean will be no problem at all,' Charlie says confidently. 'And that's not because he's a nice man – I know him better than most, and can assure you, he isn't; it's because he's at war with the dean of St John's at the moment, and he needs me as an ally.'

'What kind of war is it?' I ask, even though I can tell from his tone that he's planning to have a bit of fun at my expense.

Charlie grins. 'You're a smart girl – a private investigator, no less – and you've been around Oxford long enough to know how colleges work. What kind of war do *you* think it might be?'

'I don't know,' I admit. 'Academic?'

'No.'

'Theological?'

'No.'

'Philosophical?'

'No, it's not that either.'

I sigh theatrically. 'You know, Charlie, this could take all day.'

Charlie's grin widens. 'Indeed it could.'

'Or you could break the habit of a lifetime and give a straight-forward answer to a straightforward question.'

'It's "the War of the Two Self-Indulgent Epicureans",' Charlie says, in the manner of a stand-up comedian delivering his care-fully honed punch line.

'It's what?'

'Perhaps I should explain,' Charlie says.

'Perhaps you should,' I agree.

'Last Thursday, the dean of St John's invited our dean over to his college for dinner, and our dean made the stupid tactical error of complimenting the dean of St John's on the bottle of Château Haut-Brion *premier cru* which was served with the main course.'

I smile. Only in Oxford – or, to be fair, possibly only in Oxford and Cambridge – would anyone have bothered to say 'Château Haut-Brion *premier cru*', when 'red wine' would have done just as well.

'Why was it a tactical error to mention the wine?' I ask.

'Ah, because, as far as I can gather from our dean's long rant to me, it gave the dean of St John's the perfect opportunity to be patronizing. He appreciated the compliment, he said, but the last thing he wanted was for our dean to spend sleepless nights worrying over what wine to serve when he reciprocated the hospitality. Then, apparently, he actually patted our dean on the shoulder, and said he quite understood that St Luke's was much poorer than St John's, and in the interest of their long-standing friendship, he was more than willing to rough it for once with a much inferior wine.'

I chuckle. 'The dean must have been furious,' I say.

'He was livid. After that dinner, he did a bit of research, and he found that most experts on wine agree that a certain vintage of Château Margaux *premier cru* easily tops the Château Haut-Brion he was served, and now he wants me to lay down a dozen bottles of the stuff, so the next time the dean of St John's comes calling, *he* can be made to feel like the poor relation.'

'It must be expensive,' I say.

'It would probably be cheaper to start a real war,' Charlie admits. 'Which is why, if I am prepared to buy it for him, he'll be prepared to jump through hoops for me. And he can start by lining up these interviews with the Shivering Turn Society.' He takes another sip of his tea, and seems not to notice that by now it's stone-cold. 'Is there anything else I can do for you?'

'Do you have photographs of all the members of the Shivering Turn in your records?' I ask.

Charlie frowns, as if he's beginning to suspect – quite correctly – that he won't like what's coming next.

'Yes, I do have photographs,' he admits reluctantly. 'But they're only small ones – the sort you use for passports. And you know yourself that passport photographs never look like the real person.'

'I'd like copies of them anyway,' I say.

Charlie frowns. 'I'm not sure I can give them to you,' he said. 'Photographs attached to confidential records are, in a sense, a part of those records, and hence attain a degree of confidentiality in their own right.'

'I wouldn't want you to do anything that would make you feel uncomfortable,' I say – knowing I'm making him feel uncomfortable by the very act of saying it.

Charlie is silent for perhaps half a minute, then he says, 'Tell me a story I can live with.'

'I'm doing a montage for my next alumni dinner,' I say. 'I'm calling it "St Luke's – Past and Present" and I need some photographs of current students for the left-hand corner.'

'Fine,' Charlie says.

EIGHT

If the interviews could have been set up straight away, I wouldn't be in the public bar of the Red Lion now. But they couldn't, because, as Charlie rightly pointed out, even when it's only a gluttonous dean you are bribing, bribery can still take time. And so, with a couple of hours to kill, I have come to the pub, hoping to talk to Harry Garstead, and thereby acquire a little background information which may just prove useful when talking to the Shivering Turns.

With this aim in mind, I order myself a gin and tonic and, while I'm paying for it, I say to the barman, 'Is Harry Garstead in the pub today?'

'That's him, over there in the corner,' the barman replies, jabbing the air with his index finger, and I can tell from the sour expression on his face that Garstead has never even come close to winning his Customer of the Week award.

My eyes follow the line of the finger. Garstead is sitting at one of those brass-topped circular tables which the breweries seem to think will give their establishments a touch of class. He's a thickset man with stubby fingers. I can't really draw any conclusions about him from his face, because most of it is obscured by the copy of *Sporting Life* that he's studying, and all

I can actually see is the expanse of red skin that covers the top of his almost bald head.

I take a sip of my gin and tonic, and think about which of the dozen business cards I carry around in my bag I will use today.

There's a good reason for the business cards. One of the first things that I learned about this job of mine is that people are sometimes reluctant to talk candidly to private investigators.

I don't blame them for that. Putting myself in their shoes, I wouldn't want to open up to a person I don't know, for reasons I haven't been given (and, because of the confidential nature of the work, *can't* be given). So what I provide them with – via the business cards – is a person who they *can* see some purpose in talking to.

As I cross the room to the corner table, I've narrowed it down to two – Cynthia Joan Lee from the University of Oxford's Psychology Department, and Maggie Jones from Radio Oxford. My final choice will be made when I get a look at Harry Garstead's face, and decide whether he will be more susceptible to the public spiritedness offered to him by the earnest Cynthia, or to the money dangled in front of his eyes by the bubbly Maggie.

I reach the corner table.

'Are you Mr Garstead?' I say.

He looks up from his paper, and makes a quick assessment of me through bloodshot eyes which are both cunning and suspicious.

'I might be Harry Garstead,' he says. 'What's it to you?'

Looks like it's going to be money, then!

I reach into my handbag, take out the Maggie card, and hand it to him. He glances at it, then drops it carelessly on the table. To be honest, he does not seem overly impressed.

'It's always such a treat for me to meet one of our listeners,' I say, in an enthusiastically girlish voice.

He picks up his cigarette, which had been smouldering away in the ashtray, and takes a drag.

'Well, if that's how you get your jollies, you're right out of luck today, ain't you?' he says.

I look appropriately shocked – and perhaps a little distressed.

'Don't you listen to Radio Oxford?' I ask.

He shakes his head. 'Nah, I've got better things to do with me time than listen to all you idiots blathering away.'

'Oh, that is such a pity,' I say, 'because, you see, only our *regular* listeners are entitled to compete for the big cash prize.'

His bloodshot eyes are suddenly a deep, swirling sea of avarice.

'How big?' he asks.

'I'm sorry?'

'How big is the big cash prize?'

'Oh, didn't I say? It's five hundred pounds.'

'Then I hope my little joke won't have disqualified me.'

'Your little joke?'

'People don't always get my sense of humour, and you must be one of them. When I said I didn't listen to Radio Oxford, I was only joking. I tune into it all the time.'

I look relieved – but still a little uncertain.

'Honestly?' I say.

'Honestly,' he reassures me.

'Well, in that case, there's nothing to stop us proceeding with the first stage of the competition. Do you mind if I sit down?'

He gestures to the chair opposite him with all the style and grace of a syphilitic warthog, and I sit down.

'You're a porter at Oxford Railway Station, and you were on duty last Friday night,' I say. 'That's right, isn't it?'

'How do you know that?' he asks, suspiciously.

I giggle. 'Oh, you surely don't expect me to reveal all the tricks of my trade, do you, Mr Garstead?' I ask him. 'Let's just say that we in the media have our ways and means.'

The ways and means in this case being to go to the station and ask who was on duty on Friday night and where I'd be likely to find him.

'Yes, I was there,' he admits.

'Now, as you know, the competition we're running is called "Don't Miss a Trick". As a regular listener, you'll already be familiar with the rules, won't you?' I ask.

'Yeah,' he says, uncomfortably.

'Unfortunately, I'm obliged by the sponsors to explain the whole procedure before we begin. I know that will be boring, but there's nothing I can do about it.' I smile. 'Sorry.'

'It's all right,' he says, relieved.

'The aim of the competition is to test just how observant ordinary members of the public like yourself really are,' I continue, 'and what we're entering now is what we call the knockout stage. If you get through it successfully – and having met you, I think there's a very good chance you will – then the next round will take place at the radio station and will be broadcast live. Do you understand?'

'Yeah, yeah,' he says, with the impatience of a man who wants the money and doesn't really see why I don't just give it to him.

I take out the pictures of the members of the Shivering Turn, plus those of several other students from St Luke's College – all of which were given to me, albeit somewhat reluctantly, by Charlie Swift – and spread them evenly across the table.

'One – or several – of the people in these photographs were at the railway station on Friday night,' I say. 'To qualify for the next round, you must pick that person or those persons out. If you fail to select one who was there, or alternatively select one who wasn't, you will be automatically disqualified. Do you understand that?'

'Yeah.'

Garstead glanced down at the photographs, and then looks up at me.

'I don't suppose that you could give me a bit of a hint, could you?' he asks me.

'I'm afraid not.'

He licks his lips. 'Don't get me wrong, I'd like the five hundred quid all to myself, but four hundred is better than nothing, and if you was to, you know sort of help me out a bit . . .'

'I'll pretend I didn't hear that,' I say sternly.

Slightly disappointed, he turns his attention back to the pictures, and – since he's clearly going to have to do this on his own – studies them carefully.

'Him, him and him,' he says finally.

I look at the three he's chosen. Only two of them are members of the Shivering Turn.

'Are you sure, Mr Garstead?' I ask. 'Because, as I explained earlier, if you get even one wrong . . .'

'On second thoughts,' he says hastily, 'it was just him and him.'

He has eliminated the non-member. I give him my bubbly

Maggie Jones smile, to indicate to him that, though the competition rules mean I can't *tell him* that he's right, right is what he is.

'What time was it when you saw them?' I ask.

'It would be about eleven o'clock.'

'Are you sure of that?'

'Yeah, it was just before the London mail train pulled in.'

'And what were they doing?'

'Doing?'

'Were they meeting someone from a train? Or did they get on a train themselves.'

'Is this part of the quiz?'

'Oh yes, very much so. It's about *observation*, remember.'

'They wasn't meeting the train, and they wasn't waiting to get on it themselves, neither. They was just walking up and down – as if they was looking for somebody.'

Or making sure that somebody wasn't there!

Because this is my latest theory – Linda Corbet asked two members of the Shivering Turn to help her run away. Part of that will have involved driving her to her house (I'm sure that at least one of them will have a car), where she will have packed her bag and picked up her money. But the second part will have been to make sure that no one stopped her from leaving – and here, the person I'm thinking of is her over-protective father.

So while Linda hides away somewhere – probably in the ladies' toilets, which are a no-go zone for her dad – these two lads patrol the platform to see if Inspector Corbet does, in fact, turn up.

'Did you see this girl?' I ask, showing Garstead a photograph that Mary Corbet has given me of Linda.

'No,' he says firmly.

'You're quite sure?'

'Yes.'

In my mind, I can picture the whole scene – as the train pulls into the station, Linda comes out of wherever it is she's been hiding. But she is not exposed, because the moment she's out in the open, she is flanked by Hugo Johnson and Gideon Duffy (the two members of the Shivering Turn who the porter has picked out as being present on the platform on Friday night) and they stay by her side, giving her cover, until she is safely in the train.

'How about her?' I ask, sliding a photo of Linda's friend Janet across the table.

Why do I show him Janet's photograph, when I have already decided she played no part in Linda's disappearance?

I do it because you can be sure of nothing in my game, and when you're presented with the opportunity to cross-reference, you'd be a bloody fool not to jump at it.

'Ugly bitch, ain't she?' Garstead asks, looking at the photograph. 'I wouldn't fancy the idea of having to shag that when I got home from work.'

I imagine the feeling would be entirely reciprocated, I think.

'Did you see her on Friday night?' I ask, resisting the urge to poke him in both eyes – but only just.

'No, I didn't see her,' Garstead says.

I collect up the photographs, slide them into the envelope from whence they came, and put the envelope back in my handbag.

'Is that it?' Garstead asks.

'Yes.'

'And am I through to the next round of the competition?'

I shake my head. 'No, I'm sorry, but you're not.'

He looks gobsmacked at the news.

'Why the bloody hell not?' he demands.

'Because you missed one,' I tell him. And then, because I'm feeling particularly malicious, I add, 'You remember you picked out three photographs at first, and then rejected one of them?'

'Yeah.'

'Well, the one you rejected was also there.'

'Since I was so close, can I try again?' he pleads.

'I'm afraid not,' I reply. 'The rules of the competition are very strict on the question of second chances.'

I stand up. I had been planning to slip him thirty or forty quid of Mary Corbet's money as a consolation prize, but my dislike for him has been growing and growing over the interview, and now I have reached the point at which I would rather pull my own head off than give him a penny.

'Sorry it didn't work out, Mr Garstead,' I say.

'It was a complete waste of my drinking time,' he growls. 'And I'll tell you something else for nothing – that radio station you work for is nothing but a pile of absolute shit.'

'I'll pass your message on to my station manager,' I say. 'I'm sure he'll be devastated to learn that a gentleman of your refinement and intelligence has such a low opinion of him.'

'Are you taking the piss out of me?' he says, almost spitting the words out.

'Oh, Mr Garstead, whatever could make you think that?' I ask, in my normal – non-Maggie – voice.

*

I AM SITTING IN THE very seminar room in which I once defended my views on Shakespeare's *A Winter's Tale* to an increasingly annoyed tutor who had written a book on the play, and had clearly expected me to slavishly follow his interpretation of it. I am sitting, in other words, in the room in which my chances of ever being awarded a first-class honours degree flew out of the window.

This time, however, I am not here to get up the nose of a man on whom my academic future depends, but rather to question the members of the Shivering Turn Society whom the dean, in return for thirty pieces of silver (or rather, a case of Château Margaux) has decided to deliver up unto me.

The dean has not produced all six, as Charlie requested. In fact, there are only four of them waiting outside (does that mean he only gets two-thirds of a case of wine?), but that does not bother me, because the 'boyfriend' is there, as are the two I really need to speak to – Hugo Johnson and Gideon Duffy.

The investigation is all but over. Of course I would like to know *why* Johnson and Duffy helped Linda to run away, and I would like to know what made her decide to run away on that *particular* night, but that is just because I am a nosey parker by nature. All I actually *need* to close the case is a signed statement that they put Linda on the train.

I open the door, and look at the four young men waiting outside.

'I'll see you first, Mr Johnson,' I say.

Hugo Johnson is around six feet one inches tall. His body is well muscled (he, like the rest of the Shivering Turn, is a rower, I remember), but his face has still not quite lost its puppy fat. He moves with assurance. And why shouldn't he – he has been to a top public school, he is attending one of the best universities in the country, and when he graduates he will probably slip effortlessly into a comfortable job in a merchant bank, marry an appropriate young lady, have two appropriate children, and buy himself a country retreat where the shooting is good.

'Tell me about Linda Corbet, Mr Johnson,' I say.

'Who?' he asks, looking puzzled. 'Oh, you mean Jeff's Linda.'

'That's right.'

'She's a pleasant enough girl, I suppose, though I can't say she's really my type.'

'You mean she's nowhere near posh enough for you, don't you?' I ask.

'Well, she's certainly not a girl you would want to take home to meet the mater and pater,' he replies.

'But you were perfectly happy to have her knocking around with the Shivering Turn Society?'

'Knocking around with the Shivering Turn Society? Whatever gave you that idea?'

'She'd begun embroidering part of Cudlip's poem on her blouse.'

Johnson shrugs. 'I didn't know she was doing that – but I imagine there's no law against it.'

'So you're saying she never attended any of your meetings?'

'She most certainly did not attend. The Shivering Turn Society is strictly men only.'

'Why should a society dedicated to studying the work of a Metaphysical poet be for men only?'

'Well, there's a good deal of drinking goes on – and the language can become rather ripe.'

'She was with you when you were arrested,' I point out.

'That's not strictly true. She and Jeff only joined us a few minutes before the pigs arrived. I think they'd been to the cinema.'

'So they played no part in vandalizing the cars?'

'No, but neither did the rest of us. The pigs—'

'Do you think you could call them the police?'

'Oh, all right. The *police* fitted us up for that. Anyway, I can't see what all the fuss was about. The cars that were damaged were only tin boxes – there wasn't a Roller or Jag amongst them.'

'Tell me about Friday night,' I suggest.

'What about it?'

'You took Linda Corbet down to the railway station.'

'What an extraordinary idea! I did no such thing.'

'You were seen on the platform.'

'Can't have been me. I was in my rooms, playing Monopoly with a couple of the other chaps.'

'Look, Linda is old enough to leave home if she wants to,' I tell him, 'and there was nothing illegal about taking her down to the railway station.'

'Didn't do it,' Johnson says firmly. 'Playing Monopoly. Made a fortune out of rent on my hotel on Mayfair.'

This wasn't how it was supposed to have gone at all.

'I'm doing all this mainly for Linda's mother's benefit,' I explain. 'Her father knows what's happened, and has pretty much learned to accept it, so you have absolutely no reason to be afraid of him.'

'Not afraid of anybody,' Hugo Johnson tells me. 'Don't see why I should say I was at the railway station if I wasn't – and I wasn't.'

I push him for another five minutes, but it is clear that he is not going to budge. And the thing is, I don't really understand *why* he won't budge – what possible reason he could have for denying the truth.

In the end, I give up, tell him he can go, and ask him to send in Gideon Duffy on his way out.

Duffy has been cast in the same mould as Johnson – public school, big, muscular, self assured – and he is as adamant as Johnson that he was nowhere near the railway station on Friday night so, after a while, I am forced to give up on him, too.

I have decided to interview Jeff Meade next, but when I step out into the corridor, I find that there is only one person sitting there – and he's nowhere near handsome enough to have been Linda's boyfriend.

'You're Crispin Hetherington, aren't you?' I ask.

'Yes, I most certainly am.'

'And where's Jeff Meade?'

'Gone off for a crap. It's the third time he's been since we were all told we were going to have a cosy little chat with you. Must be something in the water, don't you think?'

A real smart-arse, even by Oxford standards.

Great – that's just what I need.

'Well, since he isn't here, I'll see you next,' I say.

'Do you know, you sound just like a pox doctor,' he tells me.

See what I mean?

NINE

Crispin Hetherington is much smaller and lighter than his friends – but he compensates for that with an air of arrogance which makes Hugo Johnson and Gideon Duffy look like understudies for Uriah Heep.

His hair is a wispy blond, his nose is relatively inconspicuous (he has somehow managed to avoid being born with the large aristocratic hooter that some of his companions are forced to carry round in the centre of their faces), his lips are thin, and his chin only just misses being a girlish oval. But none of this is of any real importance, because it is his eyes – his pale emotion-less eyes – that, despite my best efforts, I keep being drawn to.

Out in the corridor he has already shown himself to be a smart-arse *extraordinaire* and, even before I sit down, I have decided that I'm never going to get anywhere with him unless I take him down a peg or two first.

'I believe, Crispin, that you are the president of the Shivering Turn Society,' I say.

'I'd prefer it if you addressed me as Mr Hetherington, and yes, I do have that honour,' he replies.

I snort. 'It's not really that *much* of an honour, is it, *Mr Hetherington*? The Shivering Turn isn't exactly the United Nations

– or even the OU Philatelists' Association. When all's said and done, you can only muster nine members.'

'Ten,' he corrects me, 'and perhaps, when you're looking at the society, you should consider quality, rather than just quantity.'

'So your members are all quality, are they?'

'Yes.'

'In what sense of the word?'

'In every sense of the word.'

'Including Jeff Meade?'

He favours me with a thin, humourless smile.

'You were right, after all,' he says. 'We do have only nine real members – Jeff is more of a mascot.'

'Does he know that's how he's regarded?'

'Of course not. That would require some degree of sophistication, and he's about as sophisticated as dried rabbit shit.'

'I might just tell him that,' I say.

He wags his finger at me. 'Now I really wouldn't do that, if I were you,' he advises.

'Why not?'

'Because it would have completely the opposite effect to the one you intended.'

'Really?'

'Really! You would be hoping to turn Jeff against me, but he would not believe me capable of saying a single unkind word about him, so all you would succeed in doing is making him your enemy.'

For reasons not yet clear, Johnson and Duffy had spent their interviews stonewalling me, but stonewalling doesn't interest Hetherington. He not only seeks out conflict – he revels in it.

'Why is the Shivering Turn Society registered with the bursar's office?' I ask him.

'Why shouldn't it be?'

'The reason societies register is so that they can claim the grant – and you don't look as if you need the money.'

'Appearances can be deceptive,' he says. 'I come from a very poor family. Mother is poor, Father is poor, the butler is poor, the footmen are poor, the maids are poor, all twelve of our gardeners are poor . . .'

It is a very old joke, and I don't laugh. I don't even think he is expecting me to.

'You haven't answered the question,' I point out. 'Is that because you don't dare to?'

He smiles again. 'You're punching in the dark – just hoping that you'll hit something,' he tells me.

Yes, that's exactly what I'm doing.

'Will you answer the question, "Or will you, like a cold and errant coward, Abandon all and make the shivering turn?"' I quote at him.

'Oh, that really is very good,' he says, clapping his hands together slowly, in ironic appreciation. 'Very well. Let us just say that the reason I registered the society is because the bursar is a very stupid man, and it amuses me to hide something he would certainly not approve of right under his nose.'

'Would you like to expand on that?' I ask.

'No, that wouldn't be any fun at all.'

'Why do Hugo Johnson and Gideon Duffy deny taking Linda Corbet down to the railway station last Friday night?' I ask, changing tack.

'You'll have to ask them.'

'I have asked them, as I'm sure you're only too well aware – and now I'm asking you.'

'I am not my brother's keeper,' he says.

'No,' I concede, 'but you are your brother's puppet master.'

He claps his hands together a second time, then stands up.

'I've quite enjoyed our little chat, but now I'm getting bored and I think I'll go,' he says.

'I haven't finished,' I tell him.

'I cannot find the words to describe how little that is of interest to me,' he replies.

'Need I remind you, *Crispin*, that you're here on the instructions of the dean to answer—' I begin.

'On the *instructions* of the dean?' he interrupts. And then he laughs. 'You were a student at St Luke's yourself, weren't you?'

'Yes.'

'And you came from a poor but honest background, and were so incredibly grateful for the wonderful opportunity that had been presented to you?'

It's a gross distortion of my situation, but it's still close enough to make me feel uncomfortable.

'Stop pissing around, and get to the point,' I say.

'Clearly, though we are both members of the same college, our different backgrounds mean that we view it from a different perspective. To you, the dean is an authority figure who must be obeyed absolutely. To me, he is no more than a servant, just like the scouts and the kitchen scullions. So I am not here because of the dean – I am here of my own free will, in order to help you out in your search for little Jeff Meade's bit of totty . . .'

'Did I say she was missing?'

'Don't insult my intelligence,' Hetherington says. 'Feel free, by the way, to report my lack of cooperation to the dean. Who knows, he may decide to have me rusticated – though that would certainly make things rather awkward for him the next time he wants to insinuate himself into my father's box at the Royal Opera House.'

I don't try to stop him, and I wait until he's almost at the door before I say, 'Where were you last Friday night?'

He turns around, and there is a smile on his face which tells me that he's been waiting for just such a question, because that will give him the opportunity to demonstrate the full extent of his contempt for me.

'I don't know where I was last Friday night,' he says. 'I haven't worked it out yet. But I expect that by the time anyone of any importance asks me that same question – if anyone of any import-ance ever *does* ask it – I'll have a nice little story prepared which involves me being in my room with two or three of my chums.'

I wonder if a more softly-softly approach would have yielded better results, and quickly realize that it wouldn't have. Crispin Hetherington would have been just as objectionable whatever approach I'd used, because being objectionable and superior is both what he enjoys the most – and what he does best.

JEFF MEADE IS A YOUNG Paul Newman. I don't mean that he actually *looks* like Newman (for a start, his hair is dark and his eyes as black as coal) but he has the same instant effect on me as Paul Newman would have done if he'd walked in the room – the same 'Oh my God, is he for real?' sensation. And for all that Crispin Hetherington might refer to him as 'Little Jeff', he is at least three or four inches taller than his esteemed leader.

So his appearance is the first thing I notice. The second is that, unlike all the other members of the Shivering Turn Society I've talked to, he seems as nervous as hell – which might explain his regular trips to the loo.

'Take a seat, Jeff,' I say.

When he hears my voice, he immediately starts to relax.

'Your accent didn't really come through properly when you were just calling out our names, but it does now,' he says as he sits down. 'You're from up north, aren't you?'

'Yes, I am,' I agree.

'From Lancashire,' he says, narrowing it down. 'Maybe even from Whitebridge?'

'That's right.'

He smiles. 'I'm from Accrington!'

If he were still in the north, he would probably regard anyone from my home town as an alien being, to only be approached with caution – 'careful lad, they're right funny folk in Whitebridge.' Here in the south, one hundred and eighty-one miles from what all true Accringtonians know with certainty is the centre of the universe, he is inclined to embrace anyone who comes from within a ten-mile radius of that town as a next-door neighbour.

'What school did you go to?' he asks. 'Was it the Vale?'

'Yes.'

'I was on my school's football team. We played your school in the Lancashire Challenge Cup last year, and—'

'Vale's not *my* school,' I interrupt him.

'But I thought you said . . .'

'It was a school that I went to a long time ago. It's nothing but ancient history now.'

'But surely you must still have some of the old school spirit left, because, after all—'

'Look, I'd love to sit around chatting to you about the north, Jeff, but time is passing, and I've got a lot of questions to get through.'

'Yes, yes, of course, I can understand that,' he says, looking really dropped on. 'Ask away.'

'Tell me about Linda Corbet.'

'She's . . . she's sort of a friend.'

'Really? Crispin was much more explicit than that – he described her as your bit of totty.'

'We did go out a couple of times – to the cinema and that,' he agrees reluctantly.

'Where did you first meet?'

'There's a tea shop near her school called the Mad Hatter's. We met there.' He pauses, as if counting beats in a well-rehearsed script. 'Funnily enough, we might never have got together if I hadn't been such a clumsy oaf. I wasn't looking where I was going, you see, and I crashed straight into her. Her tea tray went flying halfway across the room. I apologized, bought her another cup of tea, and we got talking. And we sort of went on from there.'

Well-rehearsed, but not well-edited, I think. If you're going to lie, keep it simple.

'What made you go to the Mad Hatter's tea room in the first place?' I ask him.

His mouth falls open, as if he hadn't been expecting the question – which, of course, is exactly the case.

'I beg your pardon?' he says.

'Well, it's not exactly a student hangout, now is it? It's not close to this college, it's not close to the library – it's not even close to the shops. So why were you in the area?'

'I'd . . . I'd been out running.'

'I wouldn't have thought it was a particularly good place to run, either. The road is busy, the pavements are narrow – in your situation I'd have chosen to run down by the river.'

'Well, I didn't,' he says, clenching his jaw stubbornly, like a child who's been caught out in a lie.

'Tell me about the night you were arrested,' I say.

'That was all a big misunderstanding.'

'That's what a lot of people say when the bobbies feel their collars,' I tell him. 'So the seven of you – you, Linda Corbet, and five of your mates – had all been out on the piss and—'

'We *weren't* with them. We'd been to the pictures, and it was only by chance that we ran into them outside the Playhouse.'

In other words, he's implying that she had absolutely nothing to do with the Shivering Turn. But the more its members claim she wasn't a part of it, the more convinced I am that she was.

'Which film had you been to see?'

There is fresh evidence of panic on his face.

'What?' he asks, to give himself time to think.

'The film! What was it called?'

'I . . . I can't remember. It was a while ago now.'

'It wasn't really, you know. It was less than two months.'

'Well, anyway, I don't remember.'

'You amaze me,' I tell him. 'Carry on with what you were saying.'

'We were standing there, just chatting, and then these two bobbies came along. We weren't doing anything wrong, but they—'

'Yeah, yeah, you were totally innocent, and they were agents of the fascist state,' I say, in a bored voice. 'The fact is, you were caught red-handed, and you haven't got the balls to admit it.'

Angry men make mistakes, so I'm doing all I can to make Jeff angry – and I would appear to be succeeding.

'Look, if we'd done anything wrong, why did the police let us go?' he demands.

'I'm not sure,' I admit, 'but it could just have something to do with the fact that Linda's father is a police inspector.'

He visibly pales.

'She didn't tell me that Mr Corbet was a policeman,' he gasps.

That was hardly surprising, was it? Young girls don't like to put their boyfriends off, and to say your father is a policeman – or works in a slaughterhouse, or has been arrested on some particularly unsavoury charges – is pretty much guaranteed to do just that.

'Where were you on Friday night?' I ask.

'I was in my room. I had an essay to write.'

'You can't remember the name of the film you saw, but you can instantly recall where you were last Friday evening,' I muse. 'That *is* interesting, because if you'd asked me that very same question, I'd have had to think about it for at least a minute.'

'I'm nearly always in my room writing essays,' he tells me. 'I find the work very hard.'

It's a good recovery on his part, since it not only explains his instant recall, but also invites me to feel sympathy for him.

'What I don't understand is why it was Hugo Johnson and Gideon Duffy who escorted Linda down to Oxford railway station on Friday night,' I say. 'As her boyfriend—'

'I'm not her boyfriend.'

'That's how she introduced you to her mate, Janet.'

'She was just showing off to Janet – and I didn't want to humiliate her by denying it.'

'Then let me rephrase it,' I suggest. 'As her *friend*, I would have thought you should be the one to see her off, rather than Johnson and Duffy.'

'Hugo and Gideon weren't anywhere near the railway station on Friday night.'

'I don't see how you can be so sure of that, given that, by your own admission, you were in your room all night.'

'If that was what they'd done, they would have told me.'

'Not if they had a reason to keep it from you.'

'You don't understand. We're always totally honest with each other. We have to be. We're a band of brothers.'

Yeah, right, I think. Well, if he's going to deny that the Shivering Turn had anything to do with Linda's leaving, there's not much point in asking *why* she decided to leave.

'Moving on,' I say, 'what made you decide to join the Shivering Turn Society?'

He folds his arms across his chest – which I think means that he's suddenly gone all defensive.

'Why shouldn't I have joined?' he asks. 'Most students join all kinds of societies.'

'Yes, that's true, but they're mostly general-interest societies or societies connected with their studies – and you're a geographer.'

'Aren't geographers allowed to be interested in poetry?'

'Of course they are, but if you were going to study a poet, why choose a particularly obscure one?'

'Robert Cudlip is an undiscovered genius.'

'Is he now?'

'Yes, he is.'

'And would you care to quote one of his poems to me?'

Jeff Meade clears his throat. '"And dare you face your urges and desires—"'

'Not that one,' I interrupt. 'I'd like to hear one of his other poems.'

'I don't know any of the others off by heart.'

'Just tell me their titles, then,' I suggest.

'I haven't been a member of the society for long,' he mumbles.

'Which raises another interesting question,' I say. 'How did you come to join the society?'

'What do you mean?'

'Was there a notice in the junior common room which advertised the society?'

'No.'

'So how did you hear about it?'

He is silent for some time, and when he does finally speak, it is with a mixture of reluctance and pride.

'I was invited to join,' he says.

'Why?'

'I don't understand the question,' he says.

'I've just talked to three other members of the society. They're all in their final year, and they all come from what you might call "privileged" backgrounds, in which having an indoor swimming pool is probably considered a basic necessity of life. In addition, they were all educated at expensive public schools, and are studying either the arts or classics. That's them. And then there's you – a working-class, first-year geographer.'

'Are you saying I'm not good enough to be a member of the Shivering Turn Society?' he demands angrily.

'No,' I tell him. 'From what I've seen of the other members of the society, I'd say the Shivering Turn isn't good enough for *you*. But that's not the point. I can see why you might want to join the society. You're the only lad from Accrington in St Luke's – maybe the only lad from Lancashire – and you're feeling very isolated. So when these posh fellers offer you the hand of friendship, you make a grab at it. But what's in it for them?'

'Maybe I've got a winning personality,' he says – and I can tell that's not his own line, but one he's been fed.

'Do they ever make jokes you don't quite understand?' I ask, embarking on the course that Crispin Hetherington warned against, because I don't have anywhere else to go. 'Do you ever wonder what it is they're laughing at?'

'No,' he says, unconvincingly.

I am reluctant to press on with this line of questioning, because he is finding life difficult enough already, without me making him feel like a piece of shit. But then I remember the look on Mary Corbet's face, and realize I don't have any choice in the matter.

'Back in medieval times, they'd have given you a hat with bells on to wear,' I say.

'What do you mean?'

'You're the Shivering Turn's jester. You surely realize that. And I'll tell you something else – you'll be the only one without an alibi for Friday night. All the rest have covered for each other, but you're the outsider, and nobody cares what happens to you.'

'I know what you're doing,' he says, drawing on reserves of spirit from somewhere deep inside himself. 'You're working on the principle of divide and rule. Well, it won't work.'

No, it won't, I agree silently – at least, it won't work until I have more ammunition.

JUST AN HOUR AGO, I thought that everything was simple and straightforward. I'd believed that something had happened on Friday night which had made Linda want to leave Oxford, and some of the members of the Shivering Turn had done no more than help her.

I'm far from sure of that now. Now, as a result of all the lying and evasion from the four members of the society I've talked to, I'm beginning to think that it was not so much a case of Johnson and Duffy *helping* Linda board the train as it was of them *forcing* her to do it.

Why would they force her to leave?

Because they were afraid of the consequences of having her stay – because they were worried she might talk to the wrong people about what she'd seen!

But what had she seen?

Whatever it was, it has to be connected to the Shivering Turn – a society which is only registered with the bursary because, as Crispin Hetherington put it: 'the bursar is a very stupid man, and it amuses me to hide something he would certainly not approve of right under his nose.'

I read the extract of the poem again.

> And dare you face your urges and desires
> Embracing both the good and bad you own
> Or will you, like a cold and errant coward
> Abandon all and make a shivering turn?

Robert Cudlip is the key, I decide. The society was created in his honour, and will reflect his values.

I need to find out more about the man and, since this is Oxford, I know exactly where to look.

TEN

The Bodleian Library (or just the Bodley to us smart-arsed Oxford types) is one of the world's great libraries. It occupies a total of five buildings, the first completed in the fifteenth century and the last constructed in 1930, and even this is nowhere near enough storage space, so many of its books and documents are kept underground. Every time a new book – on any subject – is published in Great Britain, a copy of it must be submitted to the Bodley in order to establish copyright; when I last checked, it housed nearly twelve million items, including four copies of the Magna Carta and one of only twenty-one known copies of the original Gutenberg Bible. It is not a repository of the whole of the world's knowledge – nowhere is – but it comes closer than most, and if you can't find what you're looking for there, the chances are you won't find it anywhere.

What *I* am looking for is the collected works and biographical details of Robert Cudlip, who (as we know from the note on Linda's desk) lived from 1612 to 1659. Someday, no doubt, all the information I need will be stored on a computer and reached by pressing a few keys on a keyboard, but until that glorious electronic revolution arrives, it has to be done the painstaking manual way.

The first Robert Cudlip I find within the appropriate dates was a hill farmer on the Welsh borders, who came to the authorities' attention because (according to the neighbouring farmers) he had a great penchant for selling sheep at the local market which were not exactly his own property. He was duly arrested, tried at Ludlow Assizes, and found guilty of sheep stealing. The judge then placed a square of black cloth (known for some reason as a black cap) atop his wig, and sentenced Cudlip to be hanged by the neck until dead – no doubt to the great joy of the locals, whose favourite form of entertainment was a public execution. This was on 12 August 1659. If the condemned sheep rustler had ever turned his hand to poetry before he did his dance of death on the gallows, there is certainly no mention of it in any of the records.

The second Robert Cudlip was a ship's captain, whose exploits have only been noted because he was involved in a protracted legal dispute with the ship's owner over the question of how to split the profits on a cargo of slaves he transported from Africa to the New World. This merchant in human misery doesn't sound much like a poet either.

There is a Robert Cudlip the blacksmith, and Robert Cudlip the vicar of a small parish in Yorkshire, but there is no mention of my Robert Cudlip. More to the point, I can find no reference to the poetry of Robert Cudlip.

At the end of three hours, I am absolutely certain that Robert Cudlip the poet never existed.

Creating Cudlip has been an elaborate game, which was probably initiated by Crispin Hetherington, I decide, but I can discern no practical purpose to most of the process, especially composing the poem, so Hetherington probably did that just for his own amusement. The only thing that really matters – the only bit of the game which can be seen as cocking a snook at the established authorities – is the name of the society itself, because that's the only part that Charlie Swift and the dean will ever get to see.

And looked at from that perspective, the society's name simply has to be a code which, if you understand it, says, 'This is what we're doing.'

But how does the code work?

Do I have to substitute other words for the ones actually used, in order to understand the meaning?

Might the real name – the hidden name – of the society be something like 'Terrified Retreat' or 'Freezing Swivel'?

Yes, that's perfectly possible – but those names don't mean any more than 'Shivering Turn' does.

It's time to go, because the library is getting ready to close. Besides, I'm developing a tension headache, and I know from previous experience exactly what I need to do to cure it.

THERE ARE TIMES WHEN my whole being is so tightly wound that I know gin and tonic won't work its usual miracle, and the only thing that will unknot me is wild, unbridled sex. So when I feel my body starting to seize up, as I have this afternoon, my first thought is to find a suitable partner for the night.

This suitable partner does not have to be charming, interesting or amusing – although I am prepared to tolerate all those things in him as long as he only employs them in moderation.

He doesn't need to be dashingly handsome, or particularly muscle-bound, either.

What he must have – in spades – is a sexual energy which glows around him as though he's been dipped in a radioactive bath.

And detachment – I like detachment very much. My ideal partner is a lone wolf who takes his pleasure from me (and gives me pleasure in return) then lopes away into the dark night – and never thinks of me again.

Sigmund Freud, the venerated head-shrinker, would probably say this search for detachment in my sex life is evidence of a severely detached childhood.

Well screw you, you old Viennese charlatan – this is who I am, and I feel no pressing need to apologize for it.

At any rate, it is this need within which has brought me to the bar in the Randolph Hotel, a place which, in the past, has proved to be an excellent hunting ground.

I have already spotted a likely target. He's in his late thirties, and is tall and handsome – the kind of man, in other words, that gypsy fortune-tellers are always promising you you're going to meet. I'm guessing that he's a salesman – not the door-to-door sort ('If you have trouble cleaning behind your toilet, madam, this brush will do the trick'), but one of those who sign big contracts with large organizations after very expensive lunches – because he has an assurance about him which, if it's not actually genuine, is a pretty damn good imitation.

I turn my back in order to give him the opportunity to make

the first move, because experience has taught me that men are always happier if they feel they're in control.

It does not take him long. Less than five minutes later, he's sitting on the bar stool next to mine.

I hope he's not going to accidentally-on-purpose spill my drink and offer to buy me another one, because if that's the way he normally breaks the ice, I'm out of here before you can say, 'get some technique, you moron.'

He doesn't come close to threatening a booze spill.

Instead he says, 'Can I buy you a drink?'

Just that – none of the 'can I buy a *pretty lady* a drink?' crap I sometimes have to put up with.

'Gin and tonic,' I tell him.

I've dated men who've used this as an opening to show off their sensitive sides.

'Now, let me see, what brand of gin would you be likely to enjoy the most?' they tend to muse, as if they can see straight into your soul. 'You're intelligent and imaginative, and you're obviously very discerning or you wouldn't be going out with me (ho, ho!). So I would say your favourite is – (dramatic pause) – Bombay Sapphire. Am I right?'

And because he's been so nice about you (the creep!), you're expected to say that he's so clever to have guessed, and yes, Bombay Sapphire is your absolute favourite – even if you can't stand the bloody stuff.

This man doesn't do that, either. He just says, 'Would Beefeater be all right for you?'

'Beefeater would be fine.'

He holds out his hand to me. 'My name is Philip.'

Not, 'My name is Philip Curly Wurly blah-de-blah and I'm the managing director of Really Big Important blah-de-blah,' I note with some pleasure.

So far, he's registered so many brownie points with me that he's in serious danger of shooting off the top of the 'Jennie Redhead Suitable Men to Go to Bed With' Scale.

PHILIP'S FLAT IS ON St Thomas' Street.

'It's convenient for the railway station – and I do a lot of travelling,' he says, as he opens the front door.

And I'm thinking, *Oh Philip, don't go spoiling it now by bringing in personal details.*

He leads me into the living room. It is expensively and tastefully furnished, the heavy masculinity of the leather armchairs contrasting beautifully with the delicacy of the rosewood cocktail cabinet.

'Shall I mix us a drink?' he asks.

'I think we've both had plenty to drink already,' I tell him. 'Where's the bedroom?'

'This way,' he says.

It's a big bedroom, with a nice big bouncy double bed. I notice there are mirrors on the ceiling, too, which I quite like.

Since we've already done the passionate kissing stage while we were walking down the street and climbing the stairs, I move straight into the getting undressed stage, but then he says, 'Stop! You haven't decided what you're wearing yet.'

'I wasn't intending to wear anything,' I reply.

'You'll like this,' he tells me.

When men say that, I begin to feel a little uneasy, because what they really mean is that *they'll* like it.

He walks over to the fitted wardrobe, and slides it open with a magician's flourish.

'How about that?' he asks.

The wardrobe is crammed with costumes – there are French maids' outfits, nuns' and priests' habits, Nazi uniforms . . .

'I don't do that,' I say.

'You'll like it,' he promises me.

'I don't do that,' I repeat.

He reaches into the wardrobe, takes out a nurse's uniform, and holds it up for my inspection.

'How about this?' he asks.

'I've told you twice, I don't do that.'

'I never took you for an uptight little puritan,' he says, trying to shame and embarrass me into doing what he wants.

'I'm not the slightest bit uptight,' I say. 'As a matter of fact, I'm very imaginative in bed.'

'Well, then . . .?'

'But I don't like role-playing. If we're going to screw, let's screw each other, rather than pretend we're two other people.'

'I want you to wear a costume,' he says, almost sulky now.

'I'm sorry, this has been a mistake,' I say.

I head for the door, but he quickly steps in the way to block my exit.

'You're not leaving,' he says.

'You're making a mistake,' I tell him.

'Oh really? Making a mistake, am I? And what kind of mistake might that be?'

'If you don't let me go, I'm going to have to hurt you.'

He laughs. And, in a way, I can see his point, because he is at least four inches taller than I am, and considerably stronger.

The thing is, in my experience strong men place all their reliance on that strength of theirs, whereas feisty little redheads have to learn skills to compensate for their relative weakness.

As if to emphasize his power, he puts a large hand on each of my shoulders, and begins to shake me.

'You're not bloody leaving,' he says as he shakes. 'You're going to stay, and you're going to do exactly what I want you to do.'

I use my left arm to knock his right hand off my shoulder, and raise my right hand to find the pressure point on his right palm.

The first look that comes to his face is one of surprise, but that is soon replaced by pain, and his left hand drops helplessly to his side.

His instinct is telling him to pull away, but his brain is counselling him that, as bad as the pain is now, it will be much worse if he makes any violent moves.

'You're . . . hurting . . . me,' he gasps.

He wants to bring his left arm back up – to either push me away or punch me in the face – but his nervous system is so concentrated on the one spot of agony that it has no energy left for anything else.

I shift the pressure slightly, and force him to his knees.

'Do you try to rape any girl who doesn't do exactly what you want?' I ask, relaxing the pressure a little, because I don't want him to pass out on me.

'They . . . they don't usually mind,' he says.

'Well, the next time one does, will you remember what happened tonight, and just let her go?'

'Yes.'

'Do you promise?'

'Yes.'

I know that at this point he'd promise to slowly torture his own grandmother to death if it would take away the pain, but maybe – just maybe – he *will* think twice next time.

'I'm going to let you go now, and I don't want any trouble,' I say. 'Do you understand?'

'Yes.'

I release my grip. He gingerly places his injured right hand into the protective covering of his left armpit, and I step around him.

As I go down the stairs to the front corridor – where my faithful bicycle awaits me – I realize that all my tension is quite gone.

Who would have guessed?

ELEVEN

By the time I'm cycling past Queen's College, it's nearly half-past eleven. Philip has not yet been completely banished from my mind, but I've already started to forget what he looked like – which is a good start – and my thoughts have turned back to the investigation.

What kind of code *could* the Shivering Turn be?

If *directly* substituting synonyms for the words gets me nowhere, then maybe – given the way Crispin Hetherington's brain probably works – I need to expand my mental search to include synonyms that have appeared in other texts.

Is there anything in *Measure for Measure* that corresponds to 'shivering turn'? I wonder.

Or in *King Lear*?

The thing is, I don't think it *can* be *that* complicated, because Crispin (and I'm sure it *is* Crispin, rather than any of the others) must have realized that if he was being so obscurely clever that no one could ever guess it, then he wasn't really being clever at all.

No, what he will have aimed at is a code so simple that anyone he explains it to will feel a fool for not having spotted it themselves.

I cross the River Cherwell, take the right fork at St Clement's, and I'm on the Iffley Road.

Could 'shivering' stand for cold, I ask myself. And is 'turn' a punning misspelling of 'tern'?

Cold bird?

This is getting ridiculous.

Apart from the street lamps, the road on which I live is in darkness. It doesn't surprise me. A few of the houses have been converted into flats, but most of them are still single family dwellings, and the people who live in them are, by and large, quiet, conservative folk, who were probably born within two or three miles of where they ended up.

I admire them – these people with ordinary jobs who go to bed well before midnight, and wash their cars every Sunday morning. They are the backbone of the country, but I would not like to live their lives, any more than they would like to live mine.

I have reached my front door. I get off my bike, and reach into my bag – which is hanging off the handlebars – for my front door keys.

And that is when I see them – emerging like malevolent spirits from their hiding places between the parked cars.

There are three of them. They are all carrying baseball bats in their hands, and they are all – bizarrely – wearing full-face William Shakespeare masks.

Well, at least I'm about to be beaten up by someone literary, says one tiny – crazed – corner of my brain.

I look up and down the street. It is empty – and I am alone.

I could scream, in the hope of alerting someone in one of

those darkened bedrooms, who might well then call the police – but by the time the cops get here, it will be too late. Besides, if I do scream, these three Shakespearian thugs will attack me immediately, and, as things stand, it might still be possible to talk my way out of this situation.

They are approaching me from three different angles – one each side, one directly in front of me.

I could try to open the front door and seek sanctuary inside, but they are so close that I would never make it.

I could jump on my bike and make a break for it, but one swing of a baseball bat and I would be lying in the gutter.

When they get within two yards of me, they come to a halt.

'You know what this is about, don't you?' one of them asks, in what he probably imagines is a rough working-class accent, but which his posh vowels easily override.

'How did you decide which three of you would do the dirty work?' I ask. 'Did you draw straws for it – because if you did, I'd put my money on Crispin being in the toilet when the draw was being made.'

'Shut up!' says the same boy, who has obviously been chosen as their spokesman because of his skill in disguising his voice. 'Shut up!'

'What will you do if I don't – beat me up?' I ask.

They look at each other uncertainly.

This is not how it should be happening, they are thinking. I am supposed to be terrified at the mere sight of them. I am supposed to be babbling and begging them for mercy.

And, believe me, this calm front that I'm presenting is nothing *but* a front, behind which my inner core is already huddled in the foetal position. But I know – even as the fear engulfs me – that the worst thing I can possibly do is to *show* them that I'm frightened.

'Look, boys, there are three of you and only one of me; in addition, you're all armed with baseball bats, so whatever happens, you're bound to hurt me,' I say. 'We all know that. But you should also know that I'm a highly trained martial arts expert, and before I go down, the chances are very good that I could do something really nasty to at least one of you.'

They look at each other again through the slits in their masks, as if wondering what to do now it's clear I have no intention of following the script they've been carrying around in their heads.

'Go away now, and that will be the end of it,' I say, pressing my temporary advantage while it's still there. 'I promise you I won't report it to the police, and we can all pretend none of this ever happened. You can even tell Crispin Hetherington you waited for me, and I simply didn't turn up.'

Nor would you have turned up, if you'd only given into Philip's fetish, says a mockingly masochistic voice from the sick part of my brain.

For a moment, I think my appeal to them is going to work.

Then the leader of the group stiffens resolutely.

'You have to be taught not to stick your nose in where it isn't wanted,' he says.

And as he speaks, he takes a step forward.

The time for dialogue is clearly over. Now I do scream – a bloodcurdling, demented banshee scream. But it isn't a scream for help – it's a scream to set his ears ringing, to throw him off balance, if only for a second.

It works.

He freezes.

And that's when I make my move.

One hand on the saddle, the other on the handlebars, I swing my bike in an arc. The back wheel catches him on the jaw, and his head jerks backwards as if it's on a spring.

I swing round, and at the same moment move to the left, in order to avoid the blow which I'm almost certain will be coming from the right.

I don't dodge quite far enough, and I feel the baseball bat bounce off the edge of my shoulder.

I have avoided the full impact of the bat, but it still hurts like hell. Then my right arm goes numb, as my nerve endings go into shutdown mode. My right hand is no longer capable of holding on to the bike, and I feel a vibration as the back wheel hits the ground.

I throw the bike – clumsily and one-handedly – at the feet of my attacker. He steps awkwardly over it, but doesn't judge it quite right, and almost loses his balance. While he is still tottering uncertainly, I grab him by the front of his shirt, pull him towards me, and nut him full in the face.

I haven't forgotten that there is a third attacker – it's just that I only have a limited amount of arms and legs to go on to the offensive with.

And he hasn't forgotten me, either. I feel his bat slam into the back of my thighs and, despite it being the last thing I want to happen, my legs decide to collapse under me.

I am down on the ground now, and at least two of my attackers are still in good enough shape to start kicking me.

I'm not screaming any more – I need all my energy for the twisting and turning required to avoid the blows – and as each kick lands, I find myself praying that they know what they're doing, and can deliver the punishment beating without causing any permanent damage.

I notice I am suddenly bathed in bright light, then I hear the car pull up. And now there are more sounds in rapid succession – car doors being opened, voices shouting, the noise of pounding feet.

The kicking has stopped, and someone is bending down over me.

'Are you all right?' he asks, worriedly.

'What do you think?' I groan in reply.

I AM IN ONE OF the interview rooms in St Aldate's police station. I have a grey woollen blanket (with a blue stripe running down it) draped over my shoulders, and – periodically – I take a sip of the hot sweet tea from a mug which has 'World's Best Dad' written on it in bright red letters.

My rescuers – so it transpires – were three rugby-playing firemen, their combination of qualifications and outside interest making them ideally suited for the task in hand. My only complaint is that they were also such solidly responsible citizens that they insisted on bringing me to the cop shop, however much I protested that it wasn't really necessary.

So I am here, and have been examined by the police doctor, who I know from my days on the force.

'Well, Jennie, the tiny little freckles that nature has given you are going to be jealous as hell of the big black freckles you'll wake up with tomorrow morning,' he said.

He thought he was being funny – and I thought it would be amusing to stick his stethoscope so far up his backside that they'd have to send out a search party to get it back. But at least I can draw some consolation from the fact that if he could joke about it, it can't be that serious.

The door to the interview room opens, and a man walks in. I've been expecting someone to come and take my statement (I'm an ex-copper, I know how things work), but what I haven't anticipated is that it would be someone of the rank of Inspector Corbet.

I tell him so.

'Well, it's a quiet night around town, so I've not much to do,' he says. 'Besides, after our conversation at my allotment, I feel we've established a personal connection.' He pauses. 'And I suppose another point of contact between us is that you're working for my wife.'

There's another pause, to allow me to say something.

I don't.

'You *are* still working for my wife, aren't you, Miss Redhead?' he says finally.

'How are the flowers on that allotment of yours coming along, Inspector?' I ask him.

'They've not grown much since you last saw them, which is hardly surprising since that was only yesterday. *Are* you still working for her?'

Well, if he won't take the hint and drop the subject, I suppose I'd better give him an answer.

'Yes, as a matter of fact, I am still working for her,' I say.

'And have you made any progress?'

'If I have – and I'm not committing myself one way or the other on that,' I say carefully, 'I'm sure you'll be the second person to learn about it.'

'After you've told my wife,' he says.

'After I've told my client,' I correct him.

He nods. 'You're quite right, of course, it's your duty to inform her first.' He opens his notebook and produces a pen from his pocket. 'Would you like to tell me about the attack now?'

'There were three of them,' I say. 'They were armed with baseball bats, and they were waiting for me outside my flat.'

'Can you describe them?'

'Not really. It was all over so quickly.'

'Would you care to make a guess at their ages?'

'From the way they moved, I'd say they were somewhere between twenty and forty.'

'That's not really very helpful,' he says – but he writes something down anyway.

I shrug. It hurts a lot!

'I'm sorry if you think it's not helpful,' I say, 'but it's really the best that I can do.'

'Did you get a look at any of their faces?'

Ah, now here's the thing – when you're trying to catch a badger, the last thing you should do is talk about it to someone who is likely to come along and shine a bright light in the badgers' sett. And when you're investigating the Shivering Turn (in the hope of finding out exactly what happened to Linda Corbet on

Friday night), the last thing you should do is tell her father that your attackers were wearing Shakespeare masks, because that will automatically make him suspect that they were students, and from there it's only a small step to him suspecting the *right* students – and trampling all over your case.

'Well?' Inspector Corbet says – and I can tell he's doing his best not to sound impatient.

'They were wearing ski masks,' I say.

He frowns. 'That makes things much more difficult. Would you recognize their voices if you heard them again?'

'They didn't speak.'

'They didn't say anything at all?'

'Not a word.'

'Let's approach things from a different angle, to see if that gets us somewhere,' he suggests.

'All right,' I agree.

'Do you think this has anything to do with my daughter's disappearance?' he asks, trying to sound official, but coming across as a fretful father.

'Why would it have anything to do with that?' I ask.

'I don't know,' he admits, 'but I don't like coincidences.'

'All I'm trying to establish with my investigation . . .' I say. I stop. 'I'm sorry, but I can't tell you what it is I'm trying to establish. The only thing I can say is that I can see no reason why that should lead to me getting beaten up.'

I must be getting much better at lying to him, because he merely nods again.

'Can you think of anyone at all who might hold a grudge against you?' he asks.

I pretend to think about it.

'No, I honestly can't,' I say finally. 'I wouldn't claim to be universally popular . . .'

'Which of us is?' he asks, and gives me an encouraging smile.

'But though I can think of a number of people I've annoyed over the last year or so, I can't picture any of them being so pissed off that they'd hire thugs to beat the crap out of me.'

He sighs. 'So, to sum up, you can't describe the people who attacked you, and you've no idea why they would have done it.'

'That's about it,' I agree, pleased that I've been able to lead him up a blind alley.

But he hasn't finished yet.

'Baseball's not exactly our national sport, is it?' he asks.

'No, it isn't.'

'So there can't be too many sporting goods shops in the Oxford area which sell baseball bats – and any shop which sold three at the same time is bound to remember the customer.'

Oh no, I don't want him investigating the sporting goods shops. I *really* don't want that.

'It's not my business to tell you how you should be doing your job . . .' I begin.

'No,' he agrees, 'it isn't.'

'But it seems that you'll just be wasting valuable police time, because whoever attacked me was far too professional to make such an elementary mistake as to buy all three bats from the same place.'

'They're not *that* professional, or you wouldn't still be walking around,' he counters.

'They were interrupted.'

'And professionals would never have attacked you in a place where they *could be* interrupted.'

He's right, of course – one hundred per cent right – and I can only hope that I can complete my investigation before he completes his.

'I'll have a statement typed up with all the information you've given, and you can sign it in the morning,' he says.

Inspector Corbet closes his notebook and, with that action, the expression on his face changes. It is an almost imperceptible change, but now, instead of looking like a compassionate yet professional policeman, he seems to be more the kindly concerned uncle.

'The doctor tells me you're fit enough to go home, if that's what you want to do.'

'Good.'

'But I think it might be better if you stayed here for a while – possibly overnight.'

'It's never been a particular ambition of mine to spend a night in the cells,' I tell him.

He laughs. 'If you stay, I'll have a bed made up in one of the offices. You'll be quite comfortable there. There are hot showers too, and I'll assign one of the WPCs to assist you, if you think you need it.'

'That's very kind of you,' I say, 'but I'd like to go home.'

'You're sure of that?'

'Yes.'

'In that case, I'll arrange for one of my officers to drive you, and make sure you get home safely,' he says. 'I'll also instruct the patrol units to pass by your house every half-hour.'

'That won't be necessary,' I tell him. 'Whoever attacked me won't be back.'

'Better to be safe than sorry,' Corbet says. 'And it's not open for debate – I've made my judgement, and that's what's going to happen.'

'OK,' I agree.

AS WE'RE DRIVING ALONG the Iffley Road, I suddenly remember that cunningly hidden in my office is a small stash of pot to be used only in case of emergency. I debate whether or not this is actually an emergency, and reach the rapid conclusion that it's close enough.

'I need to stop by my office, and pick up something that I'll need overnight,' I say to my driver, who is a thirtyish, solidly built constable called Ben. 'Will that be all right?'

'Do whatever you want, sweetheart,' he replies. 'I've been instructed by the powers-that-be to treat you like a visiting VIP.'

When we pull up in front of my office, he says, 'Do you want me to come in with you?'

'No, I'll be fine,' I tell him. 'You stay here and have a smoke, or listen to the radio.'

'I've given up smoking, and there's nothing on the wireless at this time of night,' he says.

'You could always stick your hand in your pocket and play pocket billiards with yourself,' I suggest.

He grins. 'What, and remind myself of my tragic limitations in the genitalia department?'

'Size doesn't matter,' I assure him.

'That's easy for you to say,' he counters, but he settles down in his seat and closes his eyes.

With every step I take up the stairs, I discover a new ache, and it's going to feel worse in the morning. But that, I suppose, is the price you pay when you decide to follow the exciting career path of private investigator.

I open my office door, switch on the light, and realize that someone has visited the office in my absence.

Actually, it's not a brilliant deduction, because I'm pretty sure that before I left I didn't tip everything off the shelves on to the floor, and then turn the desk over. I'm fairly certain I didn't smash my telephone, either, yet there it lies, broken, amidst the debris.

The only thing that hasn't been flung, crushed or trampled is my chair, and that's only because my caller had a message for me, and wanted to make sure I didn't miss it.

The message is pinned to the back of the chair. It is in block capitals.

STAY OUT OF IT, it reads.

Stay out of it?

Out of what?

Could my gentle caller be referring to the Lamb and Flag?

Or perhaps he meant the public swimming baths?

No, thinking about it, it's much more likely that he meant I should stay out of the Linda Corbet investigation.

I bend down beside the fallen desk, run my hand along the bottom of the footrest, and am relieved to find my fingers making contact with the small package that is taped there.

My stash! Halleluiah, he hasn't taken my stash!

*

I MAKE THE INTERESTING DISCOVERY that walking down the stairs is even more painful than walking up them has been. I take it slowly and carefully.

One step – ouch!

Another step – ouch!

When I get back to the police car, Ben opens his eyes and says, 'You are my VIP, so I'm not complaining in any way, shape or form, but you seem to have been up there a long time.'

'A friend of mine has rearranged my office, so it took me a while to find what I was looking for,' I explain.

'Fair enough,' Ben says.

I climb gingerly into the passenger seat and stretch out my legs to test how much they hurt.

It has not been a good day.

TWELVE

It is yet another bright May morning, and as I examine the space which just yesterday I called my office – and can now best be described as a disaster area – the sun's rays stream through the window and coat the devastation in a golden glow. It is a noble effort on the part of old Sol to spread optimism – but it doesn't work for me.

I am not here alone. Standing next to me is Sergeant George Hobson, ex-lover, friend and one-time colleague, who I have asked to accompany me because I know he has the expertise that comes from serving three long, hard years in the burglary squad.

George looks around him, and then begins to slowly shake his head from side to side in what I take to be bafflement.

'What's the problem?' I ask.

'The pattern,' George admits. 'I don't think I've ever come across one like it before.'

I look around the room myself – at the broken lamp, the scattered papers, the kettle, the coffee mugs and the pens.

'I don't see any pattern,' I admit.

'Most people wouldn't see it – but then they wouldn't be looking at it through the eyes of someone applying the George Hobson Theory of Businessmen and Anarchists.'

'The George Hobson Theory . . .' I begin.

'Forget it,' George says – and I'm almost certain that he's blushing.

'I'd like to hear it,' I tell him.

He *is* blushing – there's no doubt about it.

'Look, Jennie,' he says, 'I'm just an ordinary working copper. I haven't got a degree in criminology – I haven't got *any* letters after my name – so I don't know why I even mentioned this daft theory of mine.'

'Do *you* believe in your theory?' I ask.

'Well, yes,' he says awkwardly. 'What kind of idiot would I be if I didn't believe in my own theory?'

'And do you think it could cast some light on what's happened here?'

'It might.'

'Then, for goodness' sake, tell me about it.'

'Are you sure?' George asked dubiously.

'Yes, I'm sure.'

'Well, in my opinion . . . and it is only my opinion—'

'I swear to God, George, if you don't get on with it soon, I'm going to hit you,' I say.

He smiles self-consciously, and begins again.

'In my opinion, there are basically only two kinds of burglars – I call them the businessmen and the anarchists. Now all the businessmen want to do is to make a quick profit, so they'll go through your stuff in record time, take what they think they can sell easily, and then get the hell out. They don't leave much of a mess, but that's not out of any consideration for you; they have no feelings about you, one way or the other – it's simply a result of the way they work.'

'And what about the anarchists?'

'They want to steal things, just like the businessmen, and they'll certainly try to sell what they take away with them, but, in some ways, stealing your property is not as important to them as the act of breaking into your house and causing damage. They're full of rage at the world in general – and, at that moment, in your house, they're mad at you in particular – so, more often than not, they'll take the time to shit in your bed.'

'Apart from the lack of faeces, this would seem to me to fit the anarchy pattern perfectly,' I say.

'You're quite wrong, there,' he tells me. 'You see, the anarchist doesn't have much control over the way he goes about things once he's in the house. He can be tipping out the drawers of your sideboard, when his eye suddenly falls on your display cabinet, and he knows he has to do something about that immediately.'

'*Why* does he have to do something about it immediately?'

'If you get half-a-dozen behavioural psychologists in one room, the chances are that you'll get half-a-dozen different answers, but my theory is that there's something about the particular thing he's spotted which reminds him of the source of his anger.'

'In other words, he had an unhappy childhood, and one of the things that featured in that childhood was a display cabinet.'

'That's right. Maybe he felt his mother cared more about the display cabinet than she did about him. Maybe he once accidentally broke an ornament and got the thrashing of his life. Whatever the reason, it's the trigger for a fresh wave of uncontrollable anger.'

'So he leaves the sideboard and concentrates on destroying the display cabinet?'

'Exactly! Sometimes he'll come back to the sideboard, and sometimes he won't – but if he *does* come back, then what you'll find on the floor is one layer of stuff from the sideboard, then a layer from the display cabinet, then another layer from the sideboard.'

'It's a bit like archaeology,' I say.

'It's *a lot* like archaeology.' George crouches down and sorts through the rubble. 'Aha!' he says, 'it's exactly as I thought. The coat rack is at the bottom. You see what that means?'

'No,' I admit. 'I'm not sure that I do,'

George stands up and walks over to the door.

'The coat rack was here,' he says, pointing to some gaping holes in the plaster. 'It's the first thing he will have seen when he came through the door, and it's the first thing he attacked. But it won't have been easy, because – as you can tell from the holes – the screws were set quite deep into the wall. Now do you see what I'm getting at?'

'No.'

'He tugs at the coat rack, but it doesn't come away immediately. Now a businessman wouldn't have bothered with the coat rack at all, for obvious reasons. And what are they?'

'The coat rack has no saleable value?'

'Spot on. The anarchist, on the other hand, might have gone for it, but would have given up the moment it became plain to him it was well-anchored to the wall. Because . . .?'

He looks at me questioningly.

'Because he wants to do the maximum possible damage, and the coat rack is only slowing him up?' I suggest.

'Exactly – but your man's an entirely different kettle of fish. He struggles with the coat rack until he can finally prise it away from the wall – and only when he's done that does he move on to the next thing, which is the bookcase. Then he deals with your desk, then the filing cabinet, and finally the visitor's chair.'

'So he's not a natural anarchist?'

'No, he isn't. There's no rage in it. He's a tidy, organized man. He needed to trash your office to make his point, but he didn't really *want* to do it, because – and I'm speculating even more wildly here – to him, disorder is almost a sin. But having once committed himself to being sinful, he set about destroying the office in a methodical way, just as he would have put it together methodically – because that's the only way he knows.'

I can't see Crispin Hetherington having that approach to life at all, I think – so maybe he had to send his father's butler to do the job!

The scene plays in my head – Crispin Hetherington standing in the doorway with an arrogant smirk covering his face, and the butler, tall and stately, in tie and tails, waiting for his instructions.

'I want you to destroy this office, Jeeves. Can you do that?'

'Certainly, Master Crispin. I would prefer to go about it methodically. Would you have any objection to that, sir?'

'No, not at all, Jeeves. You just carry on.'

'Very good, sir.'

I giggle. I can't help myself.

And then I see the new expression on George's face. He looks very hurt – almost crushed.

For a moment, I can't work out what's happened to bring

about this change – and then I understand. We take the piss out of each other all the time, but there are boundaries to that piss-taking which, though never formulated, are instinctively recognized. And he thinks I have gone beyond those boundaries. He has reluctantly shared his precious theory with me, and I – an Oxford smart-arse with letters after my name – can do nothing more than giggle at it.

'I wasn't laughing at you, George,' I tell him.

'What were you laughing at, then?'

'Just something that came into my head.'

'Yes, that's what people always say when they're caught out showing a lack of respect.'

'I promise you, I wasn't . . .'

'Let's just leave it there, shall we?'

In order to distract him from his sense of grievance, I tell him about the Shivering Turn, and how I'm sure it's a code for something else.

'I've tried using synonyms for both the words, and it simply doesn't work,' I say.

'Maybe it's an anagram,' George says offhandedly – as if to suggest that if I can laugh off one of his theories so easily, he's certainly not going to put a great deal of effort into propounding another one.

Looking at it from his perspective, I can't say I blame him.

I walk down the stairs to the street with him, though my body tells me at every step of the way that this is a mistake.

Once we're outside, I say, 'Thank you very much for your time, George. I really appreciate it.'

'And has my daft theory been of any use to you?' he asks, giving me another chance to redeem myself.

I want to say yes – I really do – but the problem is I can't see any of the gentlemen-oafs who make up the Shivering Turn wrecking my office in quite the way it has been wrecked.

'I don't see any practical application for it at the moment, but it might well be useful when I've collected more information,' I say.

He smiles, as if he's pleased. I'm fobbing him off, and he knows it – but for the sake of our friendship, he's willing to pretend to believe what I've just told him.

'See you around, Jennie,' he says as he's walking to his car.

'See you around, George,' I reply.

I GO TO THE VERY end of the ground-floor corridor, where I usually park my bike (this is at the request of the people who run the import-export lingerie business, who feel that the mere sight of a common bicycle would offend their refined clients intent on purchasing dirty underwear) – and it is not there.

But of course it's not there! I remember now – after I had used it as an offensive weapon against the Shakespearian ruffians, it was taken down to St Aldate's police station by the rugby-playing firemen who rescued me.

And, even if it had been there, do I seriously think I'd be able to use it, when every bone in my body aches?

I am clearly still in a state of shock, or I would neither have forgotten where the bicycle was, nor imagined that I could ride it. My best course of action is thus to forget this detecting lark for the day, go back to my flat, and rest.

Yes, that is what any sensible person *would* do.

I walk back up the corridor and out on to the street. A taxi is passing, and I flag it down.

'Where to?' the driver asks, when I have painfully hoisted myself into the back seat.

'St Luke's College,' I tell him.

REMEMBERING OUR LAST MEETING – and especially that Crispin Hetherington announced he was bored and simply walked out – I've no idea how he will react to my unexpected visit now, but when he opens his door he looks neither surprised nor offended, only rather coldly amused.

'Do come in,' he says, opening the door wider, and making an elaborate sweeping gesture with his hand.

I look around me. I have seen any number of undergraduate's sitting rooms in my time, but never one anything like this.

Some undergraduates bring the worlds they have known previously down to Oxford with them, so that once their pictures and photographs are up, the room looks almost like their old bedroom back home – but these transporters are in a minority.

For most undergraduates, Oxford represents a new beginning, and they decorate their rooms in a style which reflects the people they believe they are evolving into. The walls of their rooms are thus both a declaration of intent and an exhibition space for newly discovered radicalism, anarchism, feminism, hedonism or pure eccentricity.

Crispin Hetherington's room resembles neither of these models. Apart from the bookcase – which is positively bulging with learned texts – and the furniture provided by the college, it is absolutely bare. It contains no photographs, no stereo system, no bric-a-brac of any kind. It is as spartan as a monk's cell – as soulless as a room that is rented by the hour. I'd like to think that this asceticism of his is as much a stunt as the anarchism and eccentricity of some of the other students, but I can't be entirely sure that it is.

'Take a seat,' Hetherington says. 'I'm afraid I can't offer you a drink, because I don't keep any.'

'I'd prefer to stand,' I tell him. 'And I didn't come here for a drink. If you'll answer just one question for me, I'll be gone.'

'And what question might that be?'

'Where is Linda Corbet?'

'I have absolutely no idea.'

'I don't believe that you just forced her on to the London train and then left her to fend for herself. That would have been far too risky for you, because she might have come straight back.'

'And what makes you think we forced her on to the London train at all?'

'You already have the answer to that, because *you* know that *I* know that Hugo Johnson and Gideon Duffy were seen at the railway station late last Friday night, and the only possible reason they could have had for being there was to make sure she left.'

Hetherington laughs. His amusement sounds genuine enough, but with him it's impossible to be certain.

'Oh dear,' he says, 'you've got it quite the wrong way round. In fact, thus far, you haven't got one single thing right.'

'If I'm so far from the truth, why did you try to have me beaten up last night?' I ask.

'I didn't,' he says – and, suddenly, he is sounding distinctly uncomfortable.

Why does he sound uncomfortable? I wonder.

And then it comes to me.

'You didn't want them to do it!' I say.

'Violence is the last refuge of the incompetent,' he replies. 'Do you know who said that?'

'You didn't want them to do it, and the rest of the Shivering Turn overruled you!' I say, sticking to the point.

'It was Isaac Asimov – or, more accurately, one of the characters in an Asimov novel.'

'You're losing your control over them,' I tell him. 'You've had a good run as puppet master – I'll give you that – but now you are so clearly losing control.'

'The Shivering Turn was not responsible for the attack on you,' he says, making no attempt to sound in the least convincing. 'Each and every one of us has an alibi for last night.'

'I'm sure you do.'

I want him to say more, of course, and I know that he will – because there is nothing particularly clever about a false alibi, and showing me just how clever he can be is very important to him.

'But let us say, hypothetically and purely for the sake of argument, that the Shivering Turn *was* responsible for the attack, and that I counselled strongly against it,' he suggests.

'All right.'

'I admit it would have weakened my position if the attack

had been a success, but since it wasn't, and the fact that you are standing there is living proof that it wasn't, it's clear that it was the wrong thing to do, and that my advice was the right advice. So the next time we are hypothetically forced to defend ourselves, whose guidance will be followed, do you think?'

'You've already failed,' I say. 'And the reason you've failed is that you haven't been able to prevent the Shivering Turn from getting itself into a situation in which it is extremely vulnerable.'

'Now that is interesting,' Hetherington says. 'In what way is it extremely vulnerable?'

'I've only to tell the police that they attacked me, and they'll be all over you in five minutes.'

'You have no proof.'

'I know that one of your members has a very battered nose because I nutted him in the face, and another has a long bruise along his jaw line where I hit him with the wheel of my bike. What other proof do you need?'

'Maybe you *could* convince the police that the Shivering Turn attacked you if you really tried,' Hetherington concedes, 'but you won't.'

'Why won't I?'

'There are two reasons. The first is connected to the fact that you'll have made a statement to the police about the attack – and don't deny it, because I know you must have.'

'I've no intention of denying it.'

'And yet, despite having your statement, the police haven't come storming in and arrested us. And why is that? It's because you lied to them!'

'What do you mean – I lied to them?'

'Well, to pick just one example, you didn't say that your attackers were wearing William Shakespeare masks.'

'How do you know that they were wearing William Shakespeare masks?' I ask.

He sighs. 'Let's just say it was a lucky guess, though we both know that's not true. Now, where was I? Oh yes – you've lied to the police, which is perverting the course of justice. You can't go back now and tell them a completely different story, without getting into a great deal of trouble.'

He's right, of course.

'What's the second reason?' I ask.

'The second reason parallels the first. Simply put – your ego won't let you do it.'

'Well, if we're going to talk about egos . . .'

'You want to be the one who finds out why Linda Corbet ran away,' Hetherington says, 'and you're terrified the police will beat you to it.'

I am suddenly hit by an attack of self-doubt. Crispin Hetherington is right about me not wanting the police involved, and I've been telling myself that's because they couldn't handle this particular situation as well I can.

But what if he's right, and it isn't that – what if the real reason is that I'm terrified they'll do the job better than I could?

Am I playing dice with Linda Corbet's future for purely selfish reasons?

I don't think so. I really do believe that if they were investigated by the police, the Shivering Turn would put on an impenetrable united front, whereas by working on my own I just might be able to find a gap in their defences.

But, even as I reach this conclusion, I know that if I'm wrong, I will never forgive myself.

'Well, well, that's certainly struck home, hasn't it?' Crispin Hetherington asks.

And suddenly I've had enough of this evil little man – suddenly I can't bear to be in his presence any longer.

'Thank you for your time,' I say, turning stiffly and heading for the door.

'You've really no idea what's been going on, have you?' he calls mockingly after me. 'You don't even know what the Shivering Turn is all about, although – God knows – it's all there in the name.'

AS I LEAVE THE COLLEGE, Crispin Hetherington's last words are echoing around in my head.

'You don't even know what the Shivering Turn is all about, although – God knows – it's all there in the name.'

I walk along the Broad, hardly conscious of the fact that there is anyone else there – hardly even noticing all my aches and pains.

'You don't even know what the Shivering Turn is all about, although – God knows – it's all there in the name.'

'Maybe it's an anagram,' George Hobson had said, back there in my shattered office.

He'd never intended it to be a serious suggestion – but maybe he was right anyway!

Maybe it is as simple as that!

I am just passing the White Horse. I slip inside and order myself a medicinal gin and tonic.

Once the drink has been served, I carry it over to an empty table, sit down, open my bag, and take out a pad and pen.

S H I V E R I N G T U R N, I write.

And then, because you cannot always see patterns if all the components are presented in a linear manner, I make a rough circle of the letters.

It takes me no more than two minutes to rearrange the letters into a form that makes sense, and as I stare at the two new words I've created, I feel angrier than I can ever remember being before.

This is not about an orgy, or drug taking, or black magic rites. This is much, much worse – and if Crispin Hetherington were here right now, I am sure I would kill him.

THIRTEEN

My martial arts instructor once taught me that one of the best ways to reach a plateau of calm is to channel your rage into something else, and by the time I return to St Luke's, my rage has been channelled into steely determination. I no longer want to kill Crispin Hetherington – that would be making things far too easy for him. What I do want, instead, is to destroy everything he values – to take away the life he's known and replace it with a life he will find unbearable.

As I stand in front of the college, there are two voices doing battle in my head – the one whose wishes I want to follow, and the one which warns me I am chasing an illusion. I am starting to think of them as my good angel and my bad angel, though I know the bad angel is not really bad at all, but is only trying to prevent me from doing something which may harm me – and possibly others.

'You have no solid proof of *anything*,' my bad angel tells me. 'Everything is based on assumption – and that assumption could be totally wrong.'

'I *know* that I'm right,' counters my good angel.

'You want to *believe* that you're right – want it desperately – but that is not the same thing as *being* right,' my bad angel says. 'Tell me exactly what it is that you know.'

'I know that Linda attended a meeting of the Shivering Turn on the night she disappeared.'

'You don't know it at all – you're just guessing.'

'I know why she was asked to attend it in her school uniform.'

'That's another guess. Maybe (*if* she was there, and that's still a big "if") she wasn't *asked* to wear her school uniform at all, but just didn't have time to go home and change.'

'And I know now that her dad was probably right when he said that the reason she ran away from home was because she couldn't face her family.'

'He was *probably* right? What does that mean?'

'It means that it may not have been her choice at all – it means that the Shivering Turn insisted on her leaving Oxford.'

'Yes, that is possible. But it's also possible she may have gone to join a boyfriend she met on a school trip, and who lives in London. Or she may have discovered that some *other* boyfriend – who has nothing to do with the Shivering Turn – had got her pregnant. Or . . .'

'I don't want to discuss it any more,' my good angel says.

'Well, of course you don't,' my bad angel taunts. 'If I were in your shoes – building up my whole case on the flimsiest of foundations – I wouldn't want to keep discussing it, either.'

I walk through the gate, and the porter, Mr Jenkins, appears in the lodge doorway.

'If you're on your way to see Lord Swift, Miss Redhead, I'm afraid he's gone out,' he says.

'Actually, it's you I came to see,' I tell him.

He grins. 'Well, I am honoured. What can I do for you?'

'I'd like to know which of the porters was on the afternoon

and evening shift last Friday. Do you think you could possibly look it up for me?'

'There's no need for me to look it up. I was on that shift myself, for the whole week.'

That's a lucky break for me, because Mr Jenkins and I get on so well together, but it's still by no means certain that he'll be willing to cooperate.

'Would it be all right if I asked you a few questions about what some of the students were doing on Friday evening?' I ask.

His eyes narrow – and my heart sinks.

'What's this all about?' he asks.

'You do know what it is that I do for a living, don't you, Mr Jenkins?' I ask.

'Yes, I believe I do know what profession you follow, Miss Redhead,' he replies. 'You're a confidential inquiry agent, aren't you?'

I've always thought I was a private detective and that it was a job rather than a profession – but that's Oxford porters for you.

'Yes, that's what I am,' I agree, 'and I'm making some confidential inquiries at the moment.'

'So what you're asking me to do is become your informer, are you?' the porter says flatly.

'This isn't going to work,' my bad angel whispers gleefully. 'And quite right, too – Mr Jenkins is doing no more than saving you from yourself.'

'I know just how loyal you are to this college, Mr Jenkins,' I say, 'and I know I'm putting you in a very difficult position. I hate myself for doing it – honestly I do – but I really do believe that these students have done a very bad thing – a truly terrible thing.'

'You're right about me, I *am* loyal to St Luke's,' the porter says emphatically. 'I'm loyal to the buildings, I'm loyal to the traditions, and I'm loyal to the master, who, for my money, is the best master since Sir Hope Stanley headed the college, a hundred and fifty years ago.' His eyes mist over. 'Now there was a man who combined principle and ability, if there ever was one. He could have been prime minister if he'd wanted to be, but instead he chose to devote his mind to a much more worthwhile cause.'

Despite the gravity of the situation, I find it hard not to smile when he talks about a long-dead master as if he knew him personally.

'The students are another matter entirely,' Mr Jenkins continues. 'There are some I'm very proud of – and you're one of them – but there are others who have me seriously worried. It has to be the college that maketh the man, not the other way around, and any student who doesn't live up to the ideals of St Luke's is undermining its very foundations. Do you understand what I'm saying?'

'Perfectly.'

'And you say that these students you're interested in have done some bad things?'

'Yes, and if I don't stop them, I'll sure they'll do it again. You see, they've formed this society which is—'

'I don't want to know the details, thank you very much,' Mr Jenkins says curtly.

I can see he regrets the words as soon as they are out of his mouth.

'I interrupted you,' he says, as if he can't believe it himself. 'I have stood at this gate for thirty-two years, and never, in all that time, have I interrupted a member of coll—'

'It doesn't matter,' I tell him. 'There, you see, I've just interrupted you, so now we're even.' I wait for an artful two beats,
then ask, '*Will* you help me, Mr Jenkins?'

'What is it you want to know, Miss Redhead?'

I want him to confirm that all the members of the Shivering
Turn were out of college that evening.

But that's all it is – a *confirmation* – my good angel reminds
me, because I already *know* they will all have been out of college
on Friday.

'You don't *know* anything – you are doing no more than
supposing,' my bad angel screams.

No, I'm not – I know the true nature of their meetings now,
and because I know that, I also know that they wouldn't dare
to hold them in their rooms inside the college.

I run through the list of names for Mr Jenkins.

'Do you remember them leaving college sometime in the late
afternoon or early evening?' I ask.

'Yes,' the porter replies. 'As a matter of fact I do.'

'All of them?'

'All of them.'

I am hoping – I am *praying* – that the *reason* he remembers
so easily is because they were each carrying something.

And if they *were* all carrying something, and if those 'some-
things' were identical, then my bad angel can go and take a long
walk along a short pier.

I take a deep breath.

'Were they all carrying something, Mr Jenkins?' I ask.

'Yes, they were.'

'And what was it?'

'They all had Greenleaf & Tonge carrier bags in their hands – new ones.'

I had been expecting him to say something like 'Roman togas', because togas would add a certain *frisson* to their nasty little games, but, in a way, this is even sicker than I'd ever imagined.

GREENLEAF & TONGE, GENTLEMEN'S Outfitters, is located at 111–115, Oxford High Street. It is all that a gentleman's outfitters should be, and more, offering a wide range of jackets and trousers, suits, shirts and ties and socks for the well-dressed and discerning man about Oxford, but one of its core businesses – and one in which it has been involved for over a hundred and fifty years – is the production and sale of academic gowns.

There are a vast array of different gowns – Commoners' Gowns, Scholars' Gowns, Advanced Students' Gowns, Bachelors' and Masters' Gowns, Bachelors' and Masters' Lace Gowns, Doctors' Gowns . . .

And I am guessing – and am hopefully about to confirm – that it was gowns that the Shivering Turn members had in their brand-new Greenleaf & Tonge carrier bags on the night Linda Corbet disappeared.

There are three assistants in the department. Two of them are young, crisp, polite (without being subservient), and efficient. The third is a middle-aged man who is currently fawning over a snotty-looking type ordering a Doctor of Letters' robe and hood.

I quickly decide that if I can make him despise me enough to let his guard drop, this fawner – this snob by association – is my best bet.

I station myself by the tie rack, and become absorbed in a study of the array of university, college, social club and sporting association ties which are on offer, and I stay there until I see that the man I want to deal with me is free, and the other two are occupied.

I emerge from my hiding place as an incompetent and uncomprehending carrot top – the sort of woman who is destined from birth to end up as somebody's maiden aunt.

The older assistant spots me, and quickly looks around to see which of the other two he can foist me off on. Then he realizes he will have to deal with me himself, and assumes the expression of a man who likes to kick-start his day by drinking a pint of vinegar.

'Can I help you, madam?' he asks – unhelpfully.

'Yes, please,' I reply, all meekness and confusion. 'I'd like to buy a Bachelor's Gown.'

'Bespoke – or ready-made?' he asks – and it is plain that he expects me to choose the latter.

But ordering the former will give me more time with him – more opportunity to find out what I need to know.

'Does bespoke mean made-to-measure?' I wonder aloud.

'Indeed it does, madam,' he says, and though he doesn't actually add, 'Don't you know anything, you stupid cow?', it is clearly in the subtext.

'Then bespoke is what I want,' I tell him.

The news seems to cheer him somewhat.

'In that case, I'm afraid you'll have to wait until a female assistant is available, madam,' he says. 'I'll just go and see . . .'

'Oh, there's really no need for that,' I say. 'I've already got the measurements.'

I hand him a piece of paper. He studies it for a second, then runs his eyes – totally and completely asexually – over my body.

'Whoever took these measurements had no idea what he was doing, madam, because I can assure you that if we make you a gown to the specifications you've just handed me, it will not—'

I laugh. 'Oh, you think it's for me!'

'Isn't it?'

'Of course not. I'm not bright enough to have gone to *any* university, let alone *Oxford*.'

'Then who is it for?' he asks.

'It's for my cousin. She's a first-year undergraduate at St Luke's. That's one of the colleges here, you know.'

He wants to sneer at me for daring to assume that he wouldn't know St Luke's is a college, and he wants to express his outrage that my cousin wants the gown. He manages to produce an expression encompassing both – which really is no mean feat.

'Your cousin does realize, doesn't she, that as an undergraduate, she's not allowed to wear a Bachelor's Gown?' he asks.

'Oh dear, does that mean you are refusing to sell me one?' I say, looking worried.

He sighs heavily. 'I regret to say that it does not, because we would simply have no grounds for doing so. When the gown leaves our establishment, it is merely a piece of cloth fashioned in a particular manner. It is only within the confines of the college itself that it acquires a weighty and symbolic significance.'

He should really do this to music, I think. A Beethoven concerto, or perhaps a soaring choral work, would fit in perfectly with his 'weighty and symbolic significance.'

Pompous prat!

'Is madam still with me?' he asks.

I laugh again – I really am a dizzy type, aren't I?

'Well, you know what young people are like,' I say. 'It's fashionable among her friends to wear a Bachelor's Gown, and she wants one for herself.'

'You should tell her to be careful,' he says. 'Oxford colleges take their traditions very seriously.'

'I'm very fond of tradition myself,' I tell him. 'My mother suggested we should have roast beef last Christmas Day, but I put my foot down and insisted on a turkey.'

He looks at me as if I were an imbecile.

'I am talking about quite a different kind of tradition,' he tells me. 'If, for example, you turn up for an examination and you are not wearing the full subfusc – dark suit and socks, black shoes, white shirt and white bow tie if you are a man, or white blouse, black bow tie, dark skirt, dark stockings and black shoes if you are a woman – you will not be allowed to take that examination, however important it is to your future.'

'I didn't realize that,' I lie.

'And if your cousin is seen to be wearing a Bachelor's Gown by anyone in authority, she will be subject to what might turn out to be a rather stringent disciplinary procedure.'

'So what you're saying is that if she's going to wear it, she should be very careful *where* she wears it?'

'Exactly.'

'And is that the same advice you gave to all the other St Luke's students who bought Bachelors' Gowns last week?'

'It is.'

He realizes his mistake the second that he's spoken – but it's already far too late!

'I'm afraid I'm not in a position to discuss one customer's buying habits with another customer, madam,' he adds icily.

'Then you shouldn't do it, should you?' I ask snottily, and now I'm very much in the *grande dame* mode. 'I was told this shop was famous for its discretion, but I seem to have been sadly misinformed.'

I was right! I was bloody right! I think, as I walk out of Greenleaf & Tonge.

Almost the first thing anyone offered a place at Oxford University has to do on arriving in the city is to buy a gown and mortarboard, because you will not be recognized as a member of the university until you've attended a matriculation ceremony in the Sheldonian Theatre – and you can't attend a matriculation unless you're in full subfusc.

So all the members of the Shivering Turn will already *own* gowns and mortarboards, and the mortarboards will suit their purpose perfectly. But the gowns won't, because they are commoners' gowns – bum freezers.

What they needed, they must have decided, were much longer gowns – gowns with gravitas – if they were to play a particularly nasty game of randy schoolmasters debauching an innocent schoolgirl.

BY THE TIME I ARRIVE at the Blind Beggar pub, it is after five-thirty in the afternoon, and I have already visited more than a dozen pubs and restaurants peppered around central Oxford.

The Beggar is a slightly run-down establishment, and certainly not one I'd ever consider spending an evening boozing in, but what makes it particularly interesting to me now is that, in the Yellow Pages, it advertises itself as having a function room.

I walk into the lounge. The walls are wood-panelled, and hung around them are a series of eighteenth-century prints (presumably by Hogarth, and also, presumably, having a blind beggar as their subject matter). Aside from the walls, there has been no attempt to capture the Georgian ambience. The carpet is the usual swirl of lurid colours, the tables and chairs are only one step up from those you'd find in a greasy spoon café, and the top of the bar is covered with a padded black plastic which is doing its best to pretend it's genuine leather.

There is a middle-aged barmaid in a frilly blouse at one end of the bar counter, and a spotty youth with sly eyes at the other. After a moment's consideration, I select the spotty youth.

'Yeah?' says the youth, who is so busy using his finger to create patterns from beer spilled on the bar that he can hardly be bothered to look up. 'Do you want something?'

'I believe you have a function room for hire,' I say.

'S'right.'

'Do you think I could see it?'

'Not now, no.'

'Why not?'

'It's the governor what rents out the room. You'll have to wait till he comes in.'

'And when will that be?'

The youth shrugs. 'It might be half an hour, but then again, it might be longer than that.'

'I have another appointment in half an hour,' I tell him. 'I was rather hoping to see it now.'

He shrugs again. 'There's nothing I can do about that. Like I said, it's the governor's business.'

I take a crisp five-pound note out of my pocket and lay it on the bar before him.

'Couldn't *you* show it to me?' I suggest.

He sweeps the note up with all the speed and finesse of a professional magician.

'I'm going out for five minutes, Molly,' he shouts to the barmaid in the frilly blouse.

THE FUNCTION ROOM IS in the annexe. It is above the storeroom, and is reached via an outside metal staircase in the car park.

'Is there any other way to get in or out?' I ask my spotty guide.

'No, this is it.'

The ex-copper in me notes that the pub is guilty of a serious breach of the fire regulations, but the private detective side of me is growing increasingly excited, because although I have still had no real indication that this was the room the Shivering Turn used, it is certainly the *sort* of place they would have selected.

The room itself is rectangular. There is a small stage at one end of it, and concealed behind the curtain is a basic light board from which it is possible to dim most of the lights and activate a couple of spots. Most of the rest of the place is taken up with tables which have seen better days, and chairs in a variety of styles. It is all rather seedy, but I don't think that would have bothered Crispin Hetherington – in fact, he might even have seen that as an added attraction.

'Was this function room booked last Friday?' I ask the spotty youth.

'Might have been,' the youth replies, noncommittally. He ostentatiously consults his watch. 'We have to leave now. I promised Molly that I'd only be gone for five minutes.'

He walks towards the door, but I stay where I am, close to the shabby little stage. When he reaches the door, he seems – from his body language – to be surprised I am not just behind him.

He turns fully around. 'Listen, I've already told you once, we've got to go,' he says.

I open my bag, and take out the roll of bank notes that Mary Corbet gave me. The spotty youth notices it, and his gaze instantly becomes so intense that I'm almost surprised the roll doesn't ignite.

I sit down at one of the tables, and indicate that he should join me. His promise to Molly is discarded like an empty Coca-Cola can; he crosses the room and takes the seat opposite mine.

'We're going to play a game,' I tell him.

'What kind of game?'

'It's a very simple one, really. I ask you a series of easy questions, and if, at the end of each question, you give me an answer that I like, then you win a cash prize. All right?'

'All right,' he agrees.

'Was this room used last Friday?'

'Yes.'

I slide a fiver across the table, and watch it disappear. Then I peel another five pounds off the roll, put it on the table in front of me, and flank it with my hands, palms down.

'Who was it who hired the room?' I ask.

'I don't know.'

He makes a grab for the fiver, but I am quicker, slamming the palm of my right hand on top of it.

'That's really not good enough for a cash prize,' I tell him.

'I think they were students from the university.'

'What makes you say that?'

'They talked posh – like they had plums in their mouths.'

I slide the note towards him, and peel off another.

'Do you know any of their names?'

'No. Why would I?'

'You might have heard them addressing each other by name.'

'I didn't.' He looks down at the fiver lying on the table with real yearning. 'Can I . . .?'

'No!'

I reach into my bag and take out the series of photographs I last showed to Harry Garstead, the railway porter, in the Red Lion.

I lay the photographs on the table.

'Do you recognize any of these?'

He studies the photographs for the shortest possible time he thinks he can get away with, then says, 'Maybe if you put some more money on the table, it might, you know, sort of jog my memory for me.'

'It doesn't work like that,' I tell him. 'You have to earn it – and you can only earn it by telling me the truth.'

He looks at the photographs again.

'This one,' he says, holding up the picture of Crispin Hetherington.

'How do you happen to remember him?' I ask testily.

'It's the way he looks at you.'

'What do you mean?'

'He looks at you as if he thinks that you've just crawled out from under a stone.'

That sounds like good old Crispin to a tee.

'Any more?' I ask.

He picks out four more pictures. One of them is not a Shivering Turn, but the other three are – and that's plenty good enough for me.

'Who served the drinks?' I ask. 'Was it you, or was it Molly?'

This is another trick. If he says either of them served the drinks, I'll know he's lying – because the very last thing the Shivering Turn would have wanted was an audience.

'Nobody served them,' he says. 'They paid for all their drinks in advance, and said if we'd just leave the stuff up here before they got started, they'd serve themselves.'

'What drinks did they order?'

'Crates of beer and bottles of vodka.'

That sounds about right. No mixers, but pints of beer with neat vodka chasers. Real macho stuff.

'Bloody wimps!' the youth says. 'That's what they were – bloody wimps. They didn't drink much more than half of what they paid for.'

No, they wouldn't have, I think – because they were into something much more intoxicating.

We have come to the crunch. I peel fifty pounds off my roll, lay it on the table, and slide the photograph of Linda across to him.

'Was she here?' I ask.

'Yes,' he says.

He makes a fresh grab for the notes, but I am quicker.

'I'll want more than that before you win the jackpot prize,' I say. 'Much more.'

He screws up his eyes in concentration.

'I didn't see her in here, but I saw her outside,' he says.

'Outside where?'

'In the car park – a few feet from the foot of the stairs. I think she'd just got out of a car.'

'What was she wearing?'

'She was in a school uniform.'

'What colour was her blazer?'

He screws up his eyes again. 'I think it was a dark-red colour.'

Close enough.

'Anything else?' I ask.

'I think she'd started partying long before this party ever began.'

'What makes you say that?'

'She wasn't very steady on her feet. If it hadn't been for the bloke who was with her holding her up, I think she would have fallen flat on her face.'

I have been keeping back one photograph, but now the time is right, and I show it to him.

'Was this the lad who was holding her up?'

'Yes, that's him,' he agrees, identifying Jeff Meade.

I hand him the notes, thinking, as I do, that this is the one and only time I have used any of the money that Mary Corbet gave me.

I will not be spending the rest, because I am not working for Mary Corbet any more.

Now, I am working for Linda.

And for myself!

FOURTEEN

It's eight o'clock in the evening, on what feels as if it has already been a very long day. I am sitting in the beer garden of the Head of the River pub on Folly Bridge, watching the River Isis flow slowly and calmly by.

And it can afford to be slow and calm, I think, perhaps a little bitterly, because it knows where it is going and is pretty confident of getting there. Also, it has not been beaten up in the last twenty-four hours. I only wish I could say the same of myself – on all those counts.

There are two men with me.

One is George Hobson, who was the first person I called after I'd left the Blind Beggar.

'You argue a good case, Jennie,' he'd said back then, when I'd breathlessly outlined everything I'd done since I broke the Shivering Turn code, 'but if you want the police to launch a full-scale investigation, it's no use just convincing me – you'll have to persuade one of our big beasties to get behind it.'

And that is why I am here – to persuade the big beastie, who is the third person at the table, to get behind it.

The big beastie's name is Ken Macintosh. When I first met him, he was a detective sergeant with a bushy beard that crows could have happily nested in, and a shock of jet-black hair. Now he is a detective chief inspector, his beard has been trimmed short enough to make him a passable James Bond villain, and his hair has turned completely white.

He catches me looking at him.

'If this job doesn't turn your hair white, then you're not doing it properly,' he says in a Scottish accent which seems totally unaffected by twenty years living in England.

I am glad it's Ken Macintosh. I don't know him well, but I think I can both trust and respect him.

Macintosh picks up his pint, and takes a deep swig.

'Right, lassie,' he says to me, 'if you're willing to talk, then I'm more than willing to listen.'

'There are two sides to this – the Linda Corbet side and the Shivering Turn side,' I explain. 'From Linda Corbet's side, it all started just before Christmas. She'd been planning to read medicine, right here in Oxford – I think she might have taken that decision partly to please her father – but her best friend told her that she simply wasn't good enough to make it.'

'That's not exactly what you'd expect from someone who was your best friend,' Macintosh says. 'In fact, she sounds like a little bitch to me.'

I picture Janet as she was in the Mad Hatter's tea room. She'd been so calm and confident – and absolutely broken-hearted that, by her own actions, she'd lost the girl who she believed would be the love of her life.

'I think she meant it for the best,' I say to Macintosh. 'Anyway, instead of being sensible and accepting that she might have to lower her sights, Linda started getting depressed, and the quality of her school work fell off.' I take a sip of G&T. 'And now, before we can go any further with Linda's story, we need to talk about the Shivering Turn.'

I tell him all about the purpose for which the society was formed, how the members created a poet called Robert Cudlip, and the reasons they registered the society with the bursary.

'The two sides eventually intersect in the tea shop,' I say finally. 'That's where Linda Corbet met Jeff Meade.'

'And you don't think that was accidental?' Macintosh asks.

'I'm bloody sure it wasn't. She was targeted. And it's no coincidence that it was Jeff, of all the members of the Shivering Turn, who picked her up. He's a good-looking boy – and they used him as bait. That's the reason they invited him to join the society in the first place.'

'There could be a second reason, as well,' George Hobson suggests. 'If something went wrong, they needed a fall guy.'

'That's true,' I agree. 'Anyway, they persuade her that because she's so interested in literature, she's been wasting her talents by studying science – and maybe they've got a point, because there's certainly more literature than science in the bookcase in her bedroom. They probably told her that – though it might take a little longer than she'd been planning – she could still get accepted by an Oxford college, but on the arts side. They may have hinted that if she applied to St Luke's, they would be able to use their influence with their tutors on her behalf.'

'Isn't it possible that the only thing she was really interested in was this Jeff Meade boy?' Macintosh asks sceptically.

'Oh, I think she certainly *was* interested in Jeff – in a sort of chaste, teenage-crush sort of way,' I tell him. 'As I said, he's a very good-looking boy. But if it had been *just* Jeff she was interested in, she'd never have gone to the meeting of the Shivering Turn Society, to hear a talk about Robert Cudlip. And it would have been Jeff's name, not a supposed poem by Cudlip, which she would have embroidered onto her blouse.'

'Maybe she only did the embroidery to fool her parents into thinking that she was interested in this nonexistent poet,' Macintosh says.

'She didn't *know* he was nonexistent,' I point out, 'and she never told her parents anything at all about it. She didn't use the Shivering Turn as an alibi while she did something else. In fact, she came up with an alibi – going over to study at her friend's house – so she could attend a meeting of the Shivering Turn.'

'And you say they set up the Shivering Turn Society before they targeted Linda Corbet?' Macintosh asks.

'Yes.'

Macintosh sighs. 'It all seems rather elaborate,' he says, 'perhaps *over-elaborate*. Are you sure you're not reading into all this something that simply isn't there?'

I'm losing him, I realize in a sudden wave of panic. And if I lose him, I lose the entire Thames Valley police, because nobody – neither a lower-ranking officer nor a higher-ranking officer – is going to be willing to second-guess a detective chief inspector.

I wonder what I can do to bring him back, and realize that my only chance is to attempt to lead him deep into the alien minds of Crispin and his gang.

'Of course it's elaborate,' I say. 'That's the whole point of it. It's a game, and the more unnecessarily complicated it is, the more they enjoy it.' I can see he's still not convinced. 'They didn't *have to* invent a poet. They could have called themselves the Wordsworth Society. That would have worked just as well. But it wouldn't have been anywhere near as much fun – and it wouldn't have given them the same feeling of superiority. It's like . . . it's like . . .' I catch myself waving my hands helplessly in the air, '. . . it's like fox hunting, which is probably something else they all indulge in.'

'Go on,' says Macintosh – still sitting on the fence.

'The object of the whole exercise is supposedly to catch the fox, but in some ways that's a bit of an anti-climax, because once he's dead, it's all over,' I say. 'But the ritual and pageantry beforehand, the gathering in front of a pub all properly decked out according to your place in the hierarchy, the whipping-in of the hounds, the blowing of the post horn – ah, that's something else. And then there's the thrill of the chase, and the sense of excitement they feel when they can smell the victim's fear as they close in for the kill. What does tearing the fox apart – or virtually tearing the girl apart – matter after that?'

I stop, exhausted. But I can see it's worked – can see that Macintosh is playing the same horror movie in his mind that I'm playing in mine.

LINDA IS LED UP *the iron stairs and into the function room by her friend Jeff Meade, whom she trusts.*

She doesn't know she's been drugged. All she does know is that she's feeling a little queasy, and she hopes she won't fall asleep or be sick during the talk on Robert Cudlip, because she really wants to impress her new friends with her interest and her intelligence.

Jeff opens the door, and almost pushes her into the room.

And what does she see? She sees a group of young men – naked save for their mortarboards and gowns – who begin baying like wild animals the moment she is inside.

She tries to turn around, but Jeff will not let her pass. And then they are on her, and what feels like a thousand hands are probing and pinching her body.

DCI MACINTOSH LOOKS AS if he's about to be sick. Then he closes his eyes and takes several deep breaths.

'What do you think happened next?' he asks.

'They took her back to her home – both her parents were out for the night – and got her to pack a bag. Then they took her down to the railway station, and put her on a train to London.'

'Did she do all this voluntarily, do you think – or did they force her to do it?'

'I don't know,' I admit. 'One possibility is that she asked them to help her, because she couldn't bear the thought of facing her parents.'

'Have her mum and dad heard from her since she left?'

I shake my head. 'No. Her father thinks it will be quite some time before they do. In fact, I think there's at least a part of him that feels they'll never hear from her again.'

And her mother thinks she's dead, I remind myself – but I don't mention it, because Mary Corbet is in a minority of one.

'What's the other possibility?' Macintosh asks.

'They weren't expecting her to react as badly as she did. Maybe they've seen a few of those pornographic films in which the girl who is ravaged turns into a nymphomaniac who loves every minute of it. Whatever the case, they realize they can't just let her loose, because she'll run screaming to the police, and then they'll be in trouble. So they put her on the train.'

'And what happens once she's reached London?'

'I've been thinking about that,' I say. 'If she was liable to scream rape at any moment, she'd have been as much of a danger to them on the train as she would have been on the streets of Oxford, so I think that at least one of them must have gone to London with her.'

'And once they got there?'

'She and her escort would have met at the station, and then she'd have been taken off somewhere.'

'Kidnapped, you mean?'

'I'm sure the Shivering Turn would think of it more as providing her with a refuge until she'd calmed down, and was prepared to be sensible,' I say.

'Are you suggesting they'd put her in some sort of mental asylum?'

'Yes.'

'But wouldn't that be terribly expensive – especially in London?'

'With the greatest respect, sir, what you have to understand from the outset is that money is absolutely no problem at all to these little shits. If they've had to bribe a less-than-ethical doctor to lock her up in a clinic for the mentally unstable, they'll have had no difficulty in raising the cash.'

Macintosh knocks back the remainder of his pint.

'You tell a good story, but I'm still not entirely convinced it's

SALLY SPENCER

any more than something you've fashioned out of a series of coincidences and unrelated facts,' he tells me.

And although I once had great hopes for you, I'm not convinced you're anything more than a myopic Scottish git, I think.

But always the diplomat (hah!), what I actually say is, 'I really think you should reconsider, sir.'

'And I think you should pay more attention to the words I use, and the way I use them, Miss Redhead,' he says. 'I told you I was "not entirely convinced", which leaves plenty of room for me to be "not entirely *unconvinced*" as well.'

'So do you think . . .?'

'I think we should go and pay the landlord of the Blind Beggar a surprise visit.'

THE BLIND BEGGAR IS three-quarters full by the time we get there. Most of the customers are young, and the fact that Suzi Quatro's 'Devil Gate Drive' is being blasted out of the juke-box speakers at a volume which would probably be deemed cruel and unusual punishment under English law doesn't seem to bother them at all.

Macintosh strolls up to the bar, and signals to a podgy balding man in his early forties.

'Are you the landlord?' the DCI bawls.

The podgy balding man nods.

Macintosh produces his warrant card. 'I'd like to have a little talk to you,' he half-says, half-mimes.

'Am I being arrested?' the landlord mouths.

Macintosh shakes his head, and the landlord replies with something obviously much too complicated to be understood using any of the means of communication thus far successfully employed.

And then the music stops, and while one record is removed from the turntable and other slotted into position, a blessed peace descends on the pub.

'What did you just say?' Macintosh asks.

'I said if I'm not under arrest, then you'll just have to wait till later for our little talk – when we're a lot less busy than we are right now.'

The air is filled with the opening chords of David Bowie's 'Rebel, Rebel' and, now that he can no longer be heard, the landlord says something else which I suspect may be on the lines of, 'So stick that up your arse, copper!'

Macintosh turns around and walks over to the juke box. He studies it for a moment, then reaches behind it and pulls out the plug.

'Here, what the bloody hell's going on?' the landlord demands.

Ignoring him, Macintosh ambles over to one of the tables, where seven young men are sitting.

'Evening, lads,' he says jovially, while holding out his warrant card for them to see.

The young men, looking down at the table, all mumble something which just possibly might be, 'Evening, officer.'

'It's an offence in this country to drink in a pub unless you're eighteen or over,' Macintosh says. 'Are all you lads eighteen or over?'

None of the young men seems particularly willing to be the first to provide an answer.

'I'll tell you what I'm going to do, lads,' Macintosh says, in an almost avuncular manner. 'I'm going to walk slowly over to the bar and, once I get there, I'm going to count to ten. Then I'm going to come back to this table. Any of you still here are going to have to prove to my satisfaction that you're old enough to drink, and if you can't prove it, I'm going to haul your arses down to the station and keep you there until it's established – by some form of documentation – exactly how old you are. That's fair enough, isn't it?'

As he walks towards the bar, the young men get up from their seats and head quickly for the exit. And they are not alone in doing that – drinkers at several other tables also seem to have considered it advisable.

Macintosh reaches the bar, then turns around in a leisurely manner to inspect the room. Covered with drinks, but devoid of drinkers, several of the tables look as if they've just been tele-transported from the *Marie Celeste*.

'Well, things do seem to have quietened down a bit, don't they?' Macintosh asks the landlord. 'And I suspect that if we stay any longer, they'll quieten down even more.'

'You'd better come into the office,' the landlord says, defeated.

IT'S NOT SO MUCH an office as a storeroom with a battered desk crammed into it, but at least there is a window, looking out on to the car park.

The office only contains one chair – which is behind the desk – and Macintosh takes it for himself.

'What's your name?' the chief inspector asks the landlord, amiably.

'Mr Harris,' the landlord tells him.

'Oh, come come, we're all friends here, what's your first name?' Macintosh cajoles.

'It's William.'

'Well, Billie Boy, I'd like to see the reservations book for your functions room,' Macintosh says.

'Have you got a search warrant?' Harris growls.

'No, I haven't got a search warrant – and if you make me waste my time by going to the magistrate and getting one sworn out, that will probably put me in a very bad mood.'

Harris reaches across Macintosh, slides open the desk drawer, takes out a ledger, and hands it to the chief inspector.

Macintosh flicks through it.

'You don't seem to have had many bookings over the last year or so,' he comments.

'It's been a very quiet time,' the landlord says.

'Look, Bill, I'm not in the least bit interested in shopping you to the Inland Revenue – I just want to know who's used the room,' Macintosh says.

'It's all in the book.'

'Didn't you say the lads from the university booked the room for last Friday?' Macintosh asks me.

'Yes.'

'And yet that's not in the book,' Macintosh says, holding it up for Harris to see.

'I must have forgotten to write it down.'

'Did these lads – who probably paid cash – book the room any other time that you've forgotten to write down?'

'No.'

'You haven't got the measure of me yet, have you, laddie?' Macintosh asks. 'I'm not just any copper, I'm a *Glaswegian* copper – and if you piss me off, I'll head-butt you through that window as soon as think about it.'

'It's true, he will,' George Hobson says. 'I've seen him do it a couple of times.'

'You wouldn't dare,' Harris says.

'And after I've done that, I'll ask DS Hobson and Miss Redhead to sign statements saying that *you* attacked *me* and I was only defending myself.' Macintosh looks at the two of us. 'You will sign them, won't you?'

'Yes,' George Hobson says.

'Absolutely,' I agree. 'I'll even say in mine that, in the circum- stances, you exercised remarkable restraint.'

'And when we've picked you up off the tarmac, and extracted the glass from your wounds, I'll arrest you for assaulting an officer. But it really doesn't have to come to that, Bill,' Macintosh says in a much softer, almost seductive voice. 'All you have to do to avoid the Glasgow kiss is to tell me if these lads have used the function room before.'

'Yes, they have,' Harris mumbles.

'How often?'

'Twice!'

'More detail, man – and be damned quick about it!' Macintosh says, back in anger mode.

'Once last November, and once in February,' Harris says in a rush.

'Now you're surely not going to tell me that the February booking was for the fourteenth of the month, are you?' Macintosh asks.

'It was the fourteenth,' Harris admits.

'Valentine's Day,' Macintosh says to Hobson. 'Is it any wonder that we Scots think you English have a sick sense of humour?'

'I think the sick sense of humour in this case belongs to the Shivering Turn, sir,' Hobson says.

'You're probably right,' Macintosh agrees. He turns his attention back on Harris. 'You must have a clear view of the people going to the function room from this office, Bill.'

'I'm hardly ever in the office. Customers like to see the landlord standing behind the bar.'

'I'm sure they do,' Macintosh agrees, 'especially when they're as personable as you are.' He stands up. 'A policeman's lot is not a happy one, but when we get people like you, Bill, who are prepared to do everything they can to help us, well, it certainly makes that lot a little easier.'

WE ARE IN DCI MACINTOSH'S car, driving back to the centre of Oxford. None of us has said much since we left the Blind Beggar, but there's no doubt that we've all been having intense conversations in our own heads.

'You didn't press Harris about what he might have seen through his office window,' I say, breaking the silence.

'That's right, I didn't,' Macintosh agrees.

'Is that because you believed him when he said he was hardly ever in the office?'

'No, it's because even if he had seen something, he's too canny to admit it. As things stand, he's in the clear, the innocent landlord who had no idea what was going on; but if he so much as hints there were grounds for him to be suspicious, he'll land himself right in the shit. So he's made up his mind to keep quiet, and even somebody who's as good at intimidation as I am – and I *am* very good at being intimidating – isn't going to break his resolve.'

The traffic light ahead of us turns amber. Most drivers would put on a burst of speed, but Macintosh changes down and glides to a halt exactly behind the white line. 'They've had three meetings so far that we know about,' Macintosh says. 'One last Friday, one in November, and one in February.'

'Yes,' I agree.

'Do you think that means two other girls have been put through the same humiliation as Linda Corbet?'

'I do.'

'And what happened to those girls? Were they both packed off to London, too?

'I have no idea,' I say, because that's the simple truth.

The lights change, and Macintosh eases his vehicle forwards.

'I believe you now,' he says. 'I really do. But all your evidence is circumstantial.'

'I know,' I admit.

'And even if we could put Linda Corbet in that room – even if we could demonstrate, without a shadow of a doubt, that she had sex with all those men – we still can't prove it was rape.'

'I know,' I repeat – there doesn't seem to be much point in saying anything else.

'The only way we can put any kind of case together is if they incriminate themselves,' Macintosh continues. 'If they don't, their parents will come down on us like a ton of bricks – and they'll have the support of the university, which is very important to this town.'

'Yes,' I say, for the sake of variety.

'Anyone who tries to make the case, and fails, will be ruined,' Macintosh says. 'He might not lose his job – at least not initially – but he'll still be a walking dead man as far as the Thames Valley Police is concerned.'

He is talking about an impersonal somebody being ruined, but we both know he really means himself.

A promising career could be ruined, the force could lose a good copper, and it would be all my fault, I think.

'You have a lot to lose, and the odds are stacked against you,' I say. 'If you choose not to push this any further, I'll understand.'

'You'll understand – but will you still respect me?' Macintosh asks.

'Yes, I will, because Linda Corbet is not the only person you have a duty and responsibility to,' I say, honestly.

'So what will you do if I decide to drop it?' he asks.

'I'll find another way to get justice for Linda,' I say – with more confidence than I actually feel.

'What other way?'

I shrug. 'I have no idea at the moment, but I'm sure that something will occur to me.'

'You have no back-up – no proper resources to draw on,' Macintosh points out.

'I've got this far on my own,' I tell him. 'It's remarkable what you can achieve when you really want to.'

He signals, and pulls up at the side of the road. It's illegal to stop there, but hell, he's the police.

'I have three daughters of my own—' he begins.

'Please, there's no need for that,' I interrupt him. 'I've already said that I understand you have other responsibilities.'

'I have three daughters of my own,' Macintosh repeats, turning to face me, 'and it could have been any one of them ending up in that function room. Let's do all we can to try to nail these bastards.'

FIFTEEN

As we drive along George Street, it starts to rain, but it is not one of those glorious full-bodied downpours which clears the air and sends streams of water gurgling madly down the drains.

No, this is nothing more than drizzle – the sort of rain which hardly justifies turning on the windscreen wipers – yet, when it persists, depresses the spirit and sets the nerves on edge.

'The whole trick will be to take the Shivering Turn completely by surprise,' DCI Macintosh says. 'We need to pick them all up at the same time, so they don't have any opportunity to confer. And, by then, I'll already have search warrants sworn out, so the second they're safely in custody, I'll send some of my lads round to give their rooms a thorough turning-over.'

He sounds confident, but I don't think he is.

None of us is.

We reach the corner of the Broad, and I say to Macintosh, 'You can let me out here.'

'It's raining,' he points out.

'I know.'

'I can drive you home, if you like. I thought that was where you wanted to go.'

So did I, but the idea of being alone in my box of a flat is suddenly not very appealing.

'Here will be fine,' I say.

He pulls up at the kerb. 'Do you want to be there when I make the arrests?' Macintosh asks.

'Yes.'

'Then ring the station later, and they'll give you the details.'

I watch as he drives away. The drizzle has already begun to penetrate my defences. I turn up my collar, and walk quickly in the direction of the Oxford Union.

IT IS GENERALLY ACKNOWLEDGED that the Oxford Union (founded in 1823) is only one of the world's five or six premier debating chambers, but most of its members (and I include myself in that number) see it as standing head and shoulders above any of its rivals.

It is completely independent of the university, though to become a member of the Union you must first be an Oxford University student (and if you are, it's your absolute right to join – there is no blackballing here!)

Winston Churchill has spoken at Union debates, as have Robert Kennedy, Albert Einstein and Malcolm X.

But it is much more than just a debating chamber. It has an extensive library exclusively for members' use, a large snooker room and a full silver service dining room.

It also has a bar, which is not only cheaper than most watering holes in the city, but is open (on debating nights) long after all the pubs have closed – and since there is a debate tonight (*and* all the pubs will soon be closing), it will provide me with the sanctuary I need.

The place is full, but, as chance would have it, a space at the bar becomes vacant just as I walk in, and I grab it.

As I sip at my G&T, I find myself thinking about the Russian generals – in both world wars – who ignored the fact there were not enough rifles to go around, and sent half their men into battle unarmed.

For a moment, I wonder why such a thought should come into my head now – and then I see it. I am doing to Macintosh and his team what the Russian generals did to their men – I have shown him where the battle is, told him he should engage in it, and failed to provide him with the tools necessary to do the job.

'Aren't you going into the debate tonight, Jennie?' says Arthur, the bar steward.

I hadn't really thought about it.

'What's the subject?' I ask.

'"This house believes that democracy is no longer fit for purpose".'

Ah, that old chestnut. Every few years, a president of the Union thinks it would be a bold, bohemian move to question democracy, conveniently ignoring the fact that whether democracy is a good thing or bad thing will be decided on by a *democratic* vote.

'Who's speaking?' I ask, more for something to say than because I'm really interested.

'Take a wild guess,' Arthur says.

I think about it. 'For the "ayes", a government minister and an opposition shadow minister,' I guess.

'Spot on,' Arthur says. 'And now, for the major prize, who's speaking for the "nays"?'

'That's trickier,' I admit. 'How about a committed communist who's found an ingenious way of explaining how he can be both a millionaire and a follower of Marx, and a right-wing nutter who accepts that Adolf Hitler was a very bad man, but still thinks that some of his ideas were very sound?'

'Not bad,' Arthur concedes. 'Actually, it's a millionaire *anarchist* and a member of the National Front.'

I wish tomorrow could be as predictable as that, I think, as I take another swig of my drink.

'So are you going to watch them jump through their hoops or not?' Arthur asks.

'Might as well,' I say – because if nothing else, it might distract me from thoughts of my own failure.

THE MOMENT I ENTER the chamber, I see Crispin Hetherington across the room – and he sees me!

For a moment, I wonder if he deliberately engineered this, as he seems to have engineered so many other events, but then I remind myself that until a few minutes ago, even I didn't know I was coming here, and the fact that the idea has even entered my head is a sign of just how paranoid I'm becoming.

The principal speakers have already made their arguments, and the question has been thrown open to the floor. For twenty minutes or so, I half-listen – at best – to these earnest young men and women who are so eager to make a name for themselves as debaters, and am almost on the point of returning to the bar when Crispin Hetherington is called on to speak.

Hetherington shows none of the nervousness of some of those who have preceded him. He stands there, a small – almost frail – figure, and surveys the chamber as if it were his personal domain.

Five seconds tick by, then ten – with each second seeming like an age. Feet are shuffled, coughs are emitted, but no one seems to have the courage to shout out, 'Get on with it,' because they recognize – as I do – that he has the power.

Finally, he does speak.

'This country does not need pasty-faced democrats at all. It needs to return to its roots – to the aristocratic men of spirit, who had no fear and no compunction, and thus made Britain great. I'm talking about men like Lord Alvanley, who once gambled three thousand pounds he could ill-afford in White's Gentlemen's Club on which raindrop would slide to the bottom of the window first.'

After the tension, at least half the audience is now laughing, but not – they believe – so much *at* Hetherington as *with* him. The Union has a tradition that even in the most serious debates, there are some speakers who will deliver humorous speeches, and what they think they are hearing now is a clever parody.

But I know it isn't.

'Men like Lord Palmerston,' Crispin Hetherington continues, 'who was prepared to start a Europe-wide conflict because *one* British subject had been insulted by the Greek government. Men like Sir Winston Churchill, who would have let millions die in India before granting the country its independence. They had the courage to face their urges and desires – to embrace both the good and bad they owned.'

As he sits down, I can see from their faces that several members of the audience are trying to identify the quote he closed with. It never occurs to them that he is quoting himself.

THE VOTE IS TAKEN (democracy, it turns out, *is* quite a good thing), and I return to the bar. It's well after midnight by now, and all but the more hardened drinkers have left; so, unlike earlier, I have no difficulty at all in getting a stool.

I have only just sat down when Crispin Hetherington slides onto the stool next to mine. I am not surprised. In fact, I now know him well enough to have been expecting it.

'Good evening, Miss Redhead,' he says. 'Have you come to see me in what you fondly imagine are my last few hours of freedom?'

'You're getting paranoid, Crispin,' I tell him (the pot calling the kettle black!). 'I didn't know you'd be here, and I have no idea what you are talking about now.'

He clicks his tongue in rebuke.

'Come, come, the condemned man is at least entitled to a little honesty from his enemies, isn't he?'

'After everything you've done, you contemptible little shit, I don't think you're entitled to *any* consideration of any kind – and I still don't know what you're talking about.'

He frowns. He has scripted this encounter as verbal fencing between two civilized adversaries, and now I have gone and spoiled it all with a personal insult. For a second, he seems about to leave, but then he decides that the scene he's written in his head is a really good one, and it would be a pity to waste it.

'You're being very tiresome,' he says, 'but I suppose I should have expected no better. Very well, I'll spell it out for you. I had a phone call from William, the oikish landlord of the Blind Beggar, who informed me that you and a certain Chief Inspector MacBollock had paid him a visit and asked him how often we'd rented his function room.'

How much time had elapsed between us leaving the Blind Beggar and me entering the Union building? Twenty minutes at the most. Yet that had been long enough for Hetherington to have been informed of what we'd done.

And there, I think, goes DCI Macintosh's element of surprise.

'I can only assume that what that visit presages is that the police are now almost ready to swoop down on us, drag us off to the police station, and put us through the third degree,' he continues.

'If that's really what you think is about to happen, you're taking it very calmly,' I say.

'Why wouldn't I be calm?' he asks. 'We're all very well prepared for whatever it is you're going to throw at us. Besides, what's the point of playing the game if there isn't some danger attached to it – if there isn't, in fact, a chance that the game itself will completely destroy you?'

'Which game are you talking about?' I say. 'The game you played with Linda Corbet? Or the one you're playing with me?'

He giggles, in an almost girlish way.

'Oh, neither of those,' he says. 'Nothing so parochial. What I'm talking about, my dear Miss Redhead, is the game of life.'

SIXTEEN

It is six twenty-three in the morning, and I am in front of St Luke's boathouse, looking down at the Isis.

The sun began to rise over an hour ago, but the air which engulfs me is still cold enough to make my body shudder occasionally. Or maybe the shuddering has nothing at all to do with the temperature. Maybe it is the anticipation – half-hope, half-dread – which makes me tingle so.

That I am here on my own is DCI Macintosh's idea. It is his Plan B, now that it has become clear his Plan A isn't going to work.

'The trick in a situation like this one is to produce the unexpected,' he told me, when we first arrived at the boathouse. 'If Crispin Hetherington is expecting us to arrest all the Shivering Turn . . .'

'He is. He made that quite clear last night.'

'Then they'll also be expecting us to come in mob-handed, and when it isn't like that at all – when there's only you, a civilian, waiting for them – it will unnerve them.'

'I'm not sure that will work,' I'd said honestly.

'Trust me, lassie, I've been in this job a long time, and I know what will work and what won't,' he assured me.

Yes, I'd thought, you might well have been in the job a long time – but you don't know Crispin Hetherington like I'm starting to.

The morning mist – wispy but impenetrable – still clings softly to the river like a lover who knows his time is running out, and through this mist I hear a sound which is neither the birds, joyously heralding the arrival of a new day, nor the water, lapping gently against the bank.

The sound I hear is being produced by a voice which is clearly human, but has a strangely metallic edge to it.

At first, I cannot distinguish any individual words, but as the still-invisible boat draws ever closer, the sounds separate to create meaning.

'In . . . out . . . in . . . out . . . in . . . out . . .'

I wonder if it was the same on that terrible night in the Blind Beggar's function room – Crispin Hetherington sitting there then, watching as one after another of the members of the Shivering Turn Society violated Linda Corbet, and chanting – with the same rhythm, but with a salacious relish quite absent now – 'in . . . out . . . in . . . out . . . in . . . out . . .'

The prow of the boat bursts through the mist, and I can see the broad backs of the rowers as they heave on the oars, cutting through the water and propelling the craft forward.

'In . . . out . . . in . . . out . . . in . . . out . . .'

And now I can see the cox, sitting at the stern of the boat, with a megaphone strapped to his head.

As the boat steers in towards the boathouse, I note that Jeff Meade is not one of the crew members.

Of course he isn't! He might be tolerated – simply because

he is needed – in their sordid little society, but there is no way they would ever allow riff-raff like him to join the crew training for that holy of holies, the Summer Eights.

The rowers cannot see me, but there is no way that Crispin Hetherington could have failed to notice my presence there on the bank. Yet, despite this, he keeps his attention focused on the task in hand, and though I don't enjoy feeling a grudging admiration for him, there's nothing I can do about it.

The boat reaches the boathouse, and is lifted out of the water by the crew. This is the point at which a mistake in handling it might result in damage to the craft, and Hetherington watches the whole process with real concern in his eyes, because this is not some girl you can use for your own sick pleasure and then just throw away – this is the college's best boat.

Only when the boat is safely stowed does Crispin Hetherington finally turn towards me and say, 'So where are the police? Are they hiding behind the boathouse?'

'No, they're *waiting* behind the boathouse,' I correct him. 'They have no *need* to hide. *They* haven't done anything wrong.'

'And neither have we,' Hetherington replies. 'I must say, it was jolly sporting of DCI Macintosh to allow us to finish our practice.'

He frowns, as if something has just occurred to him. But it is an act – almost everything he does is an act.

'Or maybe it wasn't sporting at all,' he continues. 'Maybe Macintosh was just giving us the opportunity to tire ourselves out, thus making it easier for him to question us.'

The rest of the crew have gathered around us in a loose

semi-circle. They do not ask what's going on – because they already know.

I look from face to face. Even moments before they are due to be arrested, they are assessing me and imagining what they could do to me – just as they will have assessed Linda Corbet and imagined what they were about to do to her.

I am a twenty-nine-year-old woman, who knows that the police are just around the corner, yet I feel frightened and alone. How must Linda, a girl of seventeen, have felt when she realized that she *was* alone – that whatever they chose to do to her, no help would be forthcoming?

My anger for Linda overcomes my fear for myself.

'Well, I can see two of my Shakespearian friends here,' I say, looking with burning contempt first at the rower with the bruise running along his jaw line, and then at the one with a plaster on his nose. 'But who's the third of the courageous trio? If he'd care to step forward, I've got something I'd like to give him before the police arrive.'

None of them moves even a fraction of an inch.

'You seem to have your monkeys well trained indeed,' I tell Crispin Hetherington.

'Go ahead and mock as much as you wish,' he says. 'It doesn't matter who gets the first laugh; it's only the last laugh that counts.'

I was right about how to handle the situation, and Chief Inspector Macintosh was wrong. Doing it this way hasn't unsettled them. If anything, it's only tightened their bond.

Almost half-heartedly, I take the police whistle out of my pocket, and blow it as hard as I can.

*

THE MIST HAS COMPLETELY lifted, and the sun has begun its daily task of warming up the river. Most of the rowers have been cautioned, handcuffed and led away to the Black Maria vans, which are parked just up the lane, but there is still enough activity in front of the St Luke's boathouse for the crews from other colleges, out for their own early morning practice, to ignore their coxes' harsh megaphone instructions to focus, and instead to turn their heads to see what is going on.

'I'd like you to come to the station and monitor some of the interviews,' DCI Macintosh tells me.

'Is that normal?' I ask, surprised – because it wouldn't have happened in my day.

'Well, of course it's not normal,' Macintosh replies. 'Nothing about this whole bloody operation is *normal*. But you've been involved in the investigation for several days now, and we're going in cold, so you just might pick up on something we miss.'

'What do you want *me* to do, sir?' George Hobson asks.

'I want you to perform a minor bloody miracle, Sergeant Hobson,' Macintosh replies.

'Do you have any particular miracle in mind, sir?' George asks, taking it in his stride.

'Yes, I want you to find a way to stop Tom Corbet from finding out what's going on.'

'It's a bit more than a *minor* miracle that you're asking for there, sir,' George says. 'It's Tom Corbet's own nick we'll be using.'

'Do you think I don't know that?' Macintosh demands, with a hint of anger – or perhaps just frustration – in his voice. Then he softens a little. 'Look, George, just do your best. Keep him out of the loop for as long as you can – because when he does find out, God alone knows what he might do.'

Behind me, I hear a voice say, 'I'll see you at the station then, will I, Miss Marple?'

I turn. Crispin Hetherington is standing there. His hands are cuffed behind his back, which is enough to subdue the spirits of most people, yet there is a broad, excited grin on his face.

And with a sinking feeling I suddenly realize what part of me has always known – that, as far as he's concerned, this may not be part of the original game as planned out, but it's certainly nothing more than an extension of it.

I AM SITTING AT A table in the room adjoining Interview Room B. On the table sits a microphone.

'It's the latest thing,' Macintosh says, seeing me looking questioningly at the mike. 'It allows us to talk directly to whoever is conducting the interview.'

Whatever will they think of next!

I look through the two-way mirror into the interview room. There, three people are sitting around a table.

Hugo Johnson – big, beefy, and still, despite the situation he finds himself in, looking very arrogant – is one of them.

The other two are detective police constables.

'He's Norman Bassett,' Macintosh says, indicating the larger of the pair, 'the most fearless rugby prop forward I've ever seen. The little bloke with him is Gordon Hough, the Federation snooker champion. They both know about playing games and they both know about strategy – and they're the two best interrogators I've got. If anybody can get Johnson to spill his guts, it's them.'

'If they're the best you've got, then why not put them on Jeff Meade,' I suggest. 'I think he's the weakest link.'

I really *do* think that. Not only is he the youngest of the group, but he's also the most innocent or, to put it another way, the least corrupted. There might be a part of him which is already lost – the part which allowed him to lead Linda Corbet to the Blind Beggar, when he knew what was waiting for her there – but there is also the part which, only a couple of days ago, was still so childlike that he thought it would be really good fun to discuss the football rivalry between his school and my school back in Lancashire.

'I'd put Bassett and Hough on Meade if we had him,' Macintosh says, 'but unfortunately we don't.'

'What do you mean?'

'He's not in his rooms, and he's not anywhere else in the college. I've issued a general alert, which means that both the crime cars and the foot patrols will be keeping an eye open for him, but so far they've come up with sweet Fanny Adams. If you ask me, he's decided to do a runner.'

Or else he's been persuaded by Crispin Hetherington to do a runner, I think.

I'm seeing Hetherington's puppet-master hand behind everything that happens. It might sound like ever-increasing paranoia on my part – but that doesn't necessarily mean I've got it wrong.

Bassett has switched on the tape recorder, and begun the process of cautioning Johnson.

'Where's Johnson's solicitor?' I ask Macintosh.

'He says he doesn't need one.'

'What about the rest of them?'

'Apparently, they don't need one either.'

They're such arrogant little shits – but that may well turn out to be to our advantage!

The interrogation proper is about to start. I lean forwards, so I'm closer to the mirror, and then wonder why I did that, when I could hear perfectly clearly from where I was.

'**WERE YOU IN THE** function room of the Blind Beggar public house on Friday the third of May 1974?' DC Bassett asks Hugo Johnson.

'Yes,' Johnson replies.

'And was there a schoolgirl, by the name of Linda Corbet, also present that night?'

'A schoolgirl!' Johnson says, with a smirk on his face.

'What's wrong with calling her that?' Bassett wonders. 'After all, it's what she is.'

'It just makes her sound so young.'

'She *is* so young.'

'She's well above the age of consent.'

'So was she there or not?' Bassett asks.

'She was there.'

'We have a witness who says that, before Linda Corbet arrived at the pub, she had been drugged.'

'If your witness *really* says that, then he's got it all wrong. She was as clear-headed as any of us.'

'And how clear-headed was that?'

'We'd all had a couple of drinks, but we were far from drunk.'

'Did you have sexual intercourse with Linda Corbet on the night in question?'

'Oh yes, indeed I did.'

'So you are aware, are you, that you could well be charged with raping this young girl – and that if you are found guilty, you could go to prison for at least ten years?'

'I didn't rape her,' Johnson says dismissively. 'None of us raped her. She wanted it – she was gasping for it – and we were all more than pleased to give it to her.'

'CAN I ASK A QUESTION?' I say to Macintosh.

'Yes, that's what you're here for – to ask the questions that we wouldn't think of asking,' the chief inspector says.

'So what do I do?'

'There's a switch on the base of the microphone. When you're ready to ask your question, click it – but don't speak too loudly, or you'll probably shatter Norman Bassett's bloody eardrum.'

I click on the mike and say softly, 'Ask him if Crispin Hetherington had sex with Linda.'

There is only the slightest flicker of Bassett's eyes to indicate that he has received the message in his earpiece.

He asks the question.

Johnson says no, Hetherington didn't.

And the interesting thing to me is that he looks surprised to hear himself saying it. It's almost as if his mind had registered the fact that Hetherington had abstained while it was all going on, but now, for the first time, he is considering the implications of that.

'What was that all about?' Macintosh asks me.

'I'm not sure yet – I'm just feeling my way,' I say.

But I *think* that maybe I asked the question because I was testing out a theory I've been developing on exactly what makes Crispin Hetherington's sick little mind tick.

BASSETT STRETCHES HIS LEGS and yawns.

'So just to be perfectly clear on the matter, you're telling me that Linda Corbet was a willing participant in what went on at the Blind Beggar?' he asks Johnson, almost lazily.

'That's right – she was gagging for it,' Johnson replies.

'That's funny,' Bassett reflects.

'What is?'

'Well, I've been in this business for a long time, and I've certainly met prostitutes who've been willing to have sex with nine men, one after the other. I've even met a few who were prepared to let all the men watch all the other men doing her, as long as they were willing to pay for the privilege.'

'We didn't pay her anything,' Johnson says.

Bassett, suddenly no longer so laid back, slams his fist down hard on the table.

'Did I say you could speak?' he roars.

'No, but—'

'Then until I do, keep your bloody trap shut.' Bassett turns to Hough. 'Now, where was I?'

'You were saying you've known prostitutes who'd let nine men screw them, one after the other.'

'That's right, I was. I've certainly known that – more than once. But I've never known a *virgin* agree to it.' He pauses. 'Have you ever heard of anything like that, Hugo?'

'I'm allowed to speak now, am I?' Johnson asks.

'Yes, you're allowed to speak.'

'Are you saying that *Linda Corbet* was a virgin?'

'You *know* she was.'

'Do I?'

'Please don't piss me about, son,' Bassett says. 'It was only because she *was* a virgin that you and the rest of your filthy little Virgin Hunters Society were the least bit interested in her.'

'My what?'

'You heard!'

BASSETT IS ABOUT TO make a mistake, I think from my side of the glass. Instead of pinning Johnson down through a narrow line of questioning, he's going to let him take centre stage – give him the opportunity, in other words, to imitate his leader, become a mini-Crispin Hetherington – and that can only add to his confidence and make him much harder to break.

I can see it coming, but there is nothing I can do about it, because Bassett is their trained interrogator, and I am only a civilian.

*

'VIRGIN HUNTERS SOCIETY!' Hugo Johnson muses. 'Now, I must admit, that does sound like rather an intriguing society to belong to, but I can assure you that I'm not a member.'

'No, you belong to the Shivering Turn Society, and "shivering turn" is an anagram of "virgin hunters".'

For maybe ten seconds, Johnson pretends he's thinking it through – rearranging the letters in his head – then he smiles and says, 'Do you know, I think you're right. What a coincidence.'

'It's no coincidence,' Bassett says. 'Did you notice the way I phrased that? I said "shivering turn" is an anagram of "virgin hunters", rather than the other way around?'

'Yes, I did notice you doing it, but I don't really see the significance of it.'

'"Virgin hunters" is what you might call the foundation stone on which everything else rests. You looked for an anagram in which you could hide the name, and came up with "shivering turn" – and it was once you'd done that that you invented Robert Cudlip to give the phrase some context.'

'Give the phrase some context,' Johnson repeats. 'That's a rather subtle linguistic construct for a mere detective constable, don't you think? And, of course, you are quite wrong.'

It is meant to make Bassett angry, but he doesn't take the bait.

'If that wasn't the reason you invented Robert Cudlip, then why invent him at all?' he asks evenly.

'For a lark,' Johnson says. 'You do understand larks, don't you?' He frowns. 'No, you probably don't. When you were growing up, you were probably too poor to find the time to indulge in them.'

'Let's get back to Friday night,' Bassett suggested. 'What happened to Linda Corbet after you'd all finished raping her?'

'After we'd all had consensual sex with her is what you mean, isn't it?' Hugo Johnson replies.

'Sorry to have got that wrong,' Bassett says. 'I'll try again. What happened to Linda Corbet, a virgin who was so keen to lose her virginity that she virtually threw herself on to the pricks of a bunch of upper-class wankers?'

Johnson shrugs. 'I don't know what happened to her. We'd all had her, so she was of no interest to us any more. She might, I suppose, have gone down to the bus station – to see if she could persuade any of the dossers and tramps who hang around there to slip her another few inches.'

'It's interesting you should mention the bus station, and not the railway station,' Bassett says.

'All right, then, if it will make you any happier, I'll agree that she could have gone down to the *railway* station to see if she could persuade any of the dossers and tramps who hang around *there* to slip her another few inches.'

'You were at the railway station yourself, weren't you?'

'Of course not! After I left the Blind Beggar, I went back to my room in college and played a rather exciting game of chess with Duffy. Ask him, if you don't believe me.'

'Where's Linda Corbet now?' Bassett snaps.

'I have absolutely no idea.'

'She's in London, isn't she? Come on, Hugo, you must know, because you took her there yourself.'

'She may or may not be in London. I wouldn't know. But I certainly didn't take her there. As I told you, I was playing chess.'

'You're new at this game, and I'm an old hand, so I'll explain how things are going to unfold,' Bassett says, almost avuncular now. 'For the first two or three hours, you'll all hold back the truth. You might even be surprised about just how easy it is not to confess, and begin to wonder why anybody ever does. But, like I said, that's for the first two or three hours. After that, it suddenly starts getting harder. It's almost as if a weight's pressing down on you, forcing the right words – the words I'm waiting for – out of your mouth.'

'I won't—'

'I'm not just talking about you, here,' Bassett says. 'I'm speaking in general terms about everybody who finds themselves in your situation. Maybe you're right, and however long the questions go on for, you'll never crack. But one of your mates will – have absolutely no doubt about that. And now we come to the important bit for you personally. Are you listening, Hugo?'

Hugo Johnson says nothing.

'Are you listening?' Bassett growls at him.

'Yes,' Johnson mutters, reluctantly.

'Every member of the Virgin Hunters will have to be punished for what you've done – I won't lie to you about that. But the first one to confess will have a much easier time of it than the rest. And, unless I'm very much mistaken, you'd like to be that one.'

Johnson goes quiet for a second, as if attempting to recall a lesson.

Then he says, 'Linda Corbet wanted to have sex with us, and I've no idea where she is now.'

*

I AM IN DCI MACINTOSH'S office, and Macintosh himself is on the phone, talking to the chief constable.

'Yes sir . . .' he says. 'I know, sir . . . I can certainly appreciate the pressure you're under, just as I'm sure *you* appreciate the pressure *I'm* under . . .'

Sitting in a chair on the other side of the desk, I try not to listen – or, at least, not interpret what I hear – but, whatever I do, I can't help getting at least the gist of the conversation.

'Yes sir . . . I can quite understand that, sir . . . you haven't forgotten that Tom Corbet is one of our own, have you? . . . Yes, sir, I agree that was uncalled for, and you have my unreserved apology . . . No, I'm entitled to hold them for forty-eight hours without charge, and unless I receive a direct order – in writing – from you, that's exactly what I intend to do.'

He puts down the phone and takes a deep breath.

'That was the chief constable,' he says – unnecessarily. 'Apparently, he's been bombarded with calls from members of the shadow cabinet demanding to know why we're playing silly buggers with their nephews, and from captains of industry who swear that their godsons would never so much as even drop a piece of litter.'

'What does the chief constable want you to do?'

'Charge them or let them go, but we don't have the evidence to charge them yet – and, frankly, I'm beginning to doubt we ever will have.'

The problem is, they've been well prepared for just such a situation as this one, so they're showing no signs of panic, and even the words which come out of their mouths have been provided by Crispin Hetherington.

'You need to find Linda Corbet, Ken,' I say. 'You really need to find her urgently.'

'Every police authority in the country has been made aware of how eager we are to talk to her,' Macintosh tells me, 'but, even if we get her back, I'm not sure she's going to be of much use to us.'

'Not much use? How can you say that?'

'It's her word against theirs. If it goes to trial – and that's a big "if" – the defendants' daddies will hire the sharpest, most expensive lawyers in the country. And can you imagine what one of those sharp lawyers could do to Linda, once he's got her in the witness box?'

I think about it – and shudder.

He's right, of course, it would be like feeding her into a meat grinder.

THE DEFENCE COUNCIL, DEFINITELY a QC and probably a knight of the realm, rises from his seat in a stately manner, and ambles over to the witness box, where a trembling Linda Corbet is waiting.

'Good morning, Miss Corbet,' he says, in a deep rich voice – a voice that would inspire men to follow him to their deaths.

Linda says nothing.

'Good morning, Miss Corbet,' the barrister repeats.

'Good morning,' Linda mumbles.

'Now you say you were raped by all the young men sitting in the dock. Have I got that right?'

'Yes.'

'Prior to the rape, had you seen any of them before?'

'Yes.'

'One of them? Or more than one?'

'More than one.'

'How many exactly?'

'All of them.'

'All of them!' The QC turns his back on Linda, and raises a quiz-zical eyebrow to the jury, then swings round to face the girl again. 'Is it right that when you were arrested for public disorder a few weeks before the alleged incident, you were in the company of exactly the same group of young men?'

'Yes.'

The QC cups his ear. 'I'm sorry,' he says, 'you'll have to speak up a little if you want me to hear you.'

'Yes!' Linda says, and it comes out almost as a yell.

'So, on the night of the alleged incident, you arranged to meet these same young men – whom you already knew to be rather high-spirited – in the function room of a public house with a rather dubious repu-tation.'

'I didn't know the pub had a bad reputation.'

'Were you expecting to find other girls of your age there?'

'No, I knew I'd be the only one.'

'So, to sum up, you went to a sleazy pub to meet a group of young men in whose company you had been drunk at least once, and possibly – for all we know – many more times before and since.'

'I've never been—'

'So tell me, Miss Corbet, just what were you expecting to do in the function room of the Blind Beggar?'

'It . . . it was supposed to be a meeting of a poetry society.'

'A poetry society! If, as you claim, you thought it was to be a meeting *of a poetry society, didn't you ask yourself why they weren't holding it in St Luke's College, where all these young men have rooms?'*

'No, I—'

'And since it was only a harmless poetry society meeting, I assume you told your parents where you were going? Am I right?'

'No, I—'

'You didn't tell them?'

'No.'

'So what did you tell them?'

'You've got to understand, sir, that ever since that day I got arrested, my dad's been—'

'So what did you tell them?'

'I told them I was studying at a friend's house.'

'So, even though you thought you were going to attend a perfectly innocent meeting, at which you knew there would be no other women present, you went to the trouble of setting yourself up with an alibi.'

'It wasn't as simple as—'

'No further questions.'

THE PHONE RINGS AGAIN, and Macintosh picks it up.

'Yes, yes . . . I see . . . yes, as soon as possible. And thank you so much, Chief Superintendent.'

He puts the phone back on its cradle.

'That was the Dover police,' he tells me. 'They've just arrested our friend Jeff Meade.'

'On what charge?'

'He tried to bribe one of the lorry drivers who was queuing up for the Channel ferry to smuggle him across to France, but the driver was a retired copper, and he went straight to the dockyard police.' Macintosh gives the top of his head a thoughtful scratch. 'Whatever made him do it that way?' he asks. 'There'd have been some risk in pretending to be an ordinary holidaymaker, but to try and smuggle yourself out is just loopy.'

'He probably didn't have any choice – because he probably doesn't have a passport,' I say.

Why would he even *need* a passport? Lads like him don't spend their summers lolling on sunny Mediterranean beaches or jetting off to some Caribbean island. They have to work, because if they don't, they'll have only their government grants to live on – and that ain't much.

'Are the Kent police going to keep him in Dover?' I ask.

'No – they're sending him back to us. He's on the way to Oxford even as we speak.'

'How long should it take him to get here?'

'That will depend on the traffic. I'd guess anything between two and four hours.'

'When he does arrive, can I talk to him before you hand him over to your lads?' I ask.

'I'll think about it,' Macintosh replies, noncommittally.

'I understand him,' I say, in a pleading voice. 'I can get him to say things he'd never say to anybody else.'

'That may be true, but—'

There's a knock on the door. Shit – that's really the last thing I needed right now!

'Come in,' Macintosh says.

It's George Hobson.

'Have you started having problems with Tom Corbet?' Macintosh asks.

'No, sir. In fact, we've had a bit of luck there,' George says. Then, hearing his words the way that others might hear them, he hastily adds, 'Well, not exactly luck – that is probably the wrong word – but Inspector Corbet's not here because he's had to take his wife into hospital. I believe it's something to do with her nerves.'

It probably is, I think. She was teetering on the edge earlier in the week – God knows what she's like now.

'So if it's not about Tom Corbet, why are you here?' Macintosh asks.

'If you don't mind, sir, I'd like to borrow Jennie for a few minutes,' George says.

'If you want to tell her something about the investigation, then I rather think I'd like to hear it too,' Macintosh tells him.

'It's nothing at all to do with the investigation, but it *is* rather important,' George says. 'So would it be all right if I borrowed her?'

'Yes, by all means take her,' Macintosh says, in a tone which suggests he has suddenly given up caring about anything. 'We weren't achieving much in here anyway.'

As we step out into the corridor and close the door behind us, I say, 'Is something the matter, George?'

'Let's go down to the canteen and have a cup of tea, shall we?' Hobson asks evasively.

★

WHEN WE ARRIVE AT the canteen, there's no sign of any other customers – which is hardly surprising, given that all hell has broken loose at the station that morning – so we have our choice of seats.

George doesn't just suggest a table, he ushers me across to it as if I were a little old lady who's just had a nasty fall, and only when he's sat me down does he go up to the counter to order the tea.

Left alone, I watch one of the counter staff swabbing the floor, almost hypnotized by the swish-swish-swish of her mop, and the squelching sound it makes when she wrings it out in the bucket. I catch myself wondering if perhaps she might not have the right idea about life – if limiting yourself to mindless repetitive work might not, after all, be the true key to happiness.

And it is at this point that I realize that, though I do not know what I should be worrying about, I really am worried.

George returns with two heavy white mugs containing tea which, I remember from my own time here, is strong enough to stand your spoon up in.

He places my mug on the table in front of me, takes a sip of his own, and grimaces.

'This tea doesn't get any better,' he says, 'but you should have a drink of it anyway.'

'I need to know what this is all about, George,' I say.

'Of course you do,' he agrees. 'Of course you do. It's only right and proper that you should know.'

He takes another sip of his tea.

'George!' I say, exasperatedly.

'There's been a phone call from Whitebridge,' Hobson says. 'They've been trying to reach you for a couple of hours . . .'

'Who is "they"?'

'Some woman called Enid Redhead. She said she was your cousin or something.'

'She is.'

'Anyway, Enid was trying to reach you, but of course you weren't in your office, and it was only when she thought to ring the cop shop to see if we might know where you were that—'

'Get to the point,' I say, almost screaming now.

'It's your dad . . .'

Oh my God!

'What about him?' I ask, 'Is he dead?'

'No, he's not dead – but he's had a major heart attack.'

SEVENTEEN

On the first leg of the journey – from Oxford to Manchester – the railway line is electrified, and the train dashes through the countryside at what seems almost break-neck speed.

Chickety-chick-chickety-chick-chickety-chick.

Then, in Manchester, I change trains, boarding a squat, snub-nosed diesel which is really not much more than a country bus on rails.

This train – with its ker-clunk-ker-clunk-ker-clunk – holds out no promise of urgency. It does little more than trundle through the outskirts of the city and, though it picks up some speed as it passes the small towns and villages which separate Manchester from Whitebridge, there are times when it almost seems as if walking would be quicker.

Sitting in an almost-empty second-class carriage, I feel as if I am taking a voyage back in time – and, in a way, I am.

I find myself – not entirely surprisingly – thinking about my father, and search as I might, the only moment of real intimacy I can uncover is the time he apologized to his redheaded daughter for giving her the name Redhead.

We were a family which didn't really talk to each other, perhaps because we were afraid that talking could turn into disagreement, and disagreements might lead to the kind of rows the people whom my mother regarded as our more unsavoury neighbours had – rows which could be heard even from the street.

We didn't pay each other compliments, either – my father might have told me that my mother once had hair like rich dark chocolate, but he would never have dreamed of saying it to her, because that would have been to risk upsetting the emotional (or perhaps unemotional) balance of our household, and that was a risk it was better not to take.

And so we said nothing that wasn't almost perfectly neutral, thus allowing our worries and fears, our angers and resentment, to quietly fester away beneath a veneer of amiability.

FIFTEEN MINUTES AFTER PICKING up a taxi at Whitebridge railway station – a Victorian relic which stands as a reminder that this was once an important cotton town – I am standing on the street in front of my parents' house.

I can remember the day we moved in. At last we had our own three-bedroom semi in a respectable neighbourhood, with a little car in the garage. After years of wandering through the wilderness of rented accommodation and council estates, we had arrived in the Promised Land.

It was less than a year before there was trouble in paradise. It began when our next-door neighbour, Mr Hopkins – who was a senior clerk at one of the few remaining mills, and, according to my mother, 'a very nice, very *quiet* man' – announced that he was moving out. For days, Mum fretted about who might take his place, and she was right to worry, because when someone did move in, it was a man called Mr Culshaw, who was (horror of horrors!) a plumber.

It did not take the disreputable Culshaw family long to show their true colours by throwing a house-warming party.

'That music went on half the night,' my mother had said in disgust, the next morning.

'That's not true, Mum. I looked at my watch when they turned off the music, and it was only half-past ten.'

'That's as maybe – but did the guests go home once they'd turned the music off? No, they did not. They stayed around – talking!'

Talking!

With all this *talking* going on, our street was rapidly turning into a Lancashire version of Sodom and Gomorrah.

I WALK UP TO THE front door. I have a key, but somehow I would feel like a fraud to use it, so I knock, instead.

The door is opened by my cousin, Enid. She has the kind of look on her face that people always feel obliged to assume when talking to television reporters about someone else's personal tragedy.

It tells me all I need to know.

'My dad's dead, isn't he?' I say.

She nods. 'He passed away at five thirty-seven.'

Why does everybody need to be so precise about the time of death? And what does she expect me to say in response – Oh, thank God for that. It would have been simply awful if he'd died at *five thirty-nine*?

'Where's my mother?' I ask.

'She's upstairs. The doctor's given her a sedative, and he says she'll probably sleep through to morning.'

We go into the kitchen, and she brews a pot of tea.

'I've made up your bed, and a bed in the spare room,' she says. 'I will be staying the night.'

Enid is the paragon of virtue in our family. We were the first two of the Clan Redhead to go university, but she was the one who made the sensible choice, doing Business Studies at a college close enough to Whitebridge for her to be able to bring her dirty washing home. And when she graduated, she got a job in Whitebridge, like any sensible person would.

'I suppose you'll be moving back up here, now, Jennifer,' she says, as she pours the tea.

'What!' I exclaim.

'Now your dad's dead, I suppose you'll be moving back up here,' she repeats, saying the words more slowly this time, since I seem incapable of understanding plain Lancashire English any longer.

'Does my mother need looking after?' I ask. 'Has her health taken a nose dive since the last time I was here?'

'Well, no, not exactly,' Enid admits.

'What do you mean by that?'

'She doesn't need looking after in the physical sense, but she's had a big shock, and I'm sure she'll want her family around her.'

'I can't just pack up everything and move back home,' I say. 'How would I earn a living here? There's not enough work in Whitebridge for a full-time private investigator.'

'Private investigator!' she repeats, as if she thinks it's a pretend job – no more than a pathetic excuse to cover my own laziness.

And maybe that *is* what she really thinks!

We sit in uncomfortable silence for several minutes, then I say, 'Do you mind if I go out for a walk?'

She looks at me in a way which suggests that any decent person would stay where she was, cloaked in her own misery, and that only a heartless bitch would consider anything as hedonistic as *walking*.

'I intend to stay here, but I suppose you'll do what you like,' she says.

Oh, thank you, thank you, blessed Saint Enid.

I WANDER UP TO the Drum and Monkey, where I hope to see another of my small, select band of friends – Monika Paniatowski, whom I used to baby-sit for when she was first promoted to detective inspector. But, to my disappointment, Monika's habitual table in the corner of the public bar is empty.

I suppose I could go and knock on her door – I know she would welcome me in, however tired she was – but I really don't want to impose.

I drink two gin and tonics in rapid succession, and then return wearily to my parents' home.

Enid has gone to bed by the time I get there, and I go straight up to my old room, where my cousin has made the bed, tucking the sheets in so tightly that I have to prise them apart before I can climb in between them.

It is hard to believe that only eighteen hours ago I was

standing on the bank of the Isis, waiting for the St Luke's boat to arrive.

I wonder how the investigation is getting on without me.

IT IS MORNING, AND I am lying in the narrow bed of my childhood. I know that you are supposed to feel affection for your old bedroom, but I don't. The fact is, I ceased to think of it as 'my' room long before I moved out. It wasn't a sudden, dramatic dissociation or anything like that, but rather a gradual drifting, as I slowly came to realize that there were better ways to live than within the close confines of a life in which joy was sacrificed on the altar of respectability.

I go downstairs. Enid – good old Enid – is preparing breakfast, and my mother is sitting at the table.

My instinct is to hug my mother, but we have never hugged in my family, so I just say, 'Hello, Mum. I'm so sorry.'

'There has to be an autopsy,' she says, in an accusatory voice which almost – but not quite – suggests it's my fault. 'The funeral won't be until sometime next week.'

'Is there anything I can do for you?' I ask.

'No, your cousin Enid's making all the necessary arrangements. She's had business dealings with Thorburn's funeral directors before—'

'I know young Mr Thorburn personally,' Enid chips in.

'And they think very highly of her there,' my mother concludes.

I eat only a little breakfast – Enid has somehow managed to turn the toast into corrugated asbestos – then I say, 'If the funeral isn't until next week, why don't you come back to Oxford with me, Mum? You can have my bed, and I'll doss down on the sofa.'

'You're surely never going back to Oxford – with your father still warm?' Enid asks, outraged.

Actually, Enid, he won't still be warm – because they'll be keeping him in cold storage.

'You heard Mum say there's nothing for me to do here,' I tell Enid, 'whereas in Oxford, I'm involved in a case which could determine the whole future of an innocent young girl.'

'A case which could determine the whole future of an innocent young girl,' Enid repeats mockingly. 'If you ask me, you watch far too much television for your own good, our Jennie.'

'Will you come back with me, Mum?' I ask, ignoring my cousin. 'It will do you good to get away for a few days.'

'No, I will not go back with you,' my mother says firmly. 'It wouldn't be right.'

'*Why* wouldn't it be right?' I wonder. 'Who *says* it wouldn't be right?'

My mother folds her arms firmly across her chest.

'It wouldn't be right,' she repeats, as if repetition can easily kick the shit out of logic any day of the week.

I WAS NOT EXPECTING MY mother to come with me to the door when the taxi arrived, but she does.

I peck her on the cheek and pick up my bag – but she still has one parting shot to fire.

'It broke your father's heart when it was in all the papers about you and that lord,' she says. 'It did. It broke his heart.'

I want to say that was his problem, not mine – that if I had slept with Charlie I'd have been doing nothing illegal, and that I have to live my life by my own standards, not by the standards imposed by some invisible theoretic community of Right and Not Right.

But the woman has just lost her husband, and so I just say, 'I'm really sorry, Mum.'

And, to my horror, a look of triumphal vindication comes to her face.

'You may well be sorry – but that's no good to your father now, is it?' she asks.

As I climb into the taxi, I think that no one really knows when their time is due, and that if either of us should die before we can meet again, those will be the last words she will ever have said to me.

'You may well be sorry – but that's no good to your father now, is it?'

I realize I'm sobbing softly to myself – and I don't quite know why.

I SENSE THE CHANGE in the atmosphere the moment I walk into St Aldate's police station. It feels like a small boring town, the day after the carnival has departed – or like a boxing arena in which the popular champion has been unexpectedly knocked out, and everyone has gone home despondent.

'Where can I find DCI Macintosh?' I ask the sergeant on desk duty.

'He's in his office,' the sergeant replies, hardly bothering to look up. 'Can you find your own way?'

I tell him I can, and he presses a button on his desk which temporarily opens the door to the secure part of the building.

As I climb the stairs to Macintosh's office, the atmosphere of defeat begins to affect even me, and my legs feel as heavy as lead.

The moment I step into his office, Ken Macintosh says, 'I'm sorry, Jennie, I did what I could.'

My God, I think, he looks so bloody old. He's aged at least ten years in one day.

'Why did you let them go?' I ask. 'You were legally allowed to hold them for forty-eight hours.' I look down at my watch. 'It's barely thirty-six since you brought them in.'

'The chief constable asked me for some tangible evidence that they were guilty, and, of course, I couldn't give him any. That's when he called my bluff, and issued a written order that Crispin Hetherington and all his crew should be released immediately.'

'The spineless bastard,' I say.

'You can't blame him,' Macintosh tells me. 'He's a good copper and a good man, but he was under pressure from every direction.'

'Whoever was pressurizing him, he could have held them off for another twelve hours,' I say unbendingly.

'Maybe he could have – if we'd given him even a *little* something to hold them off with,' Macintosh says, 'but, as I told you, we hadn't got anything to give.'

'So you simply opened the door and let them all walk out,' I say, knowing I'm being unreasonable, but not able to help myself.

'We didn't let Jeff Meade go. He's been charged with soliciting a criminal act and an attempted breach of national security. He's being kept in the custody suite until we can put him up before the magistrate tomorrow morning.'

'Did any of them say *anything* that might just help us with the investigation?' I ask.

Macintosh shakes his head. 'What they did all say was the *same* things – over and over again. They didn't rape the girl, because she was a more than willing participant. And once it was over, she left the function room of her own volition and under her own steam. They have no idea where she went, they claim, but none of them went with her, and they have alibis to prove it.'

'If you could get me access to the transcripts, I just might be able to find something that you've—' I begin.

'You haven't quite grasped the situation, yet, have you, Jennie?' Macintosh interrupts. 'Since you've been away, this place has been besieged by reporters, and when the papers come out tomorrow morning, the Thames Valley police – or this particular part of it, anyway – will take a real battering. They'll say we arrested ten of the country's brightest and best students, on no evidence at all, and subjected them to hour after hour of unnecessary questioning.'

'There was plenty of circumstantial—'

'They'll have quotes from the students – anonymous, of course, because the wee laddies are totally innocent, and have to be protected at all costs. Can you imagine what those quotes will say, Jennie?'

'I think you're blowing this a little out of—'

'Because *I* can imagine them – all too easily. "I always believed this was a free country, but for a few terrible hours, it felt to me like I was living in a police state," said student X, who still appeared to be in a state of shock. "My nerves are shattered, I'm terrified of going to sleep in case I dream of that police station, and I have to take my final examinations in a few weeks," said student Y, in a weak, strained voice.'

'Nobody really believes what they read in the papers.'

'And then, as the real kicker,' he says, not even bothering to consider what I've just told him, 'they'll say that DCI Macintosh – and they'll use my name, because they *can* – DCI Macintosh was unavailable for comment.'

'And that's precisely why we have to fight back,' I say. 'That's why we need to—'

'It's over, Jennie,' Macintosh says wearily. 'We always knew that our only chance to nail them was to get a confession from one of them in the first few hours – and we failed. And it's something we can only do once.'

'So they're going to get away with it?'

'Yes, I'm very much afraid that they are.'

'And what about poor, innocent Linda Corbet? What the hell's going to happen to her, now?'

'I don't know, and for me – the father of three daughters – that's the hardest part of all to take. But there's absolutely nothing we can do. If she is being held in some sort of clinic, maybe they'll release her when they see the papers and realize she's no longer a danger. If she's just run away, maybe she'll read the papers and come back home.'

I scour my brain for something that I can use to turn the whole situation around.

I need a magic bullet to punch a large hole in all the obstacles that stand in my way.

I want my own personal Excalibur, to cut down the barriers behind which the guilty crouch.

But what I *do* come up with is no magic bullet or enchanted sword – in fact, it is not very much of anything.

'Let me talk to Jeff Meade,' I say.

Macintosh sighs. 'What good would that do?'

'Did he have any money on him when he was picked up by the police in Dover?'

'Yes, he had over five hundred pounds.'

'He's a working-class lad – there's no way he could have laid his hands on that amount of money himself.'

'So what's your point?'

'My point is that it must have been given to him by the other members of the Shivering Turn.'

'So?'

'Why did they give him the money?'

'You tell me.'

'It's obvious – they gave it to him because they thought he was the weak link in the chain!'

'When he was brought back here,' DCI Macintosh says, 'he stuck by the story just as strongly as the others did.'

'But that's because I wasn't here to advise you on how to approach him,' I argue. 'I know all about lads like him, because I was brought up with them. Give me fifteen minutes with him, and I'll get him to break down.'

'I don't think you will.'

'And even if I don't get a complete confession out of him, he might inadvertently let slip something we can use.'

'I've told you, Jennie, the investigation's closed.'

'What harm can it do for me to see him?' I plead. 'What possible harm can there be in giving it one last shot?'

'You can only see him if he agrees to see you,' Macintosh points out, weakening.

'I know that.'

'And if he insists on his solicitor being present, you might as well forget the whole idea, because there's no way on God's green earth that even the most incompetent legal aid solicitor in England would ever allow his client to be questioned by a civilian.'

'I know that, too,' I say.

Macintosh shrugs wearily. 'All right,' he agrees. 'I'll ask. But if I were you, I wouldn't start getting my hopes up too high.'

Jeff Meade is a decent lad who's been led astray, I tell myself.

What happened to him could have happened to me – or to any working-class kid who suddenly found himself marooned on this island of privilege called Oxford.

All I have to do now is to burrow into him a little, and bring that decency back to the surface.

'Did you hear what I said, Jennie?' Macintosh asks.

'Don't worry, I won't be getting my hopes too high,' I tell him.

But I'm lying.

EIGHTEEN

When I enter the interview room, Jeff Meade looks up at me and gives me a weak smile, but by the time I've sat down opposite him, his eyes are firmly fixed on the table again.

'Will you do me a favour, Miss Redhead – as one northerner helping out another?' he asks me.

Ah, so that's why, against the odds, he's agreed to me see me – because he wants something.

'What kind of favour are we talking about here?' I ask cautiously.

'You're Chief Inspector Macintosh's mate . . .'

'You're wrong about that – I hardly know him.'

'Well, at any rate, he listens to what you say, and you can't deny that, because I've seen him do it.'

'I'm *not* denying it.'

'So if you were to tell him—'

'I can't get the charges against you dropped,' I interrupt him. 'They're in the system now, and you'll have to appear before the magistrates, come hell or high water.'

'I know, but the magistrates have the choice of dealing with me themselves or referring me up to the Crown Court, don't they?'

'In general, yes, unless their law clerk advises them that the crime merits a sentence of more than six months, in which case they have no choice *but* to refer it upwards.'

'The thing is, my legal aid solicitor thinks I'll get a better deal in the magistrates' court than the Crown Court, so I'd like DCI Macintosh to tell the magistrates that that's where he thinks I should be tried.'

'And you want me to persuade him that's what he should do?'

'Yes. Will you do it?'

He thinks his biggest problem is facing a piddling little charge that, even without my help, he'll probably get probation for – and, depressingly, as things stand, he's probably right.

'Will you do it?' he repeats.

'That depends,' I tell him.

'On what?' he asks – and there is a sulkiness to his tone which suggests that he'd been sure I'd do it just because he was a fellow Lancastrian, and is rather disappointed that there are strings attached.

'There are other things we need to talk about,' I say.

'What other things?' he asked guardedly.

'The things that I'm particularly interested in getting an answer to,' I snap back at him.

'All right,' he agrees – though that agreement can scarcely be called very willing.

'What was it that made you decide to do a runner?' I ask.

'I didn't do a runner.'

'No?'

'No! I had no idea we were about to be arrested, and I just fancied a bit of a break.'

I stand up. It's a gamble, because Jeff might just decide to let me go, but if I'm to achieve anything from this interview – if I'm ever going to help Linda Corbet and bring the Shivering Turn to justice – then gamble I must.

'What are you doing?' Jeff asks, alarmed.

'If all you're going to do is lie to me, then I'm wasting my bloody time being here,' I tell him.

'Sit down again,' he implores me. 'Please!'

'What made you do a runner?' I repeat.

'Crispin thought that the police would be harder on me than they would be on anyone else.'

'Why?' I ask, still standing.

'Because all the other lads are posh and I'm not. He gave me five hundred pounds, and said that – for the good of the whole society – I'd better make myself scarce, and that the best way to make myself scarce was to go abroad. I've never been abroad. It all seemed like a bit of an adventure.'

I sit down again – slowly and carefully, because if I don't get it right, my body will soon remind me that I've only just recently been beaten up.

'Isn't it possible it was the other way round?' I ask.

'What was the other way round? I don't know you mean?'

'I mean that instead of Crispin sending you away to take the heat off you, he did it to take the heat off them.'

'No, no . . . it wasn't like that at all.'

'Think about it,' I say, formulating my new theory on the hoof. 'You run away, which is a sure sign of guilt, but the rest of them stay, because they want to prove their innocence. So instead of all the attention being focused on Crispin – who is so obviously the leader – it's focused on you.'

'You don't understand,' Jeff says. 'Crispin would never do that to me. We swore an oath – and that oath made us a band of brothers.'

He has invested so much of himself in the Shivering Turn that he doesn't dare to think – however obvious it becomes – that the whole thing is a sham. I understand his dilemma. I might even sympathize with it, but for Linda Corbet, who is currently absorbing all the sympathy I can spare.

'Did you all swear this oath together?' I ask.

'No,' he says, 'all the rest of them had sworn it before I joined, so it was just me.'

And I think I can just about discern the first shadow of doubt crossing his face.

'I've said this before, but it doesn't seem to have sunk in, so I'll say it again,' I tell him. 'You're not from the same class as them, you're not from the same academic discipline as them, you're not a rower, and you're younger than they are. So why would they invite you – rather than anyone else in the whole college – to join them?'

'There could be any number of reasons.'

'There's one – and one only. They did it because they needed a dupe – a fall guy!'

'No,' he croaks.

'And look what they've done to you. Think about what they've turned you into. You delivered an innocent girl to a pack of savages. Why?'

'It's part of the initiation ceremony to bring a girl,' he says weakly. 'All the others have done it.'

'*None* of them has done it,' I say, conveniently ignoring the fact that the Shivering Turn Society had previously booked the function room in Blind Beggar twice, before the night that Linda was raped. 'What happened that Friday night was an experiment. And *because* it was an experiment, they did what the aristocracy always does – they brought in a serf to do the dirty work.'

'No,' he moans.

'Come clean, Jeff,' I plead. 'Do the right thing – the decent thing. If we let Crispin and his mates get away with this, there's no telling what they'll try in the future.'

'What you're asking me to do is ruin my whole life because of one little mistake,' he says.

'Is that how you see it?' I demand. 'One little mistake? I don't think that's what Linda would call it. And she can't just leave it behind. What happened on that terrible night will be seared into her brain until the day she dies.'

I'm getting too emotional, and that's a mistake.

Worse, I've pushed Linda into the centre of things, and if I'm ever going to get him to cooperate, my whole attention has to be focused on Jeff's needs.

I take a deep breath. 'No, I'm not asking you to ruin your life,' I tell him. 'What I'm asking you to do is start *rebuilding* your life on a decent foundation.'

'What do you mean?'

'You think you can live with what you've done, but you're wrong. You're a decent lad – you have a conscience – and that means you can't just bury your guilt. Sure, you *can* lock it away for a while – but it's still there, deep inside you, slowly festering away, and it will grow bigger and bigger until it poisons every inch of you. Come clean, Jeff – you know you have to come clean.'

For one joyous moment, I think I've got him. Then a look of arrogant contempt comes to his face which turns even *his* handsome features ugly.

He has learned the lesson of the Shivering Turn well – and even before he speaks, I know what he is going to say.

'Linda Corbet must have known what was going to happen to her,' he tells me.

'What?'

'Going out alone with a bunch of lads, she must have known what was going to happen – she must have *wanted* it to happen.'

'Did she look to you as if she wanted it to happen when, one by one, you raped her?'

'She was probably pretending not to enjoy it because she didn't want to look cheap, but the more I think about it, the more I'm sure she was having one hell of a good time.'

As I start to get up, he reaches across the table and grabs my hand.

'You can't desert me,' he pleads. 'We're two of a kind – northern kids doing our best to survive in what's almost a foreign country.'

I look at his hand, which is still holding tightly on to mine.

'I really want an excuse to hurt you,' I say – and I'm not lying, 'so you just keep on holding me like that, Jeff.'

He lets go of my hand as if it were suddenly on fire.

I stand up, and head for the door.

He doesn't try to stop me.

*

THE BULLDOG IS THE nearest pub to the police station, so that's what I hit first. I order a gin and tonic, and then, as an after-thought, a neat double gin chaser to go with it.

The barman looks at me strangely.

'Just serve me the drinks I asked for, Tony – that's what you're there for,' I tell him.

He shrugs. 'Well, it's your liver.'

Yes, it bloody well is.

From the Bulldog I go to the Red Lion, and from there to the Turl. It's half-past nine when I reach the Eagle and Child. At least, I think that's the time, but I seem to be having some difficulty in focusing on my watch.

The barman, Sebastian, takes one look at me and says, 'Don't you think you've had enough, Jennie?'

'That's for me to know and you to find out,' I say, and the moment the words are out of my mouth, I realize that they are meaningless.

'I'll tell you what,' Sebastian says, 'why don't you go and sit at that empty table over there, and I'll bring your drink across to you when I've finished serving these customers.'

That seems fair enough.

I know he is still watching me, so I am determined to glide over to the table with all the grace of a very sober ballerina.

It doesn't work out quite like that. Somehow I veer from my chosen path, and my swaying hip makes fairly heavy contact with a table at which two middle-aged couples are sitting.

It's not a disaster. Not a complete one, anyway. The table wobbles, but one of the men is quick to steady it, so all that happens is that some of the contents of some of the glasses spill on to the table.

But none of the glasses falls over! I wish – here and now – to make that particularly clear.

Well . . . maybe *one* of them does – but it's certainly no more than one.

'Shorry,' I say. 'Let me get you . . . get you 'nother . . . 'nother . . . round of drinks.'

'No, that's quite all right, dear, there's no real damage done,' says one of the women, who's busy mopping the front of her dress with a handkerchief which is clearly too small for the task.

'I inshist,' I insist.

'No!' the woman says, quite firmly.

If I didn't know any better, I'd say her main priority at this moment is to get the redhead – who she wrongly assumes is drunk – as far away from her table as possible.

'I'm perfectly sober . . .' I begin.

'Just go!' she tells me.

'Please yourself,' I answer, and walk away with dignity.

I reach the empty table that the wonderful Sebastian has reserved just for me – how 'bout that! – and sink gratefully into the chair.

I'm feeling just a little bit tired, so maybe if I put my elbow on the table, and rest my head in my hand . . .

I'M BEING GENTLY SHAKEN, first this way and then that. I look up, and Charlie is standing there.

'How d'you . . . what d'you . . .?' I ask.

'The landlord called me and said you might need some help,' Charlie says. 'Goodness, you are in a bit of a state, aren't you? I think we'd better take you home right away.'

'Lan'lord had no business to be phoning anybody 'bout the state I'm in,' I mutter.

But, because I want to continue to behave in a ladylike fashion, I allow Charlie to help me to my feet and assist me to the door.

There is a taxi, with its engine running, waiting outside, but when the driver sees me, he says, 'I'm not taking her.'

'Why not?' I demand. 'Waz wrong with me?'

'Let me handle this, Jennie,' Charlie says firmly. 'Why won't you take her?' he asks the cabbie.

'Thaz just what I said,' I tell him.

'You've only got to look at the state of her to answer that,' the cabbie says. 'Likely as not, she'll throw up in my taxi.'

I want to assure him I won't – but I'm not entirely sure it's a promise I can keep.

'If she does vomit, how long would it take you to clear up the mess?' Charlie asks, 'because I'm willing to pay you for your time.'

'It would take about half an hour,' the cabbie tells him. 'But that's not the point, is it?'

'Then what is?'

'I'd have to use a lot of disinfectant, and you can't go around picking up passengers in a taxi that smells like a bleeding hospital, so I'd lose a whole night's work.'

Charlie reaches into his wallet, and takes out a lot of notes. He hands them to the cabbie.

'There must be over two hundred pounds there,' he says. 'That should more than cover any lost earnings.'

I think it impresses the cabbie that Charlie doesn't even check exactly how much money he's handing over. And, if it doesn't impress him, it bloody well should, because it even impresses me – and I know just how rich my friend, Lord Swift, actually is.

'Well?' Charlie asks

'All right, then – climb in,' the taxi driver says – as if he's doing us a real favour.

WE ARE BACK AT MY flat on the Iffley Road. I can't say I remember getting here, but since we are here, we must have done.

'I think it would be rather a good idea if I helped you to get undressed,' Charlie says.

'I'm perettly . . . perfectly capable of undressing myself,' I say, with all the dignity I can muster.

But that isn't true, alas. Someone has moved all my button-holes, which makes them almost impossible to find, and there's a buckle on my skirt which I swear wasn't there yesterday.

Actually, Charlie is pretty good at this undressing lark, and soon I am standing there stark naked, while he virtually tears the flat apart looking for my nightdress, instead of just following the clear, simple instructions I've given him.

'Here it is,' he says, after at least two days have elapsed. 'It was on top of the fridge.'

'Isn't that where I said it was?' I ask.

'Not even close,' he tells me.

He slips the nightdress over my head, picks me up and carries me to my bed. Once I'm lying down, he goes around the bed, tucking me in. He doesn't make a very good job of it, but it's the thought that counts.

'Charlie?' I say, when he's finished.

'Yes, Jennie?'

'You wouldn't fancy the idea of being a heterosexual – just for one night – would you?'

'I'm afraid, whether I fancied it or not, it's simply not on,' he says.

I suspected that might be the case.

'But if you want me to stay the night, I will do,' he says. 'I'll be perfectly happy sleeping on the sofa.'

'That's what you think,' I tell him, 'but that sofa's got a genius for being uncomfortable, and it's defeated better men than you.'

I'm joking, of course – there *are* no better men than Charlie.

'Seriously, I can stay if you want me to,' Charlie says.

'Seriously, there's no need to,' I reply. 'I'm sobering up, and I'll be perfectly fine.'

Even with my assurance, he still hesitates at the bedroom door.

'Go!' I say.

And the second he has gone – the second I hear the front door click closed – I wish he hadn't.

I've screwed up, I tell myself. I've let my client down, and let my client's daughter down. I don't know what else I *could* have done, but I should have done *something*.

But I didn't do *anything*, and now all the members of the

Shivering Turn can walk away, as free as birds and convinced they can get away with pretty much anything. So the next time one of them rapes a woman, it will be almost as much my fault as it is his – because I didn't stop him when I had the chance.

But it's not just the failure in the investigation which is making me feel so wretched.

I miss my dad!

I didn't think I would – but I do.

I look up at the ceiling and, even though I know – or think that maybe I probably know – that there's no one there, I still say, 'Listen God, why don't we do a deal?'

No booming voice suddenly fills the room!

There is no heavenly chorus!

Nor is there even a hint of celestial lightning!

Well, what do you expect from a god who doesn't exist?

But since, now that Charlie's gone, I have no one else to talk to, I suppose I *might as well* talk to Him.

'The thing is, God,' I say, 'I don't think my dad was ever happy. He doesn't even look happy in his wedding photographs. I think he got married because that was what you were supposed to do. And he got his job with the insurance company because having a job was what you were supposed to do. Then he and my mum had me, because . . . Are you getting the message, God?'

I stop, because my nose is so blocked that I can hardly talk. I reach for the tissues on my bedside table and have a good blow.

'Sorry about that, God,' I say. 'So my dad never got to do anything he really wanted to, but then, to be honest with you, there never seemed to *be* anything he really wanted to do. And

I think that, on the whole, he was content – in, of course, a slightly disappointed way.'

I really seem to have sobered up. Or is it just that I am still drunk enough to simply imagine that what I'm saying makes sense?

Whichever it is, once you've got God on the line, it doesn't do to keep Him waiting.

'And then there's me,' I say. 'I've never felt so miserable in my life, and I can't see it ever getting any better. So here's the deal – you bring my dad back to life, and you take me instead. You don't have to make any promises about what's there once I've crossed the threshold. There may even be nothing there at all. I don't care, because anything – even if the anything *is* nothing – will be better than what I've got now.'

NINETEEN

My head feels like it is about to explode every time the bloody hammer hits the bloody bell. I'm aware that I have to do something about it but, before I can, I need to take careful stock of my current situation.

I know I am not dead, because the dead can't possibly feel half as shitty as I do.

I know that I'm lying on my back, because that is just something you just *do* know.

And I know I'm in darkness, which may possibly be attributable to the fact that my eyes are tightly closed.

The hammer hits the bell again – sending shock waves ricocheting around my cranium.

I open my eyes with reckless haste, and the light streaming in through the window causes a thousand tiny burning needles to stab my pupils.

I close my eyes again.

Perhaps I should stay like this for a few hours – or maybe a few days – I tell myself.

But the bloody bell simply isn't going to let me do that.

I open my eyes more cautiously this time, and when I have

persuaded them to focus, I find myself gazing up at a ceiling which looks quite familiar.

So, I'm in my bedroom.

Good!

But where is the bloody bell?

I roll on to my side, and make two interesting discoveries. The first is that the ringing sound is coming from the telephone on my bedside table. The second is that the hammer has nothing to do with the bell, but is working independently, inside my head.

I pick up the telephone receiver, and mumble 'Go away' into it.

'Is that you, Jennie?' asks the voice at the other end of the line.

George Hobson!

'Yes, it's me, George,' I admit, with some degree of reluctance.

'I've been trying to contact you since early last evening. I must have rung you ten times. Where were you?'

'Basket-weaving classes,' I say, because that is the first thing that comes into my head.

'Basket-weaving classes?' he repeats, incredulously.

'Listen, George, just tell me what you rang up to tell me. And make it quick, because I want to do some serious suffering here, and you're just getting in the way of it.'

'Do you know, Jennie, there are times when you make no sense at all,' George says.

'Please!' I implore him. 'Just say what's on your mind, then I can go and hunt down some aspirins.'

'There's been a development in the investigation since the last time you were at the station.'

'A development!'

'Now don't go getting too excited, because it's not going to help you in your quest to bring the Shivering Turn to justice. In fact, it will probably work the other way – by making them even more untouchable.'

I wonder if my mouth is dry with anticipation – or if it's just dry.

'For the love of God, George, just tell me,' I say in a furry voice that I hardly recognize as my own.

'As you know, we've been trying to keep Tom Corbet out of the loop, but as the rumours started to fly, it was becoming harder and harder,' George says. 'Anyway, he somehow got hold of Crispin Hetherington's name, and early last evening he attacked Hetherington as he was crossing the Venetian Quad. They tell me he was like a man insane, and it took half-a-dozen students to pull him off.'

'Was Hetherington badly hurt?' I ask.

'Yes, he was – very badly indeed. The doctors say that he's going to be permanently paralysed from the neck down.'

'Thanks for the information, George,' I mumble, and before he has a chance to say anything else, I hang up.

I go to the bathroom, and force myself to drink about a pint of water. For perhaps half a minute, I feel better, then the water hits my stomach, and I realize I'm going to puke.

'But that's a good thing,' I tell myself, as I kneel down in front of the toilet bowl. 'It will get rid of all the poisons.'

In all honesty, it doesn't feel like a good thing once I've started to be sick – it feels, in fact, as if I'm vomiting up all my insides.

I stop throwing up, but I know it isn't over, because I can feel new waves of nausea building up in my stomach.

But at least I have a little time to think – and several thoughts are already competing for the brain space.

The first thought is that it is a tragedy that Tom Corbet, who I think is basically a good man, should have had his life destroyed by what happened that night in the Blind Beggar.

The second is that, as much as I despise Crispin Hetherington, I wouldn't have wished a lifetime of paralysis on him.

But it is the third which, though related to the other two, is so powerful that it dominates the centre of my brain, and sends the other two scurrying into the darker recesses. And it is this – George Hobson was quite wrong when he said that Corbet's attack on Hetherington made the Shivering Turn even more untouchable. What it has actually done is present me with an unexpected opportunity to really screw the privileged little wankers.

I throw up a second time, and then a third. I calculate there is nothing left in my stomach now to get rid of, and force myself to take a cold shower.

I towel down, go into the kitchen, and make a cup of strong black coffee.

I will never drink alcohol again, I promise myself – not if I live to be a hundred.

The coffee does its work. I no longer feel as if my death is imminent, and though the hammer is still at work in my head, it is now pounding cushions rather than anvils.

I pick up the phone and ring Charlie Swift.

'I thought about calling, but I didn't want to disturb you,' he says. 'How are you feeling?'

'I'm feeling fine,' I lie. 'Listen, Charlie, I need a name – and I need it right now.'

'Steady on, old girl,' Charlie says.

I didn't think anyone said, 'Steady on, old girl,' any more.

'Look, I'm sorry if I'm sounding a bit abrupt, but this is really important,' I tell him.

'Any particular sort of name you have in mind?' he asks 'A Welsh name? An exotic name? One of the secret names of God? Or are you just collecting a ragbag of any old names?'

I love Charlie dearly, but there are times when I could kill him – and this is one of them.

'I need the name of a student at St Luke's who is quite small, quite light and quite sporty,' I tell him. 'And if he is also someone Crispin Hetherington dislikes, that would be a bonus.'

A MIDDLE-AGED COUPLE are standing in front of the reception desk for the intensive care unit of the Radcliffe Hospital. They are respectably – but not expensively – dressed, and they remind me in some ways of my own parents.

The man has his arms draped comfortingly over the woman's shoulder, and the woman is talking with painful intensity to the pretty nurse behind the desk. It is clear to me that the woman is not imparting any sort of vital information, but merely feels compelled to talk, and the nurse – knowing that she needs this release – is listening sympathetically.

I try not to eavesdrop, but the woman has a voice which carries. I could walk away, I suppose, but I am on a mission, and the moment the woman has stopped talking to the nurse, I want to have a word with her myself.

'He's always been such a good boy – never any trouble at all,' the woman is saying. 'He studied damned hard at school, and even now he's in university, he gets a job in the summer—'

'And at Christmas,' her husband chimes in.

'And at Christmas,' the mother agrees. 'Easter too, some-times – and all so he can pay part of his own way through college.'

'I'm only a window cleaner, you see,' the husband says, apolo-getically, 'and Oxford does seem to be very expensive – *much* more expensive than any of the universities that Christopher's school friends have gone to.'

'We used to worry that he had no time for fun,' the mother says, 'but he told us we shouldn't concern ourselves, because he was investing in the future – but now he hasn't got a future, and all that sacrifice was for nothing.'

'He seems a very determined young man, and that will certainly help him in the difficult years ahead,' the nurse says.

'It doesn't seem fair,' the mother says.

'It never does,' the nurse replies.

The father looks at his watch. 'We'd better go now, or we'll miss the train home.'

The woman stiffens. 'I don't want to go home,' she says. 'I want to stay here in Oxford.'

'It's not about what you want, love,' the man says with a gentleness that it almost breaks my heart to hear. 'It's about what Christopher wants. And what *does* he want?'

'He . . . he wants us to go home.'

'That's right. He says it's distressing for him to see us so upset. He says we should go back to Coventry, and then, in a week or so, he'll call and tell us when we can come again.'

'But he can't call us, can he?' the mother asks, on the verge of hysterics. 'He can't even make a simple phone call.'

'You know what he meant,' her husband says. 'He'll get the hospital to call.' He pauses. 'Christopher's feeling helpless enough as it is – how much worse is he going to feel if we won't even respect his wishes?'

The mother nods. 'But I want to take a later train,' she says determinedly. 'Before I leave Oxford, I want to see his college.'

'All right, love,' her husband concedes. He turns to the nurse. 'Could you tell us how to get to St Luke's College?'

'Haven't you been before?' the nurse asks, the surprise evident in her voice.

'No . . . we . . . Christopher said none of his friends' parents visited them in college, so he'd find it embarrassing if we did.'

The nurse gives them directions to the college.

'Goodbye, Mr and Mrs Hetherington,' she says.

'Goodbye,' Mr Hetherington says, over his shoulder.

And Mrs Hetherington, her head sunk so low that her chin is almost touching her chest, says nothing.

I AM IN THE HOSPITAL cafeteria. Around me sit all manner of people, united only by the single fact that, at this moment, they are all connected – in one way or another – to illness.

Under this broader canopy of sickness and malfunction, each table is its own little theatre, and the actors sitting around it are playing out a drama which God, or nature – or perhaps just blind chance – has written specifically for them.

At the table to my left, for example, an old man is talking earnestly to a middle-aged woman who could be his daughter, perhaps persuading her that there's a good chance her husband will pull through.

At the table to my right sit a man and a woman who are about my age and, though they are holding hands, it is plain that each is swimming in a thick sea of personal misery.

And then there are a group of nurses, all looking very tired and drawn, and setting an example of healthy living by chain-smoking their way through their short break.

I have – for obvious reasons – postponed my personal drama for an hour, and I am now thinking about names. If I had not been a redhead, born with the name Redhead, it seems to me unlikely I would ever have thrown myself into the martial arts with such vigour. And perhaps if Crispin/Christopher had been born a Sidebotham – rather than the posh-sounding Hetherington – he would never have felt impelled to pretend to be a member of the upper class.

I look at my watch. The hour has passed, and now it's time for me to attempt to con the arch-conman.

I APPROACH THE NURSES' desk, and smile sadly at the pretty nurse.

'I'd like to visit one of your patients, if possible,' I say.

'Could you give me his or her name?' the nurse asks.

'Christopher Hetherington.'

'Poor Christopher,' she says, shaking her head. 'Are you family?'

I want to say we're friends, because that's likely to make her more receptive, but, try as I might, I just can't bring myself to do it.

'No, I'm not family – we're from the same college,' I say – and hope that's enough.

'We normally like our patients in intensive care to have as many visitors as possible, if they feel up to it,' the nurse says, 'but I have to tell you that Christopher doesn't even want to see his mother and father, so I doubt very much that he'll be willing to—'

'I think he'll want to see *me*,' I say earnestly.

'Well, all we can do is ask,' the nurse replies, philosophically. 'Could I have your name, please?'

'Jennifer Redhead.'

'And do you have any means of identification, Miss Redhead?'

'There's my driving licence,' I say, taking it out of my bag and offering it to her.

She examines it carefully, then hands it back and says, 'Would you please wait here, Miss Redhead,' before disappearing through a pair of swing doors and leaving me with my thoughts.

I've known right from the start that Hetherington relishes conflict, and that he likes to live on the edge, but now I've learned he's not the man he pretended to be, I think I know why he created the Shivering Turn. And it wasn't about sex – it was *never* about sex.

The nurse has still not come back. It's always possible, I

suppose, that Hetherington will refuse to see me, but I will be surprised if he does, because even in his present pitiful condition, I don't imagine he'll be willing to turn away from a good fight.

The nurse returns, with a slightly bemused expression on her face.

'He'd like to see you,' she says. 'Would you please follow me?'

CRISPIN HETHERINGTON HAS COUNTLESS wires and tubes attached to him, and these wires and tubes run into several machines that I wouldn't even try to name. He is pale and fragile-looking, but it is clear from his eyes that he is more than willing to do battle with me.

Neither of us risks more than a neutral 'hello' while the nurse is still there, but the moment she has gone, he says, 'I really am rather disappointed in you, Miss Redhead.'

'Are you?'

'Indeed I am. I've always considered you a worthy adversary, but now it seems I was wrong, because if you really were worthy – if you had anything like the spirit I have – you would never have lowered and degraded yourself by coming here to gloat.'

'I'm not here to—' I begin.

'I haven't finished,' he says fiercely. 'Not only have you diminished yourself in my eyes – and, when you have time to think about it, in your own – but you haven't even achieved your pathetic objective. You have no grounds for gloating, because we both know that while I may be paralysed for the rest of my life, I'll always be a gentleman, whereas you, with control over your body, will never be any more than a piece of working-class scum with an education.'

I have to admire him for his sheer nerve – his determination to extract some kind of victory from even the most devastating of defeats. I could, of course, easily rob him of that victory with a few well-chosen words about his parents, but I don't want to – because I hate to kick a man when he's down. Yes, he is still the vicious little bastard he's always been, but now he's a tetraplegic vicious little bastard, and if it will help him through the remaining years of his life to think he's had me fooled, then I'm more than willing to go along with it.

'Can I speak now?' I ask.

'Yes, you may.'

'I'm not here to gloat. I'm here to keep you up to date – courtesy of your local police force – on what your good friends in the Shivering Turn have been doing since you were admitted to hospital.'

'What are you talking about?' he asks.

'Most people would have expected them to sit around in shocked silence after what happened to you, but we both know they're made of stronger stuff than that,' I say. I take my notebook out of my pocket, and turn to a blank page. 'Let me see . . . John Teale and Gideon Duffy went down to the Grapes last night, and they picked up two good-looking nurses from this very hospital. They all left together, and Gideon used his credit card to book two rooms in the Randolph Hotel—'

'His daddy's credit card, you mean,' Crispin interrupts me bitterly.

And then he realizes that, for the first time, he has shown me his envy of the wealthy – and that simply will not square with the idea that he is wealthy himself.

'Gideon has to go begging to his father for every penny he spends,' he continues. 'I have had drawing rights on all the family accounts since I was fourteen years old.'

It's a good recovery – I have to give him credit for that.

'Yes, they booked into the Randolph, so it's likely that they got their ends away – and without having to resort to tranquillizers,' I continue.

'I think I'd like you to leave now,' Crispin Hetherington said.

'Fair enough,' I agree, turning and walking towards the door. 'I certainly wouldn't want to distress a man in your condition.'

'You're not distressing me,' he says.

'Of course not,' I agree. 'You're not in the least distressed. The only reason that you're telling me to go is that you have so many better things to do with your time than listen to me.'

'Come back here,' he says – and it's an order, rather than a request.

I turn, and go back to the bedside.

'Do you want me to carry on?' I ask.

'Yes.'

'You're sure?'

'Say whatever it is you've got to say.'

'Where was I?' I muse. 'Ah yes, it's more than likely John Teale and Gideon Duffy ran into Richard Tennyson and Hugo Johnson at the Randolph, because Tennyson and Johnson were in the restaurant – treating Rupert Congreave to a slap-up meal.'

'Rupert Congreave!'

'They're probably looking to recruit him as their new cox, don't you think?' I ask. 'Some people might feel that they could have waited a little longer, if only out of respect for you, but hey, life's a race, and you have to keep running – if you can run, that is.'

'Is that the best you can do?' Crispin Hetherington asks.

'It's ironic, isn't it?' I say. 'Everyone else got to screw Linda Corbet, but only you get to pay the price. Still, I expect you'll draw some comfort, in the endless tedious years that stretch ahead of you, from the odd snippets of news about how well your old friends are getting on.'

'It won't work,' he says, and now there's a smile of triumph on his face. 'You're simply not good enough to manipulate me in the way that—'

'In the way that you manipulated the Shivering Turn?'

'Exactly.'

He's left me little choice. I want to spare him, but Linda Corbet – poor, defiled Linda Corbet – is still missing, and she has to be my priority.

'Yes, you certainly did manipulate the Shivering Turn,' I say. 'By the way, I ran into your parents outside.'

'Oh Jesus,' he moans.

'How did you pull it off?' I wonder. 'How did you persuade these public schoolboys – who share so much common background – that you were one of them? My guess is that you came up with a convincing story to explain away why you hadn't been to Harrow or Eton. You probably said something like . . . I don't know . . . that you attended a very expensive and very exclusive American boarding school, because your father's extensive business interests meant that he had to spend most of his time in the States. Am I right?'

He doesn't say anything, but from the expression on his face, I can tell that I am close enough.

'You really admired them – those poncy public schoolboys with their stately homes,' I press on. 'You wanted to be exactly like them. And then you realized that you never could be – that there'd eventually come a point at which you were unmasked and, when that happened, they would despise you. So you needed a reason to despise *them* – and it couldn't be because of what they were, because, despite everything, you still envied and admired them for that. No, to be able to despise them, you had to bring them down to a level at which you *could* despise them. And that's when you came up with the idea of the Shivering Turn. It wasn't about sex. It wasn't even really about exercising power for power's sake. It was about dragging them down – putting them in a position where they would willingly degrade themselves.'

'You should have seen the way they fell on the girl,' he says. 'They were like animals. They were worse than animals.'

'Why don't you tell the police exactly what happened that night in the Blind Beggar?' I suggest.

'You'd like that, wouldn't you – because it would mean that you'd won,' he says.

'It's not about me winning,' I tell him. 'It's about seeing that the right thing is done.'

'I may not have been born a gentleman, but now I have the opportunity of proving, if only to myself, that that is what I really am,' he says.

'And how do you propose to do that?'

'By protecting the members of the Shivering Turn – even though I know they're not worthy of my protection.'

I have one shot left in my arsenal, and if that fails to hit the target, then I'm lost.

'I might go down to the college tonight,' I say. 'Yes, I think I'll do that. I expect I'll find the rest of the Shivering Turn in the bar, celebrating their lucky escape. Can you imagine what a good laugh they'll have when I tell them that haughty Crispin Hetherington – whose disapproval they lived in trepidation of – is really called Chris, and is the son of a window cleaner?'

'Please don't,' he gasps, his face a picture of perfect agony, 'please, not that.'

'It's up to you, Chris,' I tell him. 'I will definitely be in the bar, but if the members of the Shivering Turn are not there, I won't be able to talk to them, will I? I wonder if you can think of a reason why they might *not* be there.'

If he could bang his head against a wall at this moment, I'm sure he'd do so. I'm sure he'd keep on banging until the wall was stained with his blood.

But he can't do that.

He can't move a muscle from the neck down.

He closes his eyes, so that he can no longer see me.

'When you get back into town, you can tell DCI Macintosh that I want to make a fresh statement,' he says.

TWENTY

It is three-thirty in the afternoon, and beyond the confines of St Aldate's police station shopkeepers are minding their shops, students are slaving desperately over essays they know they should have started weeks ago, alcoholics from the Salvation Army hostel are falling over, and young men in newly purchased striped blazers are punting their girlfriends up and down the River Cherwell (and praying they don't make a mess of it). It is, in other words, an Oxford day like any other Oxford day.

It is not a normal Oxford day inside the police station. Here, there is an electric tension – a teeth-grinding, nail-biting nervousness. Unexpectedly, and against all the odds, the police are getting a second bite at the cherry – and they know there will be no third bite.

I am sitting next to DCI Macintosh in front of the two-way mirror, and studying the occupants of the interview room. There are four of them. On one side of the table sit DC Bassett and his partner, on the other side Hugo Johnson and his solicitor.

Johnson is so nervous that sweat is trickling down his normally self-satisfied cheeks, yet at the same time there is a certain arrogant set to his jaw which suggests that he is still finding it hard to believe that he should be in this situation, and that surely – surely! – he must come out of it relatively unscathed.

It is the attitude adopted by his solicitor – Bartlett Townshend – from which I draw the most hope. Townshend is known to be a Rottweiler of a legal representative, yet today he does not look as if he expects to pull his client clear of the morass he has landed himself in, but rather is prepared to settle for whatever concessions he can squeeze out of Bassett.

DC Bassett switches on the tape recorder, and, in a precise and emotionless tone, lists those present in the room and issues the required caution.

'Tell me about the Shivering Turn,' he says to Johnson, when the routine has been completed.

'What do you want to know about it?'

'Well, we could start with whose idea the whole thing was, and exactly how it came about.'

'WHY ISN'T HE ASKING about Linda Corbet?' I ask Macintosh.

Because Linda is what matters to me – it is only thoughts of her which have kept me going when the situation seemed hopeless.

'Patience, Jennie, patience,' Macintosh replies. 'We have a saying where I was brought up – "If you want to keep the winkle in one piece, then you have to coax it out of the shell".'

Great – Scottish homespun philosophy! Just what we needed!

But he is right – I know from my own experience that it is the interviews which are carefully structured which produce the best results.

*

'HOW DID IT START?' HUGO JOHNSON asks, on the other side of the glass. 'I suppose it started with Crispin. He's our coxswain, and a bloody good one he is, too. When he's in charge of the boat, you completely forget you're an individual – you become just a part of a powerful, unstoppable machine. He's been the main reason we're so successful, and—'

'I think the officer would like you to stick to the point of his question, Hugo,' Townshend says.

'Oh, sorry,' Johnson said. 'Crispin got this video from America – he went to school there, you know. It was called *Behind the Green Door*, and what happens, you see, is that this woman is abducted and ravaged. It seemed like bloody good fun. And Crispin suggested we could do the same thing.'

'Did you ever think that perhaps Crispin wasn't quite – how should I say it – "one of you"?' Bassett asks.

'Well, once in a while, he did say something that none of the rest of us would ever have said, but I just put that down to him having been brought up in America. And now I come to think of it, Gideon Duffy did once say that he thought Crispin wasn't "quite right" – but that's Gideon for you. He gets all kinds of strange ideas in his head.'

'And was it shortly after Duffy said he wasn't "quite right" that Hetherington suggested forming the Shivering Turn?' Bassett asks.

'Do you know, I rather think it was,' Johnson says, sounding slightly surprised.

'Was Linda Corbet the first girl you abused?' Bassett asks.

'Yes . . . no,' Johnson replies.

'Which one is it – yes or no?'

'We had girls before, but they were prostitutes, who were paid to pretend that they were virgins.'

I BLOODY KNEW IT! When Jeff Meade told me that taking a virgin to one of the Shivering Turn meetings was part of the initiation ceremony, I knew it was a load of bollocks – because if that's what they normally did, they wouldn't have had any need to recruit Jeff.

'**DID YOU ALWAYS DRESS** up as schoolmasters when you hired the prostitutes?' Bassett asks.

'No, there was a different theme every time. Once we dressed up as eighteenth-century lords, and the whore had to pretend to be a peasant girl. And then there was the time we blacked up as Negro slaves, and dressed the girl as a southern lady.'

'But you got bored with using professionals, did you?' Bassett asks.

'No, not really.'

'So why didn't you just keep on hiring them?'

'Crispin said the real thing would be much better.'

'And was it?'

'Of course not!' Hugo Johnson says. 'It was disgusting and wrong, and I'm most terribly ashamed of it.'

THAT'S HIS OFFICIAL LINE – the line he's been schooled to adopt by his solicitor. But the look of pure lasciviousness which flashes briefly across his face as he recalls that night tells quite a different story.

I wish I could have charge of him for just ten minutes. I'd whip him down to the vet's office and have his balls cut off before he knew what had hit him.

'**HOW DID YOU GO** about selecting Linda Corbet as your victim?' DC Bassett asks Hugo Johnson.

'Crispin was the one who chose her. He went to that tea shop near the school, and listened in on what the girls were saying to each other. He thought this one would be perfect because—'

'Linda!' Bassett says harshly. 'She's not a "this one". Her name is Linda, you filthy deviant!'

'Sorry,' Johnson mumbles, and though he's heard what Bassett has just called him, he doesn't dare to object – and nor, apparently, does his solicitor consider that it would be wise to.

Hugo Johnson takes a deep breath. 'Crispin thought *Linda* would be perfect because she seemed so interested in literature, and we were already known as the Shivering Turn Society . . .'

'Which you'd created because you thought it would be fun to dangle a clue to what you were doing before the eyes of the dean and the bursar?'

'That's right. Crispin called the game "Hoodwinking the Hog and the Homo".'

'Was it after you'd targeted Linda that you recruited Jeff Meade into your jolly little society?'

'Yes.'

'*Why* did you recruit him?'

Johnson shrugs his powerful shoulders helplessly. 'Well, you know . . .'

'No, I don't know,' Bassett counters. 'So you're going to have to bloody tell me, aren't you?'

'We . . . we thought he'd find it much easier to talk to her than we would have done.'

'And why was that? Was it because they're both so *common* – both such peasants?'

'I wouldn't say that.'

'Then what would you say?'

'I'd prefer to say that they probably shared certain cultural and societal attitudes that differed from ours, and—'

'Oh Jesus, what crap you can come up with,' Bassett moans, burying his head in his hands. Then he slowly opens in his hands, and in his normal voice, he says, 'And, of course, another advantage to recruiting Jeff Meade was that, in his rough working-class way, he was quite handsome. Isn't that right?'

'Yes, that was part of the calculation.'

'He'll be very popular in prison – a pretty boy like Jeff. And you're not so bad-looking yourself.'

'Oh, please, no!' Hugo Johnson says. 'Not that.'

'We are cooperating fully,' Bartlett Townshend says, 'and our expectation is that this cooperation will be taken fully into account.'

'You're quite right to point that out, sir,' Bassett agrees. 'Some members of the Shivering Turn will soon be finding out what it feels like to be Linda Corbet, but if Hugo here keeps on being such a good boy, I'll do my best to see that he isn't one of them.'

'I'll tell you anything you want to know,' Hugo Johnson promises, in a voice which is close to a sob. 'I really do want to help.'

'Fair enough, son,' Bassett agrees. 'Was Linda drugged when she arrived at the Blind Beggar?'

'No, she—'

'Remember what I said about everything depending on your being a good boy?' Bassett asks. And then he repeats the question. 'Was Linda drugged when she arrived at the Blind Beggar?'

'Yes, she was a little bit drugged.'

'You can't be a little bit drugged, any more than you can be a little bit virginal. She either was or she wasn't. Which is it?'

'She was drugged. Before she got there, Jeff Meade had slipped a few mild tranquillizers into her drink.'

'And how did he get hold of them?'

'Crispin bought them, from one of the technicians in the chemistry labs.'

'What's his name?'

'I don't know.'

'That's not the answer I was hoping for – nor is it an answer that's likely to do you much good.'

'I don't know his name,' Johnson says, in a voice which is almost a shriek. 'I swear I don't know.'

'All right, son, calm down,' Bassett says. 'Let's go back to what happened that night. You're all waiting in the room. You're wearing academic gowns, because this time it's going to be a schoolmaster-schoolgirl fantasy. But it's not *that much* of a fantasy, is it – because Linda really is a schoolgirl!'

Hugo Johnson says nothing.

'So Jeff brings her into the room,' Bassett continues, 'and you all rape her. Is that right?'

'Yes.'

'Let me be clear on this – did every single one of you rape her?'

'Yes – apart from Crispin.'

'Now think very carefully before you answer the next question, Hugo,' DC Bassett says, 'because what you tell me could determine whether you spend your prison time in a nice open prison, with bent accountants as your neighbours, or whether you go through the next ten years with a very sore bottom. Do you understand what I'm saying?'

'Yes,' Johnson says, in a voice that is little more than a whisper.

'It's a very simple question, Hugo, and it's this – where is Linda Corbet now?'

'I don't know,' Johnson says.

Bassett slams his hand down on the table with some force.

'Stop pissing me about!' he shouts. 'We already know that you and Gideon Duffy took her to London on the mail train, so what did you do with her once you got there?'

'We didn't take her to London.'

'Then what were you doing on the platform at Oxford station?'

'We were there to make sure she *didn't* get on the train – but she never went anywhere near the station.'

'Then where was she?'

'I don't know. She escaped.'

'But you were planning to take her to London – or, at least, get her away from Oxford?'

'No.'

'Then how in God's name did you imagine you were going to get away with what you'd done to her?'

'The woman in the *Behind the Green Door* video liked it by the end of the evening.'

'Jesus, are you seriously trying to tell me that you thought real life would turn out to be just like a pornographic film?'

'It could have done – but if it didn't, we had contingency plans.'

'And I can't wait to hear them,' Bassett says.

'Crispin said that once it was over, we'd all be very nice to her, and tell her how good she'd been, and how much we'd enjoyed it. And if that didn't seem to be working, we'd tell her that she'd be well advised to keep her mouth shut about what had gone on, because nobody would ever take her word against ours. But whichever way it went, we were going to give her the money.'

'What money?'

'We'd all put five hundred pounds into the kitty – all except Jeff Meade, that is. That's four and a half thousand pounds.'

HOW HARD HETHERINGTON MUST have worked during his summer holidays to earn that five hundred pounds, I think. What hours of backbreaking overtime he must have put in – on jobs so unpleasant that no one else wanted to touch them – in order to come anywhere near that amount. And then he handed it over as if were nothing – because that was what he had to do if he was going to continue playing his role.

'CRISPIN SAID THERE ARE some people who would consider four thousand five hundred pounds a lot of money,' Johnson tells Bassett.

'And are there?' Bassett asks.

'Are there what?'

'Are there are some people who would consider four thousand five hundred pounds a lot of money?'

Hugo Johnson shrugs. 'I suppose there must be.'

'My mortgage is around four thousand five hundred pounds,' Bassett tells him.

'Oh!' Johnson says – though it's clear he doesn't see the point.

'So what went wrong with this plan of yours to either sweet-talk or threaten this helpless schoolgirl you'd just violated?' Bassett asks.

'We told Jeff Meade to help her – to help Linda – to get dressed. She looked as if she was still well doped-up, but she can't have been, because the moment she had her clothes on, she headed for the door, which, in all the excitement, we'd forgotten to lock.'

'Didn't any of you try to stop her?'

'We couldn't – not immediately.'

'Why not?'

'She was fully dressed, but we weren't. And you can't go chasing round a public house car park wearing just an academic gown – not without drawing attention to yourself.'

'No, I don't suppose you can,' Bassett agrees. 'So what was your next step, after your brilliant master plan had collapsed?'

'We knew that we had to catch her. Not to hurt her – you must believe that – but just to talk to her, and offer her the money. So we put our clothes on as quickly as we could, and then went looking for her. Toby Fortescue and Jeff Meade got into Toby's Jag and went straight to her house, Gideon and I went down to the railway station, on the off chance she might be there, and all the rest went to the other places she might have gone to.'

'But you didn't find her?'

'No, we didn't.'

'So where did she go?'

'I don't know,' Johnson says, indifferently.

'And you don't bloody care, do you?' Bassett explodes. 'You don't care now – and you didn't care then. As long as she wasn't around to get you into trouble, you didn't give a damn *where* she'd gone.'

Hugo Johnson, realizing his mistake, tries his best to assume the proper look of anguish.

'Of course I cared,' he says. 'I'm desperate to know where she is, if only so I can go and see her and apologize from the bottom of my heart for what we did to her. But the fact is, she's simply vanished.'

'You really are a thoroughly nasty piece of work, aren't you, Hugo?' DC Bassett says in disgust.

IT'S HALF-PAST FOUR. Hugo Johnson has been taken down to the cells – I hope he's tripped on the way, and broken his bloody neck – and his place at the table has been filled by Jeff Meade and his solicitor.

Meade's solicitor is no Rottweiler. He has been provided by legal aid, wears a shabby suit, and already looks bored out of his mind.

I feel no sympathy for Jeff. I gave him his chance and he blew it, and now he must learn to live with the fact that he is being represented by a deadbeat, while the rest of them have the best advice that money can buy.

'THE SECOND YOU WERE dressed, you and Fortescue got into Fortescue's car and drove to Linda's house,' Bassett says. 'Is that correct?

'Yes,' Jeff Meade agrees.

'How did you know where she lived? Had you been to Linda's house before?'

'No, if I'd been there before, I'd probably have found out that her dad was a bobby, and then we'd never have . . .'

'Never have what?'

'Nothing.'

'Never have selected her as your victim?'

'I suppose so.'

'So how *did* you know where she lived?'

'She left her school bag behind when she made a dash for it, and it had her address on it.'

'So the plan was that the others would try to find her, but if they failed, you'd be waiting in ambush for her when she arrived home.'

'I wouldn't put it quite like that.'

'Then how would you put it?'

'We just wanted to talk to her.'

'You just wanted to *threaten* her, you mean.'

'No, we thought that if she'd just listen to us for a minute, we could persuade her to be sensible.'

Bassett shakes his head in contempt. 'Tell me what happened when you got to her house?'

'The house was in darkness, so Toby parked a little further down the street. About an hour later, her mother arrived home, parked her car in the garage, and went into the house.'

'So that was when you left?'

'No, we didn't dare leave, in case Linda turned up.'

'Carry on.'

'Her father drove up about an hour and a half later. I told Toby I was going to ring Crispin . . .'

'Why?'

'Why? Because Crispin would know what to do. Crispin always knows what to do.'

'He certainly does,' Bassett agrees. 'Do what Crispin says, and you can't go wrong – except that it's by doing what Crispin said that you've ended up here, isn't it? So did you make the phone call?'

'No. Toby said that Linda might turn up while I was looking for a phone box, and he couldn't handle her on his own.'

'A big lad like Toby – and he couldn't handle a little girl like Linda?' Bassett asked incredulously. 'Didn't it occur to you at the time that what he really meant was that if anybody was going to humiliate themselves in front of Linda, if anyone was going to beg her to keep quiet, it was going to be you, because he has his pride, he has his dignity, but you're only a peasant, so you're not entitled to either.'

A look of deep sadness fills Jeff Meade's face. 'No, it didn't occur to me,' he says. 'Not then. But I'm beginning to see it now.'

'So you didn't go to make the phone call,' Bassett says. 'What did you do instead?'

'We just sat there – waiting.'

'Did anything else happen?'

'Linda's father went out again, but he was back within the hour, and he went to bed.'

'What about Linda's mother?'

'She stayed up all night.'

'Are you sure of that?'

'Yes, she hadn't drawn the curtains, and we could see her pacing up and down.'

'When did you two eventually leave?'

'It must have been seven o'clock in the morning.'

HOUSE IN DARKNESS . . . MOTHER comes in . . . father comes in . . . father goes out for an hour, then goes to bed . . . mother stays up all night . . . Jeff Meade and Toby Fortescue leave at seven in the morning.

Tears are pouring down my face now – great big, bitter, salt tears.

'Is something the matter, Jennie?' Macintosh asks.

'Yes,' I say.

Something is very much the matter, because I've just realized that Mary Corbet was right all along.

TWENTY-ONE

I've not seen today's papers – to be honest, I've been rather busy with other matters – but it would surprise me if they aren't pretty much as DCI Macintosh predicted they would be in that dark despairing period now known as yesterday afternoon. They will, I am sure, have called the Oxford police vindictive and incompetent – and they will have been screaming for blood.

Tomorrow's newspapers will be different. The more honest of them will probably confess they were a little hasty in their condemnation; the less scrupulous will try to insinuate that when they said heads should roll, they only meant that *other* papers thought heads should roll.

And it is all down to little me. I am the heroine of the hour, and when Macintosh and I walk into the police canteen, the officers already there actually stand up and applaud.

I should feel a warm glow coursing through my whole body – but I don't. Instead, I feel the weight of my own stupidity pressing down on me – almost crushing my ribs.

'Do you want to tell me what the problem is?' Macintosh asks.

'I will tell you,' I promise, 'but first I need to talk to Inspector Corbet – alone.'

'That's an unusual request,' Macintosh says. 'Can I ask *why* you need to talk to him alone?'

'No.'

'Tom Corbet's been charged with attempted murder. I really can't let you see him.'

'Is that because of the regulations?'

'Yes, it is.'

'I just pulled the Thames Valley police – and you in particular – out of the shit,' I say. 'To hell with the regulations!'

Macintosh hesitates for a few second, then he nods and says, 'Yes, to hell with the regulations.'

WHEN I OPEN THE door to the interview room, I see that Tom Corbet is already sitting at the table.

I sit down in his direct line of vision, but though his eyes are on me, I don't think he's actually registering my presence. If I had to guess, I would say that what he is actually watching is a series of tragic scenes – spanning generations – which are playing in his head.

I turn to the uniformed constable who is standing by the door.

'I'd like you go now, please,' I say.

'Are you sure?' he asks.

'I'm sure,' I tell him.

I wait until the constable has left, then I say, 'They tell me that you'll be appearing before the magistrates this afternoon, Mr Corbet.'

The eyes flicker, finally showing recognition, if not interest.

'Yes,' he says. 'By tonight, I'll be safely behind bars in a real prison.'

'You won't be asking for bail?'

'No.'

'Why not?'

'There'd be no point, because they'd refuse it. And so they *should*, because whatever I promise them, if they let me loose, the first thing I'd do is hunt down the rest of the young bastards.' He pauses. 'I'd hunt them down, and I'd kill them, but I know it's really all my fault – everything that's happened, right from the start, has been my fault.'

'What makes you say that?' I ask.

'I knew Linda was interested in literature and art, but I pushed her into the sciences. I wanted her to study medicine at one of the most outstanding universities in the world. I told myself I was only doing what was best for her, but I see now that wasn't what was making me push her at all. Do you know what was?'

'No.'

'I'm ashamed to say it, but I come from a family of parasites, who've always taken whatever they could – and contributed nothing. And we have to break that cycle – we just *have* to. I've managed to do some good – law and order is important to people's lives – but if Linda had become a doctor, she could have made a *real* difference.' He wipes a tear from his eye. 'And she went along with it all, because she wanted me to be proud of her.'

Yes, that was what she'd wanted, and when her best friend, Janet, had told her that she'd never get into Oxford – would never live up to her father's hopes for her – she'd felt a crushing disappointment of her own. And that was what had made her so vulnerable to the Shivering Turn.

'But you're not here to listen to my confession, are you?' Tom Corbet asks. 'At least you're not here for *that* confession.'

'You're right,' I agree, 'I'm not.'

'Then let's move on to what you're really here for. Let's just get the whole thing over with.'

'When your wife told me that she was absolutely convinced that Linda was dead, I thought she was just being hysterical. I mean – just look at the facts. Some of Linda's clothes were missing, so it was obvious that she'd run away. Of course, there were a couple of things that didn't seem to quite fit. One was that she'd taken her least favourite clothes and her school uniform with her. Another was that she'd left her teddy bear behind. But the money she'd earned at the pharmacy had gone, too, and that was the real clincher for me. Is there anything you'd like to say at this point?'

'No.'

'But from what I've learned this morning, she couldn't have packed her bag, because there simply wasn't time for her to do it. She left the Blind Beggar on foot, and, a couple of minutes later, two of her rapists jumped in a car and drove to your house. There was no way she could have got there before them. They stayed outside your house until the next morning, and she still hadn't come home. So when was the bag packed – and who packed it? It was packed later that night or early in the morning – by someone who had no idea which clothes she'd have chosen if she had really been running away. And that same person removed the money from its hiding place in the bookcase in

Linda's bedroom. How many people, other than Linda, knew about that money?'

'Two,' Corbet says. 'Her mother and me.'

'Where did you bury her, Tom?' I ask. 'Was it on your allotment?'

'You know it was.'

'And then you planted flowers on the grave?'

'Yes.'

'Why don't you tell me what happened that night?' I suggest.

'Why should I?' he asks.

'Because you need to tell somebody and, since I'm here, it might as well be me.'

'You're right,' he agrees. 'The night . . . the night it all happened . . . I was supposed to be attending a meeting at the lodge, but as I was driving there, I noticed Linda's friend, Janet, walking down the street. She was all dressed up, and was obviously going out for the evening.'

'But Linda had told you that they would be studying together?'

'Yes. I realized she'd lied to me – that all the promises to behave she'd made after she was arrested with those vermin on Beaumont Street meant nothing. I drove around. Maybe I was looking for her, or maybe I was just driving for the sake of driving. I no longer know.'

'But you did eventually find her.'

'Yes, she was down by the river. I asked her where she'd been and what the matter was. She told me she'd been raped. I asked if her "rapists" were the boys she'd been arrested with, and she said yes. I'd never raised a hand to her before – I swear I hadn't – but I hit her then. I didn't think about it – I just did it. In some ways, it almost felt as if the fist that struck her didn't even belong to me.' He shudders. 'She fell backwards. We were standing close to a park bench, and her head hit the metal armrest. She must have died instantly.'

'You buried her on your allotment, then you drove home, and while your wife was ringing all her friends, you packed her bag with some of the clothes.'

'Yes.'

'What did you do with the bag?'

'I went out to the allotment again, and buried it, too.'

'You're no coward – I know that,' I say. 'So what I can't understand is why you weren't prepared to face up to the consequences of what you'd done – why you decided to protect yourself by making it look as if Linda had run away.'

'Is that what you think?' Tom Corbet asks, with genuine surprise in his voice. 'That I did what I did to protect myself?'

'Maybe you did it partly for your wife – because you thought it was better for her to believe that her daughter had run away than to know for certain that she was dead – but mostly, yes, I think you did it for yourself.'

'I can count on the fingers of one hand, the number of times in my life I have done something for myself – and this wasn't one of them,' he says.

'Then who *did* you do it for?'

'For Linda.'

'For Linda!'

'If I'd turned myself in and confessed, the whole story would have been all over the newspapers, wouldn't it?'

'I suppose it would.'

'And it would have besmirched her memory for ever. When people thought about her, they wouldn't remember the sweet, caring girl who was always willing to listen to them, or offer a helping hand – they would remember the cheap slut who was more than happy to give herself to any man who wanted her. And I couldn't have that because – however badly she'd behaved – she was still my little girl.'

'But she *hadn't* behaved badly!' I say, keeping my voice low and reasonable, though what I really want to do is scream at him. 'She'd been raped! She *told you* she'd been raped!'

'I know that's true, now. I've known it was true from the moment I was told that DCI Macintosh had arrested those animals from St Luke's College. But I didn't believe it *then*.'

'What kind of man are you, who wouldn't believe what his own daughter said?' I demand.

'I'm the kind of man whose view of women has been warped and distorted by his own childhood,' Corbet tells me.

'What does that even mean?' I ask sceptically.

'I told you my mother was a street-corner whore, didn't I?' Corbet asks. 'Well, from the moment I was old enough to understand what she was doing, I absolutely hated it. I begged her – down on my knees – to stop. And do you know what she said? She said, "It's not that I want to go with men, but if I don't, who's going to put food on the table and keep a roof over our heads?" I told her I'd rather starve than have her prostituting herself, and she said that was easy to say when I'd got a full belly.' He pauses. 'Are you following me?'

I nod.

I *am* following him. I may even be ahead of him.

'I had a newspaper round and a Saturday job,' he continues. 'I ran errands in the evening. I worked all the hours God sends. And when I handed the money to my mother, she didn't even thank me. She just looked at it and said, "Sorry, darling, this is nowhere near enough."'

My heart goes out to him. I desperately want to offer him a few comforting words, but I also want to get through this ghastly story as quickly as possible – for both our sakes. And so I say nothing.

'There was a middle-aged man who lived in a big house on my newspaper round, and who'd made it quite plain that he was interested in me,' Corbet says. 'I went to see him. I . . . I offered my services to him. He did some terrible disgusting things to me, but he paid well, and so when he asked me if some of his friends could join in, I said yes. That was even worse, as you can imagine. At times, I didn't know how I could endure it for even a second more. But I *did* endure it – so that my mother wouldn't have to. I saved up the money until I'd got nearly a hundred pounds, which was a small fortune back then. I gave the money to my mother. And do you know what she said?'

'No,' I tell him – though I think I could make a fair guess.

'She said, "That's wonderful, darling, but we can't live on it for ever. Will there be more?" I said yes. She never asked where I got the money from, but given that I was still only a kid, she must have had a fair idea, mustn't she?'

'Yes,' I agree, 'she must have had a fair idea.'

'She promised me she'd come off the game, but just a few nights later, I saw her in an alley, screwing a drunken soldier. That was when I realized that there are some women who, whatever they may *say*, like to be humiliated – who take pleasure from rolling around in the filth and degradation of their own making. And when Linda told me that she'd had sex with all those boys against her will, I didn't believe her – because I thought she was as immoral and duplicitous as her grandmother.' A tear rolls down his cheek. 'But even at that moment – even as I despised her – I couldn't help loving her. You have to believe that.'

'I do believe that,' I tell him. 'I'm so sorry.'

'For Linda and Mary?' he asks 'So am I.'

'For you as well.'

'Don't be sorry for me,' he says. 'I won't be suffering long.'

'What do you mean?'

'They've got me on suicide watch at the moment – but they can't keep that up for ever.'

EPILOGUE

It is a mild Sunday evening, towards the end of May, and I'm sitting at one of the wooden tables in the Head of the River's beer garden. The last rays of the setting sun cast a blood-red glow across the wide sky, the birds are singing their farewell to the day, and the river laps gently against the shore. It is all very peaceful – all very calming.

I have just returned from Whitebridge, where I went to attend my dad's cremation. When my mother asked me if I wanted to bring some of his ashes back to Oxford with me, I was surprised to hear myself say yes, but I'm glad I did, because, in a way I still don't quite understand, I find them comforting.

'Ground control to Jennie Redhead,' says a voice, quite close to me, in a Scottish accent. 'Are you receiving me? Over.'

I turn to face DCI Macintosh, who is sitting opposite me. I wonder, not for the first time since we arrived at the pub, exactly what we're doing here. We might, I suppose, be called friendly acquaintances, but we are certainly not friendly friends, so there is no reason I can think of that a fairly senior officer in the Thames Valley Police should have called me, out of the blue, and suggested we go for a drink. And that, you must admit, is slightly disturbing.

'Jennie?' he says again.

'Sorry, I was miles away,' I admit. 'What were you saying?'

'I was asking you if you thought it was Tom Corbet who wrecked your office?'

'He certainly didn't tell me that he was the one who did it – and now we'll never know,' I say.

Poor Tom Corbet. He was a good man – a man who always tried to do the right thing. It was tragic that he should have ended his life hanging from a pipe in a prison cell.

And poor Mary Corbet. I went to see her after her husband had confessed to me – and all the time that she was sobbing in my arms, I was struggling to hold back my own tears. It was not an experience I ever want to repeat, and when I eventually left her in the capable hands of Linda's best friend, Janet, I took the wad of notes that was to have been Linda's university fund, and dropped it in the box at the Oxfam shop.

'I've lost you again, haven't I?' DCI Macintosh asks.

'Sorry,' I say, for a second time.

'Tom Corbet didn't *tell* you he wrecked your office, but what do you *think*?' Macintosh persists.

And I'm beginning to suspect that the question is less about Tom Corbet, and more about why we're here now.

'It was certainly wrecked in a neat and orderly way, and since Tom was the only neat and orderly man I know who had anything to gain by wrecking it, I suppose it must have been him,' I say.

'He thought that might frighten you off – but he didn't know you like I'm getting to know you,' Ken Macintosh says.

Is he making a pass at me? I wonder in a mild panic.

Is it a case of flattery first – and knickers off second?

And then I relax. Macintosh put his career on the line in the Linda Corbet case, and he did it because he has three daughters, so he's certainly not going to risk having his contact with those daughters limited to two weekends a month just for the sake of a bit of illicit nooky.

'You've got a good degree from an excellent university, haven't you?' he asks.

'A goodish degree, at any rate,' I say, wondering what this change of direction indicates.

'So whatever made a young woman with your qualifications join the police force?'

I have a standard answer for that question – one that, I think, succeeds in being both amusing and in signalling to whoever asked the question that it's something I'd rather not go into too deeply.

But Ken Macintosh, while he is still not quite a friend, is at least a comrade with whom I have stood side by side in battle – and I think he deserves an honest answer.

'I used to babysit for a DCI in Lancashire, and she once told me that before she adopted her daughter, her work was the only thing that had stopped her from coming apart at the seams,' I say. 'And it seemed to me then – and it still seems to me – that any job which can do that is one you should seriously consider.'

Macintosh looks at me strangely – and that's the trouble with being honest, people *do* look at you strangely.

'Do *you* worry about coming apart at the seams?' he asks.

'Doesn't everybody?' I wonder.

'The reason I asked about why you joined the police,' Macintosh says (leaving my last question diplomatically unanswered), 'is that I've been talking to the chief constable recently, and he's been very impressed with the way you handled yourself during the investigation.'

'That's good to know,' I counter, noncommittally. 'Because I'm not proud – I'll take fans from wherever I can find them.'

'And he's instructed me to tell you that if you apply to rejoin the force, not only are you very likely to be accepted, but your years on the outside will be counted as relevant experience, so you won't lose any seniority.'

'That's very generous,' I tell him, 'but I left the force for a reason, and that reason hasn't gone away.'

'I think we're talking about Chief Superintendant Dunn here, aren't we?' Macintosh asks.

'Are we?'

'Yes, I rather think we are. Well, I have reason to believe that the chief superintendent will soon be in no position to cause you any grief.'

'He's being investigated, isn't he?' I ask, with a slight flush of pleasure which is probably unworthy of me. 'And it's more than likely that he's going to be booted off the force – if not jailed.'

Macintosh shifts uncomfortably in his chair. 'I didn't exactly say that, you know.'

'You didn't exactly have to.'

'So will you consider reapplying?' Macintosh asks.

I feel that I should take time to seriously consider the offer – but I don't want to.

'No,' I tell him.

'Why not?'

'I quite like the job I've got now.'

'You're mad,' Macintosh says.

There's no denying he has a point.

'Yes, I probably am,' I agree.

'You're a good investigator, Jennie, but there's only so far you can go working on your own. Rejoin the force, and you could be a DCI in a few years. Stay where you are, and you're doomed to frustration, because you simply won't have the resources available to you in the police. It'll be like banging your head against a brick wall.'

'Maybe you're right,' I agree. 'But there are brick walls in your job, too. Once you'd released the members of the Shivering Turn the first time, there was nothing more you could do. Isn't that right?'

'I suppose so.'

'But I *could* do more – and did – because the only boss I have to listen to is me.'

'Even so—' Macintosh begins.

'Let's be honest, we all end up banging our heads against brick walls whatever job we do,' I interrupt him, 'but at least, in my case, I get to choose my own bricks.'